ROGUE ANGEL

SINNERS & SAINTS
BOOK 2

LANA SKY

Rogue Angel

Rogue Angel By Lana Sky

Cover Design and Interior Formatting by Charity Chimni
Editing by Charity Chimni
Alpha Reading by Jessica Rita Rampersad

ACKNOWLEDGMENTS

Thanks so much to everyone who supported this draft along the way, including the many beta readers who provided encouragement! Please keep in mind that this story includes dark, graphic, and explicit content matter that may not be suitable for readers under the age of 18—or for readers who are uncomfortable with the following subject matter: drug use, mentions of suicide, cultish behavior, explicit sex, and graphic depictions of violence.

IT'S TERRIFYING when all you know is pain. Pulsing agony floods my skull with every breath, and for a moment, I can't even remember my own name. Gradually, snippets of clarity come back to me, but they feel disconnected, like facts about a stranger.

I'm Frances Heywood. Twenty-three. I'm...

Where am I?

I blink my eyes open, but something's wrong. A scratchy material brushes my eyelids, weighing them down. A groggy part of my brain voices a term for it—*blindfold*. That's not the most troubling realization, either. I can't move. My arms are tied behind my back at awkward angles, and the air smells...wet. Like rust or mildew.

My body feels dry, at least, though I'm cold. A gritty substance under my bare feet makes me think of concrete. My teeth are chattering, and the surface I am sitting on is hard and frigid. A metal folding chair? Maybe. Kicking my legs against the floor and rocking back, I hear a metallic squeal echo off the nearby walls. Could I be in a basement?

Whatever the case, I'm not in Daze's apartment—the last place I remember being. I strain my ears but don't hear a hint of his gruff laugh or coarse murmur. As a chilling silence echoes in his place, I try like hell to remember more. What happened?

We were asleep, and then...

Without warning, a dozen disjointed images flood my head, and I wince at the speed of them. *Me and Daze in his bed. A noise. Him trying to protect me from someone. A man. Silas. He and his goons dragging me into a van. Being blindfolded...*

I must have gotten knocked out after that.

God, they could have taken me anywhere...

No. I can't panic. *Think, Frey!* "Hello?" I shakily call out. "Is anyone there?"

All I hear is my own shrill voice echoing back at me. It's childish to hope that Daze is here with me, but I do. I call out again.

And again.

Eventually, I fall silent and put my focus into moving, rocking the chair back and forth to shift over an inch. Another. Maybe somehow, I can find a way to the exit. Wait... A faint murmur draws my notice, and I freeze. Voices?

They sound muffled, as if coming from another room, and I don't know whether to be hopeful or terrified.

Surprisingly, my own safety is the least of my concerns. I can't stop thinking of Daze. Silas hit him, from what I remember—hard. The kind of blow that could have killed him. I won't ever forgive myself if it did. Oh god... Wallowing in guilt won't help me, but it's all I can do to push the prospect to the back of my mind and keep breathing.

After Hale, I can't have another death on my conscious. Because I know in my gut that whatever this is about has to do with me. My father. *He wants you unharmed,* Silas said.

I want to believe he was lying or playing a sadistic mind game at my expense. Father mingles only with trusted politicians and the loyalist members of his congregation. I can't imagine him knowing someone like Silas apart from a good campaign sound bite regarding his fight against crime.

But Daze knew him, enough to warn me not to trust him.

Or Colton.

With my skull on fire, I don't have the ability to concentrate on idle speculation. *Focus, Frey!* I squeeze my eyes shut, feeling the blindfold chafe against my eyelids. Wherever I am, I can't stay here. Sucking in a breath, I open my mouth to scream—but it's like I hear Daze's voice in my head before I can make a sound, hissing—*Don't tire yourself out. Wait until you know what you're up against.*

There appears to be more than one person. As if on cue, three distinct baritone voices trickle into my ear, emanating from somewhere in the distance. They seem to be arguing— heatedly. It's hard to make out more than a handful of words, but what I can discern paints a grim picture.

"...weren't supposed to be seen... No matter, though. I'll make sure she knows better than to talk." I recognize that voice. Deep with an unmistakable gruffness. Silas. "When I'm through with that little bitch, she won't say a fucking word."

"And how do you plan to do that?" someone demands, but him I don't recognize. "You may have Heywood's balls in a vice, but I don't think he'd tolerate you threatening his kid—"

"Did I ask for your opinion? No. Then shut the fuck up. I'll handle this."

Abruptly, the voices fall silent, replaced by the unsettling thump of footsteps advancing in my direction. *Thump. Thump.* My heartbeat surges with every deliberate thud until it's all I can hear, nearly drowning out the harsh sigh that echoes next. The culprit is close enough to ruffle the edges of my hair with a second ragged exhale. I tense, anticipating a physical touch that never materializes.

Why? What do they want? An explanation comes to me when a guttural chuckle teases the air—he's toying with me.

"Oh dear," my tormentor finally drawls, having grown bored with his game. "Your daddy is going to be very disappointed when I tell him where I found you, little girl. You were supposed to run home last night and go to sleep in your safe, secure bedroom. It would have been far more believable that way. But you had to go and make it difficult—"

The blindfold is ripped free by a harsh tug. I blink, struggling to comprehend the sight before me—a man standing tall, his grin contorted in cruel, unwelcoming fury.

Silas. He's dressed head to toe in black, barely visible in the dim lighting drifting in from a nearby window with wooden slats nailed over most of it. The room beyond him is large and above ground—contrary to my initial suspicion—but empty. A warehouse or a garage, perhaps? The floors are concrete, and the walls are water-stained and coated in grime.

"Wakey-Wakey," Silas taunts, snapping his fingers. "Keep your eyes on me."

I look up, squinting to observe him more closely. Despite the animosity between them, he and Daze carry themselves with the same confident swagger. The only difference is Silas, with his mature features and scraggly five-o-clock-shadow ghosting his chin, lacks Daze's charm. His gaze is ice-cold, taking me in without an ounce of compassion.

"Now we've gotta go through the effort of forging security footage and spreading gossip to make it all legit," he says, shaking his head with obvious annoyance. "You know, I wouldn't go through the trouble if your daddy wasn't so very friendly. But he won't stay sweet on me for long if you go around spreading nasty little rumors. What did Daze tell you?"

The statement stirs a response in me; I can't hold my tongue. "You're working for my father..." My voice comes out slow and garbled. Like I'm trying to talk with my mouth full.

"Working?" Silas frowns, but I think it's the way I phrased it rather than the implication that bothers him.

"The Saints work for no one, missy," he says, crouching to my eye level. His breath reeks of a sickly sweet, alcoholic substance. Beer? If so, he's drunk a lot of it. That must be why his eyes are bloodshot. "Not anymore. It's your daddy who does *our* dirty work. Laundering our sins to keep his pious hands clean. I'm sure Daze told you that much."

I stay quiet.

"Oh?" He raises an eyebrow at whatever he sees in my expression. "I guess not."

A shiver runs down my spine as I contrast his sudden frankness with Daze's evasiveness. Daze could have been deliberately misleading me, withholding information at every opportunity, but I think there is more going on. Silas' motive for telling the truth now isn't out of mercy. It's to scare me—but not only that.

He seems too cocky. As if... As if he's convinced that, no matter what he might say, I won't be able to tell anyone else.

"Are you going to hurt me?" I ask him outright. My voice a hollow rasp in the face of his.

I can't help but stare as he flexes the fingers of his right hand to deliberately crack each knuckle. *Crack... Crack!*

After the unsettling musical display, he shrugs. "Of course, I'm not gonna hurt you, honey. Why would I go and do a silly thing like that?" He reaches out and strokes a tangle of hair from my cheek. Although I cringe at the contact, my hands are tied, and I can only move my face a few inches away. He lets me go, regardless, issuing a harsh laugh.

"My secrets are safe with you, right?" he adds, winking. "Because if I get so much as a whiff that you've been running your mouth, I'll snatch you again, personally—only it won't be a fake little ruse meant to boost your daddy's poll numbers. Then I'll have Daze's sweet sister, Lyra, lure him somewhere under the guise of meeting with Samuel. Only I'll be there..." His smile falls, rendering his expression feral. "Waiting to blow his fucking brains out while you watch."

Horror almost robs my ability to speak. "What are you talking about?"

"I'm talking about your only purpose," he says, crooking his finger to caress my chin. I hate the way he feels. Too smooth, as though he's never done a hard day's work in his life. He has others do his dirty work for him—except when it comes to violence. Sizing me up, he smirks at my reaction. "That of the good little pawn."

The insult irritates something inside me—some rebellious instinct that Daze Keaton alone woke up. "Don't fucking touch me!" I recoil again, making the chair rock backward.

Silas just shakes his head, clicking his tongue. "Naughty. Naughty. Ah, such bad manners. Any other little girl might have to be punished..." His voice dips to a dangerous octave, sending a shiver down my spine. *Be careful, Frey.*

I go still, hating how pathetic I feel. My heart seems liable to pound its way out of my chest. God, I can barely breathe.

But... To my credit, I don't look away from him. "Where is Daze?" I demand. "I know you hurt him, you coward!"

"Were you any other bitch, I'd slap the shit out of you for that," Silas warns. "For you, I'll make an exception. Do you want to know why?" He tilts his head as if waiting for a response. When I say nothing, he runs his tongue along his lower lip and shrugs. "Because your daddy really needs to win this election, and he needs his beloved, obedient daughter by his side to do so. Optics and shit. Don't tell me you thought your little disappearing acts had gone unnoticed?"

My expression gives me away—eyes wide with shock. So many chilling actions on both the part of my father and Colton click into place. Their faux concern and supposed patience with my lies had been all an act. All along, they knew.

"Oh yes," Silas says as if reading my mind. "You've had your fun pouting around and sulking these past few months, but the pity party is over. It's time to play ball. Don't you agree?"

I can't tell from his expression just how serious he is. He has the same virtual poker face as Daze. Only God knows what they're really thinking. Still, he waits patiently as if giving me all the time in the world to reply. Then, he snaps his fingers in a sudden motion designed to make me flinch.

And I do.

"Tick tock," he scolds. "I need an answer, little girl. Or maybe I didn't make myself clear before? Perhaps we should go back to your friend Daze and see if he has any brains left in his skull to put a bullet in—"

"Play ball," I croak the second he moves to take a step toward the shadowy doorway behind him. "How?"

"Good girl." He turns back and claps his hands. "First, you will be miraculously rescued and returned to your doting father by the Westpoint P.D. Then you will appear by his side at every political shindig, smiling and happy. You'll hold hands and sing and pray or whatever the fuck it is you people do."

"And if I don't?" I jut my chin, infected by a sudden surge of bravery. Maybe Daze has rubbed off on me more than I thought.

At least until Silas smirks, and my heart twitches ominously in response. "And if you don't?" he repeats with a haunting chuckle. "Well, if your daddy even suspects that you know more than you should, *Frances*, I get to make your ordeal far more real. Understood?"

Craning my neck, I see a shadow flicker in a small hallway beyond this room. He isn't alone. Just how many men does he have here with him? Does he truly intend to let me go? And is my father really aware of this...

My mind has gone to some dark places since Hale died, but even that level of betrayal is a step too far.

I can't believe him. "You're lying—"

"I thought you might say that." Silas cups my chin without warning, forcing me to meet his gaze. The second I tense, his nails dig in, scraping into my flesh, so hard tears well behind my eyes. "I'll make one thing clear—you don't know shit, little girl. Not about one damn thing. Daze might have run his mouth about what a bastard I am, but I bet he hasn't told you the full truth, has he? Like how he rushed to do your daddy's dirty work when it paid him well enough. How he begged me to help him dig the Saints out of the hole his dear old dad left us in. What we're not going to do, is play dumb. Do you understand?"

I bite my lip rather than let him know how confused I really am. *Your daddy's dirty work?* Picturing Daze, I somehow doubt he would be involved in passing out church pamphlets or volunteering during sermons.

What is he talking about?

"I want an answer," Silas growls, wrenching my head back and forth.

"Yes," I choke out.

"Good." His voice is too loud, and my skull is pounding worse than ever. I can't deny that his insinuations about Daze gnaw away at what little composure I have left. God, I feel seconds from breaking. Screaming...

"Okay." Silas sighs and taps his forefinger against my jawline. "Let's go over things one more time. After this conversation, you'll wake up again, probably in a hospital. You'll then perform your role as the traumatized kidnapping victim and do everything your daddy tells you to with a smile. Otherwise, your friend Daze's body will find its way to your doorstep. Then I'll sneak into your bedroom while your daddy is out. You'd like that, wouldn't you? I'm sure I could teach you a thing or two that he wouldn't dare, little girl."

My cheeks flame at the implication. "You're disgusting!"

"Yeah? Well, I'll do you a favor, just to show how nice I am. I'll teach you exactly what your daddy expects. Let's try practicing now. Smile. Like this—" He brutally digs a finger into the corner of my mouth until I grimace.

"That's a girl. Keep doing that, and we won't have any further problems."

I wrench my neck as hard as I can to escape his grasp. Then I blurt, "How do I know you won't hurt Daze?"

His eyes darken, betraying a hint of the real rage he's hidden until now. "If I wanted him dead, he would be. As much as he likes to strut around like he's hot stuff, Daze is a threat to no one. I've kept him around out of pity, but for now, he can be my gift to you. Be a good girl, and he can stay alive. But if you step out of line..."

He leans in, blowing air into my face, and I gag at the disgusting odor.

"I won't be so nice anymore, darling," he says. "In fact, if you try to talk to your daddy about our little conversation or run away to Daze, I will have to make my disappointment very, very clear. You have no idea how badly I want you to disobey. Punishing you would give me great pleasure, little girl. In fact, I *dare* you to—"

I flick my tongue along my dry lips, toying with the thought of pushing him further. The more information I can get out of him, the better—but angering him could backfire.

"Well," he prods, waving his hand in front of my face. "Do we have an agreement?"

He waits, though I can tell he doesn't expect an answer. In response to my silence, he chuckles. "Good girl. Now sit tight. You'll be sent home shortly. Oh, and one more thing—"

He stands to his full height, and I only have a split second of warning as his arm shoots out. *Wham!* I jolt sideways, bringing the chair down with me. A high-pitched ringing echoes in my ears as pain sears through my left cheek—at the same time, agony rips through my right side and into my shoulder.

"We need to make this believable," Silas says from above me, his voice disjointed. Dazed, I crane my neck in time to watch him still shaking out his right hand. "You never saw your attackers either," he warns as I connect the dots behind his actions to the source of my pain—he punched me. "And you'll be sure to tell the investigators some juicy headlines about them wanting to teach your old man a lesson. Blah, blah, blah. And, just in case you need one more reminder to play for the right team, here it is—your daddy has already been willing to throw away more than one of you precious Heywoods to preserve his image. Don't think he won't hesitate to get rid of another."

His wording itches at me. *More than one?*

"And," he adds, drawing my attention back to him. "If you think that sad bastard, Daze, is on your side..."

Something hard taps my left shoulder—his boot. He lets the square toe dig into the tender joint brutally enough to rip a gasp from my throat. I strain to get away but only tug on my bound wrists, sending fire up and down my arms. Right when the sensation borders excruciating, he withdraws.

"You're wrong—" His foot shoots out, connecting against my ribcage. I groan, watching him loom above through streaming eyes. I barely hear him growl, "He only ever looks out for himself. I'll let you in on a little secret. You aren't the first girl he's used in a petty game of revenge. You won't be the last. He killed *her* when he got bored of her, though. I doubt a preacher's daughter will fare any better. Ta-ta, for now, darling. Think about what I've said."

He strolls from the room, leaving me tangled with the folding chair, wheezing for air, and tasting blood.

"Oh, and Frances?" His voice sounds distant, as if coming from a nearby hallway. "Next time you see Daze, ask him how much he planned to ransom you for. I'm sure that's the only reason the bastard kept you around in the first place. One look at you, and he probably saw dollar signs. Like father like son..."

I'm forced to lie there, my cheek throbbing and blood dripping down my face as I puzzle over what he meant. He was lying, of course. Taunting me.

But Daze has kept more than a few secrets from me already.

What else could he be hiding?

Do I even want to know?

TWO

DAZE

I'VE HEARD that true desperation can only be understood when you've hit rock bottom. Funny. I've been there, done that. I even dusted myself off and climbed to the top once upon a time. That being said, there's something worse about this latest fuckup, but I'm not sure why.

Maybe it's the guilt, enhancing the usual sting of defeat. My fucking head may feel like it's splitting open but failing her hurts more. And, of course, there's the whole lying to her from day fucking one bit to take my self-pity up a notch.

Damn. Frey was never meant to be part of this shit. Despite her brother's best efforts, the irony is that he still couldn't protect her from the truth. Hell, he died rather than let her in on the secret that had driven him to the brink of insanity.

And what a secret it is—that their dear old father, Michael Heywood, isn't who he pretends to be. He has his holy hands wrapped around a crime syndicate stretching throughout every inch of Westpoint City—not that I have any proof.

Contrary to his image as the poster boy of peace and purity, he's damn good at covering his tracks. With his impending election on the horizon and the influence he already wields over the local police, the bastard is practically untouchable.

I wasn't sure when I first met her, but it is clear now that Frey has no idea who he is, walking around, repeating his holy spiel. She's the cliché of a perfect, churchgoing girl—the kind who makes a man's dick hard from afar, but never ventures beyond her safe, distant tower. *Shit...* I wouldn't have believed she were real if I hadn't seen her in action.

No one in the world is *that* damn good.

In Silas' grasp, she won't last long. He'll break her down, but to what end? That's what worries me. I have no damn idea what he's up to.

Or what he might tell her in the meantime.

I'm a selfish bastard to give a shit about having my cover blown—but I do. Spun the wrong way, the lies I've told can be made to sound so much worse. Silas will make sure of that, though it's not like I can stop him. The bastard's got himself roped into something big by working with Heywood. The only way to counter them is to make a few alliances of my own—no matter what it will cost me in the end.

Some might say I've already sold my soul to the devil, anyway. At least now I have a good rationale for the eventual destruction I'll cause. A reason sanctified enough to risk being picked off by one of Silas' goons and venturing to the outskirts of the city merely to wait in a shitty alley reeking of piss. Considering I didn't clean up, I'm a walking target with fresh blood dripping off my skull, attracting worried looks from anyone I pass.

An unwelcome thought sneaks in as the wind blows an empty soda can past me—if Frey were here, she'd make some prissy little comment about how I need first aid. How unsanitary it is to traipse around alleyways with an open wound. She'd fuss over my throbbing head and probably bitch about me needing to go to the hospital. Without her, I just wipe the back of my hand over my forehead and try to ignore how it comes away coated in red. Gritting my teeth, I keep moving, even as the world starts to pitch and sway beneath me.

There's plenty of time to wallow in agony later. Staying a step ahead of Silas is all that matters. Though the truth is, I'm not taking him on out of selfish pride, or even revenge. I'm doing this for her...

Fighting back is the one way I can atone for the sins I've already committed. That has to account for something, right? As the seconds tick by, doubt sets in. What was I even thinking by calling someone like him out here?

I should turn around and forget this entire fucked-up plan.

Only, it's too late. A sudden noise draws my notice ahead, and a shadowed figure steps around a nearby corner. With a cock of their head, they beckon me closer. From this angle, I can't tell if they're friend or foe.

"Daze," they say.

I tense, even though I know at a glance he isn't one of Silas' goons. He's not wearing a vest, or Saints' colors, for one. Whoever he is, he's well trained, too. I didn't even hear him approach. As he steps from the shadows, his hulking form reveals his identity. His size paired with the havoc he caused in the ring back in the day, more than earned him his nickname—*Mayhem*.

"Damien," I say, eyeing him from head to toe. The last time we met was in a jail cell, and he looked almost as fucked up then as I do now. His face has healed, at least. His green eyes are crystal clear, sharp as flint, and narrowed to slits.

"You said you'd have my back when I needed it," I add, cutting right to the chase. "I need it now."

Damien scoffs. With his head cocked, the tattoo of a snake creeping up the side of his neck is visible above the collar of his black tee. Since our cage fighting days, he's bulked up some, seeming more like a crazy motherfucker than when I first met him in the ring years ago.

"It's about damn time you called in that favor I owe you, Day," he replies. "I've been waiting. Though fuck..." He sizes me up with a questioning glance, his gaze lingering on my face. "You look like shit. What happened?"

Apart from the muscle, he hasn't changed much in the past few months. The same disheveled, blood-red hair sticking out at all angles. Angular features. Piercing green eyes and ebony tattoos everywhere, from his knuckles to his neck. All in all, the kind of bastard who will fit right in around Westpoint City. Ignoring his question, I continue, "You came.

That's all that matters. I know you aren't affiliated with the Saints—"

"Damn fucking right, I'm not." He hisses through his teeth and then spits onto the pavement between us. His anger is warranted. God knows that some days I feel the same. "Surprised you were still running with those fuckers," he adds. "I thought you'd turned your back on them after your daddy croaked and left you his shit to clean up."

Damn. I'd almost forgotten just how much about my past Damien knows—and he's one of the few people in the world who isn't afraid to throw it all in my face. "I don't run with them anymore," I clarify, clenching my jaw. Then I wince as agony sears through my skull. I have to press my heels into the ground to keep from swaying. "Since you don't either," I grate out next. "You won't have any problem with tailing their members, would you?"

"That depends." He smirks, tilting his head to the side. "What did you have in mind?"

I exhale a breath I didn't realize I'd been holding. "I need to find someone they took. A woman. Blond. Average height —" With every descriptor of her, the more guilt I feel piercing my gut. She's out there because of me. Hurt because of *me*. The thought stings like hell, but Damien takes in every bit of info without batting a fucking eyelash. Gritting my teeth, I add, "Her name is Frances Heywood—"

"Ah," he cuts me off mid-sentence with a smirk. "It's about a woman."

I shrug off his amusement. "It is. I need you to find her," I press. "She's the key to taking Silas down. You can start by tailing him and his crew. I'm sure they'll lead you to wherever he's stashed her."

And then I'll break in no matter what. Unarmed if I fucking have to.

"Got it," Damien remarks, straightening his posture. "I'll see what I can do, but you're asking for a tall order, Day. You're lucky you had my back in lockup, or I might tell your ass to go to hell—"

"You're the only one I can trust to do this right," I interject. Since he left cage fighting behind, I've heard the rumors of what he's done to make his money. Mercenary work. Cold, cruel shit that some bastards wouldn't be able to sleep at night after carrying out. Finding Silas' hideout will be child's play for a man like him—as long as he doesn't chafe at being kept on a leash. "Look, I just need intel. I don't know where Silas could take her, but if he lays a hand on her..."

"Relax. We'll find her." Damien nods to himself, making up his mind on the fly. "What's your game plan?"

I wince at the question and ball my hands into fists. Eyeing the battered knuckles, I have no choice but to come clean. The honest truth is... "Nothing concrete yet, but things could get fucking messy. I need a base and a way to determine Silas' next move." I rake my hands through my hair and wince. "Doesn't fucking matter what we do. I need to find Frey. He went too far this time."

"This girl. She wouldn't happen to be the daughter of some big-shot churchman, would she?" Damien asks.

"What?" I whip around to face him and instantly regret the sharp movement. *Fuck.* It feels like my skull is splitting in half, but I shrug off the pain. To his credit, Damien's expression doesn't reveal much, but it wouldn't surprise me if he gathered his own intel before coming here. It's what I would do. "Yeah. Why?"

He juts his jaw, keeping his gaze sharp but blank. "Because a woman fitting that description is all over the news. Her father reported her missing last night."

Shit. I should have known better than to think she'd go unnoticed, even in disguise. It's probably why Silas held back in the first place. The fucker had to be planning this for a while.

"Damien, I might need another favor—"

"Already done," he says, his tone as unnervingly calm as ever. "I'll have my boys watch the family. Case their house. If she turns up, we'll know before anyone else."

I raise an eyebrow. "Your boys? People I can trust, right?"

"Damn right, you can," he says with a sly smirk. "Ex-cage fighters, too, though they didn't run in our old ring. One's an ex-Marine, and the other's a damn good tracker. You'll meet them soon enough. Even the three of us alone can take down a few Saints, no problem."

I grimace at the reminder of his original promise. "Look, I know that we agreed you can do things your way, but..."

That was before I came to my fucking senses and remembered one key thing—Frey. The sheltered little princess is naïve as hell, but she won't like it if I paint the city red just to get her back—no matter how badly I want to. "If we can keep the violence contained, for now, I'll owe you one. I swear on my life. Just bring her back to me in one piece."

Damien shrugs. "I warned you. We don't do shit nice and clean—"

"Think of it as a challenge then," I bite back. "Help me find her, but keep it subtle. Dropping bodies every damn where means police. FBI. The fucking SWAT team. I need her safe, Damien. She's not from the streets like us. She won't understand if things get out of control."

And, if they do, Frey will never look at me the same way again.

"You're the one who called me here," Damien says. "Your turf, your rules. For now."

I don't know what to make of that, but I nod anyway. "Good. Thanks."

In that unsettling way, he laughs again. "Don't thank me yet. I warned you when you called, Daze—we don't sit around on our fucking hands. If you want this done nice and neat, we aren't the right men for the job. Don't think you can keep us on a leash for long."

Only a stupid man would try. Silas has a reputation for brutality. Maybe in my heyday, I'd earned my own street cred.

Combined, our records don't come anywhere close to the chaos this man gets up to just for fun.

"I'm done with playing nice," I say. After dealing with Silas for as long as I have, it's about damn time I met him tit for tat.

The bastard's had it coming—for more reasons than just Frey.

"Well then, it sounds like you'll have your work cut out for you."

Given the overall influence of Michael Heywood and Silas, he has no fucking idea.

I don't have a choice but to face this shit head-on. For years, Silas has wanted to pick a fight with me.

Well, he got it.

IF YOU THINK *Daze is on your side... You're wrong.*

Bound, with no way to move, Silas' words echo in my skull on an endless loop. Pain is the only thing strong enough to rival them. God, I just hope nothing's broken. My shoulder throbs badly enough to be. I can only rock back and forth to relieve the pressure on it as my hands remain tied behind my back, tethered to the chair. I don't know how long I'm left like this before someone new enters the room. Their steps are slow. Cautious.

"Hey, sweetheart..." The masculine whisper sends terror through my veins.

I tense, scrambling for enough purchase to sit upright. Move. Do something! One detail I notice provides a small tendril of relief—this person isn't Silas. Their footsteps aren't as heavy as his, approaching from behind. All I can see is a length-ening shadow painting the floor in front of me. When I strain to turn around, something dark falls over my face, and I'm blind again.

A harsh voice cuts over any cry I start to make, "Don't move —" I gasp in relief as my hands are freed from the chair, but both of my wrists are seized, and I am yanked upright.

"Where are you taking me?" I croak, swaying to find my balance.

"Easy, little girl," a man drawls. I feel his hands paw at my shoulder. Then a pinching sensation. I flinch, but he just grips me tighter. "Enjoy the ride," he snarls while easily manhandling me toward an unseen direction. He's moving quickly, unconcerned about whether I can keep up.

I can't. The second I lose my footing, my captor surges forward, even as my knees hit the floor. For what feels like an eternity, I'm dragged over the bare concrete by my wrists. The harsh surface bites into my skin, rubbing my shins raw.

"You stupid bitch," my captor hisses, wrenching me upright. "Walk—"

"Easy," another man growls. He sounds further away, his voice unfamiliar. "He said not another scratch on her."

"Yeah, well, he's the one who gave her a shiner. Come and help me. Let's get this over with."

More footsteps approach, and another set of hands grab me from the side, lifting me off my feet completely. I do my best to fight. Kick. Scream. But with each passing second, every movement gets ten times harder than it should be. My limbs feel too heavy, weighted down...

I'm so dizzy.

"Damn, the shit's already kicking in," one of the men says, sounding garbled as if I'm hearing him from underwater. "Help me get her into the truck."

Suddenly, the air changes, feeling cooler on my skin. I can hear the faint sounds of distant traffic, but it's nothing like the roar of the city. Somewhere on the outskirts of Westpoint? But where?

Before I can comprehend what's happening, I land on a hard surface, and the air whooshes from my lungs. A thud echoes like that of a car door slamming, and then the world lurches forward.

My ears ring. I can't even tell up from down, and the strange sensation weighing me down becomes stronger. Bit by bit, I feel my consciousness seeping away.

Until everything goes black.

The air feels so heavy. Every breath takes monumental effort, and I give up trying to open my eyes within seconds—but I'm not alone. Nearby, someone gasps.

"Praise be," they exclaim with audible relief. "She's waking up."

"Yes," a man agrees, his tone grave. "Praise be to the Lord."

That voice. The low cadence sends a shockwave through my entire body. It's...wrong. Untrustworthy. As hard as I wrack my brain, I can't come up with a name yet. Everything is groggy. Blurry.

I try again to open my eyes and only manage to crack them halfway. Through a sliver of blinding light, I can't make out much. Just formless shadows and bright, painful white.

"Frances? Can you hear me?" Someone gently grasps my hand, squeezing each finger one by one. They feel warm, their touch persistent. Still, some part of me internally cringes. I don't like it.

After a few more attempts at blinking, my blurred vision finally clears up enough to make out the face of someone sitting next to me. Colton? He looks exhausted, his hair tousled, his usually neat button-up shirt wrinkled. Framing him is a backdrop of pristinely white walls. Alarm jolts through me, giving me the strength to sit up. This room doesn't look like it belongs in my apartment or even my father's uptown house.

Except for a narrow bed I'm lying on, a tray table, and two plastic-looking recliners, it's sterile and mostly empty. On one of the chairs sits a figure whose face is obscured, but I recognize his tall, lean shape right away.

Father. Seeing him makes my chest tighten. It's as if, overnight, my body reclassified him from a neutral authority figure to...

Someone dangerous. A man who smiles warmly at me even though he knows exactly why I'm here—I remember that much. Silas taunted me—*Play your role, little girl*. My newest stage is a hospital room, I realize once I get both eyes open. Panic has me glancing down, scanning what little of my body is exposed above a light-blue blanket. My legs kick out on command, and my arms react the same way. Thank goodness.

"You're okay," Colton says, stroking the length of my forearm. "Apart from this, anyway—" He gestures toward my left eye. It feels sore when I blink. Something hit me? No, *someone*. Silas. "And a few minor scrapes and bruises. The doctors say you'll be fine. No long-term damage."

I try to speak. "What... What happened?" My mouth is so dry I can barely muster up a hoarse whisper.

"You were attacked. The police are doing their best to track down who did this," my father says, his voice as commanding as ever. I turn to see him approach my bedside. My breath catches as his features come into view, his eyes hooded. "They will be punished to the full extent of the law. I can promise you that."

"What were you even doing in that part of town?" Colton asks, still gripping my hand. "You should have told me if you were going to do outreach on your own. I would have—"

"I think Frances needs some rest," my father insists. His stance is polite enough, but there is no mistaking the authority in his voice. Instantly, Colton sits back, wringing his hands together.

"Yes... Of course," he mumbles, eyeing the floor.

"The doctors say she will be released tomorrow," Father continues. "Colton, you can visit her then. I think I speak for us all when I say that home is the best place for her right now."

"Yes." Colton nods in deference before he stands and moves toward the door. "I will visit you tomorrow, Frances."

The second he's out of view, Father steps closer to the head of the bed, his hands clasped behind him. "You've been through quite the ordeal, Frances," he says. His expression is so utterly blank. I can't tell even a hint of what he's thinking. Doubt starts to sneak in among the pain and fear clamoring for attention in my skull. What if I was wrong and he isn't the vicious monster Hale and Daze seem to believe he is?

There isn't time to waste, either way. I run my tongue along my lower lip. "F-Father—"

"You should rest," he says over me, raising a graying eyebrow. "I've held off the investigators for now. You can talk to them tomorrow once your recollections are clearer. Do you remember anything?" A rare note of hesitation creeps into his voice, and alarm bells go off in the back of my mind.

If Daze were here, I know what he'd say—*Lie.*

"No." I shake my head. "It's all so blurry…"

I slump into the pillows behind me for emphasis and watch his reaction to every word I've said. The strange part is how normal he seems. Standing tall, with his stern frown, he appears the way he always has—as the strict, guiding force in my life, never to be challenged. His blue eyes don't betray a hint of malice.

But as the seconds tick by, I realize something else that raises the hairs on the back of my neck.

There's no warmth in them, either.

"That's to be expected." He nods and takes my hand, clasping both of his around it. "You had us worried for a moment. If anything happened to you... I don't know what I would do."

"I'm sorry," I croak.

"I should be the one who apologizes. With everything going on, I haven't done my duty as your father. That changes now —" He pats the back of my hand, but each seemingly reassuring blow is harder than the last. "Starting tomorrow, you will return home. I want you at Covenant more, by my side where you belong."

His directives sound eerily like what Silas ordered me to do. Be the good daughter. Smile. Preen. I bite the inside of my lip so hard I taste copper—anything to suppress my reaction. I can't let him know that I'm uneasy.

Thinking fast, I try to change the subject. "I'm so tired..."

"You were drugged," Father explains. "The doctors aren't sure with what, but it should be out of your system soon. You are safe, my child."

But I don't feel very safe.

I feel trapped.

Compounding that feeling is a commotion near the doorway to my room. A new figure attempts to cross the threshold only to be stopped by an officer—I hadn't noticed until now —standing guard. While the cop appears stiff and serious, the other man, dressed in dark-blue scrubs, seems very relaxed and along for the ride. He's slender, with a friendly, disarming smile that contrasts sharply with the calculation flashing in his eyes as the guard inspects the plastic food tray he's carrying. Just as quickly as the serious look came, it's gone before the officer glances back up to usher him into the room.

As he nears, I take him in fully. He's wiry with black mussed hair and a baby face. He looks barely older than I am, but judging from how his clothing clings to his frame, he's all muscle.

"Her dinner is here," he says tersely, his gaze on Father.

"You may bring it to her," Father commands, unsurprised by the arrival. To my questioning look, he says, "From now on, you will be protected at all times. Frankly, I should have arranged a security detail for you sooner."

"S-Security detail?" I stiffen in alarm as the orderly steps in front of Father to place the tray on a side table and arrange it over my lap. Before he withdraws, he notices me eyeing his badge and the name and photo displayed—Jet. When I look up at his brown eyes, he pointedly looks at the tray he's positioned in front of me. Is he trying to tell me something? Before I can question him, he's stepping back.

"Enjoy your meal," he says while eyeing the tray as he walks backward toward the door before retreating into the hall. I turn my focus back to Father and his demand for guards.

"I don't... Is that really necessary?"

"Necessary?" Father's voice deepens, and a sense of foreboding washes over me. I'm on dangerous ground. "Keeping you safe is my main priority," he says. "Never again will I forsake that duty. Try to eat. I will discuss your discharge with the doctors. Excuse me."

He leaves, closing the door behind him, and I deflate, utterly confused.

Did you think your little disappearances had gone unnoticed? Silas had taunted.

This was as sure a sign as any that he hadn't been bluffing. For whatever reason, he conspired with my father. To what aim?

Desperate for a distraction, I inspect the food tray, finding nothing appealing. I start to push it away, but it doesn't slide the way it should. Puzzled, I lift the edge of it and find a bulky slip of paper taped to the underside. This must be why the orderly, Jet, kept staring at the tray. Did he leave this note behind?

My fingers tremble as I peel it off. Somehow, I doubt it's a menu displaying tomorrow's meal choices. Sure enough, as I unfold it, a block of unfamiliar handwriting spells out a simple, blunt message—*Daze is alive. Stay put. He'll come for you.*

FOUR

DAZE

SILAS IS MANY THINGS, but brave isn't one of them. He spent most of my old man's tenure bitching from the sidelines, but he never had the balls to step up. If anything, this past year proves how incompetent he truly is. Despite finally having the control he craves, you'd never know it from the outside looking in. The coward keeps close to Saints' territory and never makes a move without a handful of boys to back him up. This newest partnership with Heywood only proves how much of a coward he truly is—too chickenshit to take over the city on his own. He needs a puppet master to put a battery in his back. On its face, him barging into my apartment could have been a brazen move to show he's stepped up his game.

I know better. I know *him*. Like any cornered animal, Silas becomes reckless when backed against the wall. Something has him spooked, and I'd bet my ass that it has everything to do with his deal with the devil. The dumb son of a bitch has gotten himself in deep.

Any other time I'd sit back and watch him burn...

If it weren't for Frey. It would have been easy for me to write off the entire Heywood clan before she came along. Even Hale had turned his back on them, desperate enough to beg an ex-con for help. It hurt him just to mention his sister's name. I think he blamed her for failing to see what he had so clearly.

Now that I have a new perspective, I realize the truth is much more complicated than he thought. Frey isn't callous, and she isn't stupid, either.

She's too damn good. Someone too pure to even begin to fathom the shit her father is responsible for. The lies she's lived under. The danger she's really in.

Not that I'm some hero. No, I let her walk around in blissful ignorance, too damn selfish to let her in on the big bad secret everyone except her knows. Without batting an eyelash, I looked her dead in the eye and lied to her.

I'd do it all over again, too.

In my defense, she can't stomach the truth that her family has more skeletons in their closet than mine does—and that's saying something. It would break her to know the harsh reality. The thought of those pretty green eyes hollowed out with pain guts me. Maybe it's the soul I didn't realize I still had. Whatever the source of the emotion is, she alone calls to it like a goddamn siren. It's strange. I've never felt this way about anyone.

As if thinking of her conjured an update, my phone lights with a text from Damien. *My boy found your girl. She's at the hospital, but security is tight—the dad's got a guard on her 24/7. We got word to her that you're ok. Stay back for now. Will keep you posted.*

Thank fuck. Somehow, I'll make it up to Frey for having her dragged into this shit. As I type a reply of thanks to Damien, I hear a rustling outside.

"Daze?" The side door to the gym opens, letting in a mixture of fresh air and gray daylight. I tense, but before I can lurch into a defensive stance, Ben inches inside, his expression wary. "You in here?"

I go limp with a sigh and call out. "Over here."

His slow, cautious movements tell me what he's thinking. *How much has he drunk to sound this shitty?* When he spots me near the practice mat, his eyes narrow, and he stalks forward, his hands in fists. "You crazy son of a bitch. I figured I might find you here, which means Silas won't be too far behind me. Do you have any idea how badly he's gunning for you now? A smarter man than you would have already skipped town. Instead, you're here like a sitting duck."

He comes within striking distance only to back down.

"Shit, Daze… You look like hell."

"Feel like it, too," I say, pressing a wet towel to my skull. It's all I could find by way of first aid. Without a pretty blond to patch me up, I know I should be worried about long-term damage. A concussion definitely—maybe worse. Still, I don't feel half as concerned as Ben seems to be. He spins on his heel and starts hunting for a roll of paper towels he tosses to me.

"Shit, you need to put ice on that or something. Where the fuck have you been, anyway?" he snarls while marching around, rummaging through the scattered equipment until he finds a bottle of water that he also throws my way. "I tried calling you." He looks at me questioningly while I re-read Damien's update for the umpteenth time. If he did try to call me, I must have missed it. When I say nothing, he continues, "Then Chris got a hold of me and said I should keep an eye on you. That Silas is on the warpath. I was shitting bricks, worried about your ass, only to find you lounging in here—"

"You seem riled up, Ben," I say, manipulating the paper towels into a makeshift rag. I wet the wad with water from the bottle and dab blindly at my skull. It doesn't do shit to lessen the pain, but hell, it's better than nothing. "Riled up, more so than usual, I mean."

"Riled up?" He looks at me the way I figure I'd look at him were he in my shoes—like I'm a fucking idiot. "Very Funny. Is that your idea of a joke? Daze, I'm sure you realized since you've had her hanging onto you since day one, but your little girlfriend? Her face is plastered all over the news right now—"

"What are they saying?" My head shoots up. Damien mentioned a hospital, but what if Silas wanted to make his point crystal clear by attacking her again—she was always collateral damage.

"Calm down," Ben says, shooting me an odd look. "She's alive, from what I heard. Basically, they're using her as the poster child for the 'rising crime in Westpoint.' If you ask me, she didn't seem unwilling to be with you. What the fuck happened?"

Shit. If Silas let this get into the press, he was either sloppy as hell, or that was part of his plan all along. It's a clever move on Heywood's part. He can rally the city to his cause after yet another family tragedy and demand his daughter's loyalty through fear.

The funny part? I could have prevented all of this... Like a dumbass, I was too chickenshit to tell her the whole truth. Making it up to her solves only half of the mess this new dilemma presents. Frey got taken, but who else might have been in on the plan?

I hate the doubt that gnaws at me as I cast Ben a searching look. He's dressed in jeans and a jacket, as if he just got off the truck—overtime would be a fitting excuse for why he wasn't there when I got jumped. Not a very convincing one, though.

To stall for time, I refocus on my cell phone and flip through the stream of call notifications. What a coincidence—Ben hadn't lied about trying to reach me, but he only started roughly an hour after I got my ass handed to me.

"You asked me what happened," I echo coldly, my eyes on the screen. "You mean you weren't there?"

"Of course, I wasn't!" He's frowning when I look up. "What the hell are you talking about?"

"Well, you live two doors down, Ben," I say. In my voice, I can hear the anger I don't fully feel. Based on appearances alone, many men would jump to conclusions without giving Ben a chance to explain himself. That being said, most men haven't put up with my shit as long as he has. Maybe that earns him the benefit of the doubt—but not by much. In any case, he's lucky I'm too busy holding my own skull together to take a swing at his.

So, I settle for asking outright, "Do you really want me to believe you didn't see Silas and his men barge into my fucking apartment and take her this morning?"

"Shit, Daze..." He steps back, his hands at his sides. Thank fuck, his confusion doesn't seem fake. "Like hell, I knew about that! I went out in the truck earlier than usual. I didn't think... He really came onto your turf? I thought you two had a truce or something—"

"Had," I echo through clenched teeth. My makeshift compress has gotten too dry to be much use. I toss it aside and snatch another handful of paper towels. One-handed, I keep manipulating the cell phone—there's a notification for a new text message from Damien. I open our conversation thread while saying to Ben, "I should have known better than to think the bastard would honor his word."

As it turns out, I can still trust a handful of men. Damien has another update it seems, sending a text that simply reads— *Doctors say she'll be fine. They're discharging her from the hospital in the morning. Under heavy guard. Will update.*

How relieved I feel just reading those words catches me by surprise. I have to bite my lip to suppress the emotion before looking up to meet Ben's gaze. Do I still trust him? Hell yeah —when it comes to my life, at least. Regarding Frey, he seems skeptical, rightfully so. I'll have to play my cards right to convince him she's worth protecting.

"Silas has become too big of a threat to ignore anymore," I say carefully. To Damien, I type—*Let me know where we can meet up.*

"Ya think?" Ben shoots me an odd look. "Playing devil's advocate, you haven't been too nice on your end of the truce, either. Didn't you beat one of his men to death the other day?"

A fair point, not that I'm in the mood to go over that now. "The shit he just pulled is the last straw. No more Mr. Nice."

"Big words for someone who looks like he got his ass kicked to hell and back." Always honest to a fault, Ben leans against the wall, his head cocked at an angle. "But you aren't one to make idle threats, Day. Just what are you saying?"

"I'm *asking*..." I toss the now-bloodied paper towels aside and stare him down. "Can I count on you, Ben?"

"Something tells me you don't mean 'count on me' to get you some Band-Aids the next time Silas comes after you."

"No. I'm saying..." There's no beating around the bush anymore. "I know you technically aren't a Saint, but you've stayed on Silas' good side until now. Does that mean that when push comes to shove, you'll stand with him over me?"

"Do you even have to ask?" Ben raises an eyebrow and steps from the wall. "What the fuck is that supposed to mean, anyway?"

I just shrug. "It means, are you with me or not?"

"You must not know me at all, Day. Who else has been by your side all this fucking time, even if it meant getting pushed out too?"

"You," I admit. "I just need to be clear. With what I'm planning... If you're still on my side, I don't think Silas will see you as a neutral party any longer. You'll be deep in the thick of it, Ben. There's no going back. If you don't want any part of that shit, I won't hold it against you—"

"You always were a dumb son of a bitch," Ben snarls, curling a fist. Rather than strike me with it, he presses it to the nearest wall and sighs. "I've been with you from the jump. If you're finally going to take on Silas like you should have done the second you got out of lockup, you bet your ass I'll be there. The fact that you could even think I wouldn't... You've become that damn paranoid, Day?"

"Maybe," I admit, but Ben's vote of confidence has robbed the suspicion from my voice. "I wouldn't blame you if you did turn your back on me. You were right. I've played nice too damn long. No more. Not after what he's just done."

"Stealing your little girlfriend, you mean?" His grunt of annoyance proves just what he thinks of that insinuation. "Trust *that* to be what tips you over the edge—him messing with your dick, and not your pride, your livelihood, your reputation—"

"You think this is funny?" I snap. Though hell, if anyone has the right to crack a joke, it's probably Ben. After all, he's one of the few who stood beside me when I lost everything he just so casually listed out.

"Yeah," he snaps back. "I find it *funny* that your change of heart happened because of some girl, and not because Silas has been strutting all over town like he owns the city you and your dad practically built from scratch. Not because he stabbed you in the fucking back, destroyed your life, and nearly got you thrown in prison. Not because he sold you out to Michael Heywood on a silver platter and let you take the fall for his screw-up. Yeah. Whatever floats your fucking boat, I guess. At least you're done wallowing in misery and ready to do something about it."

Some girl. I don't know why the way he says those words irritates the hell out of me. Could be that anyone else would have taken one look at me and gone running. Anyone but her. She flitted around like a moth drawn to a flame, sizzling alive without realizing it. She had no fucking clue about the damage her family has done to me.

The damage I'd fantasized about doing to her in return. Before I knew her, that is. Before I felt her soft hands on my skin and heard her delicate voice whisper three words without understanding the power they have—*I trust you.*

Frances Heywood isn't just some girl.

"Earth to Daze," Ben calls, snapping his fingers. "It isn't like you're a wanted man or anything. Or is fantasizing about your little romance more appealing than staying alive—"

"It isn't like that," I grunt out. "She isn't the only reason."

"Though she is a big damn part of it," Ben interjects. "For more reasons than you've told her, I bet."

Damn it, he's right. Why is that?

I've had more women than I care to remember. Tough as nails broads who grew up on the outskirts of the Saints and outfits like it. They knew what they were getting into by fucking with me. They knew the risks and were always angling to hop to the next man with power the second I lost mine.

Frey comes from a different world than they had—and for that reason, she possesses one trait few people do. Innocence. Her perception of people is limited to the surface level. What they pretend to be—the stray bits of goodness they might have left over after a lifetime of wallowing in shit. It's all she sees, and she is blind to everything else.

It doesn't hurt that I've only told her a fraction of the truth. A shitty part of me doesn't want to come clean yet, either. I enjoy that soulful way she looks at me too damn much. It only takes one glance from her for a man to forget what a bastard he is. In a strange way, that has power. She can make someone rethink the choices they thought were their only options before.

Even me.

"Mock me all you want. You're right. I walked away from everything I had once," I tell Ben, craning my neck to find him watching me, still skeptical. "I thought then I was doing the right thing. Now? I see what a fucking fool I'd been—"

"You wanted what was best for your kid, Day," he admits, staring down at the floor. "What was best for all of us. I know that."

"Maybe," I concede. "But now I see that what's best for Sam is having his dad in a position powerful enough to protect him from anyone. Silas. Heywood. Anyone."

Ben whistles through his teeth. "It sounds like you're talking about more than just clawing back a few pieces of territory, Daze. Are you saying what I think you're saying?"

"You're damn right," I hiss through gritted teeth. "I'm talking about taking over the city. But not with the Saints. It's time for me to step out and start something new."

"You mean a new outfit, all on your own." He runs his thumb along his chin—this isn't what he expected to hear. "You would really walk away from the Saints for good? Walk away from everything your old man built?"

"Yes," I reply without an ounce of hesitation. "I'm not him. I never should have pretended to be. If I'm going to do this, it'll be my way. On my terms."

To his credit, Ben doesn't laugh outright. I'm not sure I'd have the same restraint if I were in his place. Instead, he sighs again. "That's ballsy of you. Where are you going to get the men, land, let alone collateral to do something like that?"

A strange thought worms into my skull—if Frey were here, she'd probably suggest something innocent like pray, or hold hands, or some shit.

Looking Ben dead in the eye, I voice the truth. "Via any means necessary. We don't have the time to dabble in politics. Silas needs taking down a peg yesterday."

"Okay. Now we're talking." He swallows hard as both of his eyebrows shoot up. "How in the fuck do you plan on doing something like that?"

"I'll worry about the details later." I shrug, waving off the question. "For now, I need a favor. Frey... You said you saw her on the news. What else are they saying? Anything about the Saints being involved?"

Deep down, a part of me wants to pretend that I know the full extent of what Silas is capable of—but I don't. After all, he let his own sister be used as collateral damage. The truth is, he'd take pleasure in crushing a girl like Frey.

I hate to admit it, but there are plenty of ways he could, too. Threats. A beating. Worse...

"If he hurt her," I start, seeing red, "I'll fucking kill him."

"Slow your roll, Day. Damn." Ben winces and raises his hands in a placating gesture. "Chill. From what I saw, they're spinning it as a botched blackmail attempt, but she's in the hospital."

"About to be discharged in the morning," I say, thinking out loud. Damien's intel was solid. Good. "They'll probably take her home after."

To Heywood's private estate. I know the place, and I doubt there's been time for them to ramp up security too much. A good disguise and a few keywords might be enough to get me in. And if not... I'll improvise. No matter what, the second Damien sends word that she's home, I'm there.

"That sounds like more than just a lucky guess," Ben surmises. He looks me over and scoffs. "Oh no. I know that look, Day. Hold up. You wouldn't be stupid enough to think you can waltz up to that place with a damn get well soon card? They'll shoot your ass on sight. Not only that, but Silas won't let you get close to his newest moneymaker. Not twice."

Probably. Is a bullet to the skull preferable to not knowing if Frey's okay? Maybe.

"Waltzing in wasn't exactly my plan," I admit, cocking my head his way. "But do you still have that cousin who does security for that nightclub?"

"Why?" Ben raises an eyebrow. "What the hell are you planning?"

"Something fucking stupid. If you want no part in it, I'd understand—"

"You're a crazy bastard, but..." He holds my gaze for a long time. Then he exhales, shaking his head. "I owe it to ya, for what happened with Silas. You were right. I should have been there."

"Good." This part of my plan is going better than expected, at least. Then I look down and realize I'm still wearing a pair of bloodstained sweats. Definitely not an ensemble that would impress the Heywood household. "Well, first, I'm gonna need some new clothes."

"That's not all you'll need," Ben says. "If you find your little girlfriend, you need to figure out what the hell you'll tell her. That is, if Silas didn't beat you to the punch already. She's naïve, but I think it won't be long before she puts the pieces together. Like that you know far more about her father than you've let on, and you've been stringing her along all this time—"

"Silas sure does love his vengeful fairy tales," I agree. Hell, the bastard wouldn't even need to feed her lies to turn her against me. I think I've been avoiding the possibility all this fucking time—and the reality is I didn't hold back the truth entirely out of concern, either.

I've gotten used to that reverent way she looks at me. Sooner or later, her sweet little expressions are gonna turn to hate.

Am I ready for that?

Hell no, I'm not.

"I'll think of something," I say, more so to myself than to Ben.

"You better," he counters. "Something better than the truth, at least. Maybe then you'd have a shot in hell that she'd ever forgive you."

"Maybe." Don't know if I believe it, though.

It's just after noon when I set out, leaving Ben behind. Waiting for the hospital to release Frey was torture. I feel exposed as hell, moving out in the open like a sitting fucking duck. Luckily for me, I'm well beyond Silas' territory, though the well-manicured lawns and sprawling mansions around me seem more sinister than the seediest parts of Westpoint.

This is Frey's world—a pretty, gilded cage in the uptown section of the city, far from the riffraff of the lower side.

Honestly, I'd rather be in hell. Teeth gritted, I keep one eye on my phone—re-reading the text I got from Damien an hour ago with a nearby address—while keeping the other peeled for any trouble. When I near the secured entrance of some fancy gated community, I hear a lone whistle ride the air.

It comes from the direction of a small security shack by the gate's entrance. Square and squat with blacked-out windows, it's probably where Heywood has part of his guard duty stationed to monitor the traffic coming in and out. Shit. I keep my head lowered and attempt to keep walking.

I've barely gone a step when the whistle comes again. Followed by a gruff, "Daze, you dumb motherfucker. Over here."

My head jerks up, and I'm instantly more alert—luckily, the intimidating figure who steps out into view from behind the shack isn't wearing the typical security guard attire. Damien. I lope toward him and spy the open door of the hut. Inside are two other men who look as far from capable of upholding the law as I figure I do.

"Damien, you crazy son of a bitch," I address the smirking figure leaning against the shack's entrance, dressed head to toe in camo. Behind him, one man sits with his feet propped against a desk covered in coffee cups and old donuts while another crouches in the corner, his back to me. The scent of copper mingles with the overpowering aroma of fresh coffee. I know that smell. Fuck.

"So much for being subtle," I say. "Damien—"

"No real names," the man at the desk scolds, his almond-shaped brown eyes narrowing. He runs a hand through his jagged black hair, brushing it off his round face. "We agreed. Though, fuck. I guess we're breaking all the rules today. You Daze?"

I nod, but my attention is on the third man who stands, wiping his hands on the front of his fatigues. His brown hair's been shaven close to his head, his amber eyes sharp as they inspect his ruined disguise. The simple attire is similar to Damien's—only he has a smear of red where his hands have touched. Behind him, the poor bastard, I assume is the real security guard, lies slumped on his side, bleeding from his nose.

"Got the intel we needed," the third man says, turning to face me fully. "This dumb fucker told me he's due to swap out with another guard and patrol the house. That's your cover, and your way in. I bought us an hour tops. We should move."

"So much for keeping shit contained, Damien," I say, grimacing at the body. "What the fuck?"

"Relax," the man standing instructs. "He's just knocked out."

"Lex. Kane. This is Daze," Damien says curtly, nodding in my direction.

"I know who he is," the man called Lex says, flexing his shoulders. "I've heard of that gym of yours back in the day. Damien says you had his back in lockup. If you weren't the one beating on that psychotic son of a bitch, that makes you alright in my book." He chuckles and swings his feet from the desk, planting them on the floor. In a fluid motion, he stands, moving with an easy grace I recognize. Compact and wiry, he's the smallest of the three. If I met him in my fighting days, I'd know better than to underestimate him based on size alone. Though, compared to the hulking man behind him, he seems barely a hundred pounds wet. He must be the tracker Damien told me about, which means the tall man—Kane—is the ex-marine. I can't get a gauge on him. His face reveals nothing as he watches me, his head at an angle.

Damien clears his throat. "Daze, Lex and Kane, also known as Jet and Hellion in the ring. Lex's the one who got to your girl. Nice and fucking clean."

I look the black-haired man over, impressed. "Thanks."

"No problem. Well then." Lex heads for the door. "Now that we got that shit out of the way, let's get this show on the fucking road."

Thinking of Frey, I just nod. "Let's do this."

On a plot of land near the back of this gated community, Heywood is sure living fucking large. Considering how deep his ties to organized crime must go, he should be. Unfortunately, his stolen money and increasing paranoia doesn't make my job any easier.

He has at least ten guards out in the open, swarming around the house like bees in a hive.

"Damn." Lex whistles through his teeth as we scope the gated property from the backyard of an empty estate nearby. He rakes a hand through his hair, his smile feral. "These rich bastards must piss in a gold fucking toilet." He scoffs at a carved statue of an elephant posted near the edge of a marble patio.

I have to agree with him. The bastards who own this place must be on vacation, but they have a fortune almost as big as Heywood's. It took all of Kane's skill to hack the security system so we could infiltrate the backyard unnoticed. From here, it's merely a skip, hop, and a jump over a perimeter fence to enter the Heywood property from behind.

I grit my teeth, picturing Frey behind those pretty, fancy walls. Lex said she looked okay, though bruised. *Fuck*. The need to see her gnaws away at the logical part of my brain that knows stealth is called for now. Barging in guns blazing won't help anyone.

"Let's split up here," I suggest. "I'll go in. You guys wait for me along the back fence and make sure the coast is clear."

"Got it," Lex replies. "Just make sure none of those assholes look at you too closely." He eyes my uniform with a frown.

Ben came through, and his cousin was able to secure me a security uniform—the downside is that said uniform is navy blue. Heywood's security, on the other hand, seems to prefer black. Oh, fucking well.

I flash a smile. "I've been known to charm my way out of a shitstorm or two. Don't worry."

"We'll be here just in case," Damien says, though it comes across more like a warning. The look in his eyes warns that he's craving the worst-case scenario.

But I doubt Frey would think much of me if I left a few dead bodies on her doorstep.

"Let's go," I say, starting forward.

After scaling the wrought iron fence separating the two properties, I'm on the outskirts of Heywood's mansion, and no one seems the wiser. Relief is the last thing I feel. Infiltrating the compound should be harder than this. The suspicion itches at me as I crouch behind a row of hedges and advance toward a fancy-looking pool at the back of the house.

If Michael Heywood truly intended to protect his daughter, I wouldn't be able to grab a spare uniform and waltz right through their backyard. Either the bastard has gotten sloppy, or his impending election win has him believing he's untouchable.

Or, he doesn't give a shit about protecting Frey. His only goal, in fact, is to keep her locked inside.

In any case, I'm more than ready to ruin the motherfucker's day.

"...area clear." Static from a radio draws my attention to the hedges on my left. With a wary glance around, I stand upright and approach, hoping like hell I blend in enough to avoid a second glance.

When I round a curve in the gravel pathway lining this section of the yard, I find the source of the commotion just a few paces away.

Damien, Lex, and Kane stand out of view, monitoring this poor excuse for security as they patrol the grounds. It's strange, watching the three interact together. They all seem calm as hell, as if breaking into a guarded fortress undetected is second nature to them.

"Hey." Kane observes the device in Damien's hand with a raised eyebrow. "Where'd you get the radio?"

Damien shrugs, his eyes glittering. "Pulled it off a guard. Here, listen—" He angles the radio so that the sound from it is clearer.

"Outer perimeter clear," a man says, his voice garbled by more static. "Inner perimeter, clear."

"You hear that, Day?" he asks, his eyes on me.

I nod. "Yeah." Apparently, the guards have a system of verbally checking in after a few rounds of patrols. Interesting.

"If you guys stay here and listen in, you can give me the all-clear," I say, feeling my upper lip quirk. Maybe breaking in to save this princess won't be as hard as I thought. "Smart thinking, Damien."

Kane chuckles. "But who did you steal it from?"

"And what happened to not drawing any attention?" Lex adds.

"Who said I did?" Damien brushes off their concern with another shrug. "Now, are we doing this shit or not?"

"Oh, we are doing this," I say, narrowing my eyes with the house in view. "Now tell me when the fuck I can go in."

"Alright," Damien starts as we observe two men passing by. "As soon as these fuckheads pass on their next round, you should be good to make it through the rear door. We'll hang back here and monitor the radio transmissions for trouble."

"Copy." I adjust my cap and put on my dark shades as I wait for my opening to stroll in. The thought of Frey is all I can seem to think about. Her beautiful face. The sound of her voice. The feeling of her small, delicate body against mine.

She's so close, I can almost feel her.

And I'll fight like hell to get her back.

FIVE

FREY

"WE'RE HOME," Father declares in the gravelly voice usually reserved for his sermons.

I look over, unable to suppress a shiver. *Home.* Just a few months ago, that word had such a different connotation it brings tears to my eyes. Once, it meant safety. Joy. A haven from the cruel world rivaled in purity only by my father's church.

Now...? The beautiful Victorian-style dwelling in the heart of the city's affluent district resembles something colder and more unfeeling. It isn't until we pull into the driveway that an actual term comes to mind, though—a jail cell.

Or a prison.

"It's good to have you back," Father continues from his position beside me. He has my hand clasped in both of his, and I can't stop looking from the house, down to my trembling fingers, swallowed in his grasp. Lost in grief over Hale, I had barely noticed the various ways his campaign had changed our lives.

Now, there is no hiding from them. One of the many differences is Father himself, and how vainly he's cultivated his public image. Gone is the modest preacher of Salvation who sometimes frequented public transport when Hale and I were children. Lately, he's taken to being chauffeured in an expensive SUV composed of a gray steel exterior and a spacious, dark leather interior. Dressed in a matching shade, Father sits beside me, and across from us are his trusted advisor and a man I assume to be a bodyguard. Both eye me sternly without any trace of warmth.

"I've decided that you don't need to speak to the investigators after all," Father says. "Following the doctor's suggestion, you will rest here until a press conference next week. The police can interview you then. I've made the arrangements."

"Oh?" My shock is feigned. I'm not surprised by the shifting timeline. His sudden "protectiveness" tracks with what Silas warned me would happen. Any taste of freedom I once had is long over.

After all, what need is there for me to speak with the police? Father has already gotten exactly what he needed from my supposed kidnapping—an eye-grabbing headline. On the drive here, I didn't miss the throng of reporters stationed outside our gated community, desperate for a glimpse of me, freshly released from the hospital.

"What if they need my help to find the culprits?" I ask, making my expression as wide-eyed as I can.

Father doesn't even look my way. "Every officer in the city is out looking. You can believe they will find the monsters soon enough. I hear they already have a suspect."

"Did they say who?" I croak.

He angles his head to shoot me a penetrating glance. "Some criminal, I'm sure," he says. "You look exhausted, sweetheart. Go inside and rest. Catherine will help you settle in."

"You aren't coming?"

"No." He faces forward and motions for the driver to open the door on my end. "I need to see to it personally that what happened to you will never happen again." His voice takes on a malicious tone I've never heard before. "I'll be speaking with the police commissioner personally to devise a joint statement about this savage attack. You will be there, of course. This city will soon learn what happens to those who dare to touch the anointed."

"A statement," I echo.

One that will no doubt be televised and designed to use my ordeal for the maximum impact on his campaign. Suddenly, that conversation with Silas feels less like a delirious nightmare and more...

Like an awful truth I don't have the space of mind to process at the moment. Instead, like a meek little lamb, I allow myself to be led inside, where my stepmother, Catherine, lurks near the door, wringing her fingers together.

"Oh, Frances, we were so worried! I'm so glad you're okay." She throws her slender arms around me, and it's apparent that we're the same height. In fact, Catherine is only a few years older than me, barely twenty-nine. She looks exhausted, though her hair is perfectly coifed in the ringlets I know my father prefers for her to wear. They make her look angelic and beautiful in his shadow, a quiet accessory to such a powerful politician.

For the first time, it hits me that the same descriptor might have applied to me all this time.

"Frances?"

"Huh?" I blink to find Catherine watching me.

"I said that I had your bed prepared for you," she explains before heading up the stairs. Slung around her waist is a delicate pink apron that she wipes her hands on. "Your father has had most of your stuff already brought over from your apartment, but I think he would prefer for you to wear the clothes you left here. There are some lovely pajamas. Do you need me to help you?"

She skips to my side and guides me up the stairs while prattling on about my freshly-stocked closet. "...and here we are!"

We're poised just outside the charming, beautifully decorated bedroom I'd grown up in. For a horrifying second, I wonder if I have a more serious concussion than the doctors feared. I don't even recognize the pink walls and elegant furniture. It looks like the perfect furnishings of a dollhouse, meant to be admired but never lived in.

"Get some rest, sweetheart," Catherine chirps before kissing my cheek. "We're both very glad to have you home—"

Suddenly, a man dressed in black rounds the hall from the direction of the master bedroom. With a curt nod toward Catherine, he heads down the stairs and out the front door.

"Oh, and don't mind all these strangers wandering around," she says with a nervous laugh. The way she tugs at the sleeve of her charming sweater reveals just how uneasy she is. "Your father was already paranoid about security, and after what happened... I'm surprised we don't have the SWAT team camping on our lawn. Well, here is your room, just as you left it, though I did tidy up a bit." Awkwardly, she gestures to the open doorway.

Cleanliness aside, this room looks just as I left it—minus the strewn clothing I know I dumped all over the floor in my fog after Hale's death. I barely remember those disjointed few weeks. Returning here after learning what I know now feels different than I thought it would—it's suffocating. I can't breathe without the weight of the memories threatening to weigh me down. The strange part is that not all of them have to do with Hale.

Daze is a new painful figure on my psyche. I can't stop seeing his face—or hearing the sound he made when Silas struck him. God, I pray he's okay, like the note on my tray claimed. If he isn't...

I don't think I can stomach that. I really don't.

I can't even re-read the message for reassurance. Out of an abundance of caution, I threw it away and prayed my father or his men didn't find it. For all I know, Daze could have written it himself. As things stand, I probably won't hear from him ever again.

My throat feels so tight that I approach one of the windows to get some air. One glance from it, and I better understand what Catherine meant. Father didn't merely increase our security. He's turned our home into a fortress.

Our usually serene backyard has been overrun by at least three men dressed in black who walk near the perimeter on guard and alert. My heart sinks watching them. Judging from their orderly patrol of the yard, it becomes clear that securing the house isn't their only missive. One of the men keeps looking directly toward my room. Toward me. A black baseball cap obscures most of his features, and a pair of sunglasses cover his eyes. I can't even tell his hair color from here.

Something in his stance unnerves me, though. He doesn't move like the others, who mainly keep to the perimeter of the gardens and pool. He stays closer to the house, his head tilted upward, his gaze fixed on my window.

I shudder and back away, out of sight. First Silas, then my father, and now this. I toy with the idea of trying to leave anyway. Maybe even begging my father to let me return to my apartment. I might even be desperate enough to ask Colton to put in a good word for me.

Or...

I'm being the naïve, stupid idiot that both Hale and Daze accused me of being. To Daze's credit, he made it seem like a good thing. A...sexy thing—though even utilizing the word as he did makes me feel strange. Hot all over. Too suffocated to stay in this room.

When I retreat to the hall, I feel a twinge on the back of my neck—as if the stranger below is still watching me. *Focus, Frey. Paranoia won't help you now.* With a stern shake of my head, I struggle to push him and everything else from my mind. Lord, I need to think. Aimlessly, I find myself in my father's study, pacing before a view of the front walkway. He doesn't use this room much anymore, preferring to operate from his office in the Covenant building though he publicly stepped down as the Shepherd.

Once upon a time, these four walls contained the heart of the home. My brother and I would play in here or spend the evenings studying at our father's feet. He was different in those days. Less concerned with image and mainly focused on the joy of reciting scripture.

Mother had been happier, too, back then, at least for the most part. She used to pop in and out to read us various stories and bring us warm milk to drink. Goodness, those memories sting. I swipe at my eyes as I approach the desk and run my fingers across the polished surface.

I'd give anything to go back to that time. Back when she was here. Anything...

Even the memories I have of her are fragile, hard to recall. I remember that she used to find me here when it was time for bed and would walk me back to my room, humming all the while. Retracing those steps now, I try to recall her voice as I cross the threshold.

"Ready for bedtime, sweetheart?"

The truth is, despite those small gestures, she was rarely around during my childhood. In her place, Hale strived to do the best he could, no matter what. My eyes burn as I pass the room next to mine. I've avoided looking at it until now. God, it hurts so much to realize that he isn't behind the polished wood, drawing in his journal, or brooding over a piece of scripture. I miss him so, so much.

And now it hits me—the truth as to why I meekly let father bring me here. I'm not afraid of Silas. I'm afraid of failing Hale again. His room may be my last chance to find something to solidify my suspicions regarding his death. Did father really...

Focus, Frey. Sucking in a breath, I steel myself to step toward that empty room. *I can do this. I can...*

There is no other choice.

SIX

DAZE

I'M HALFWAY across the back lawn before meeting the first guard. He pauses when he sees me, his expression obscured by a pair of black sunglasses. Shit. I keep moving without slowing down. Then, fuck it, I get cocky.

"How's your shift going?" I call out. When push comes to shove, I find that most people are less suspicious the more confident you appear.

In this case, it seems I made the wrong move. *Shit.* The man stiffens, and I form a fist. Then his shoulders relax, and he laughs. "Same as yours, I bet. All this fucking overtime is killing me, but I've had worse assignments."

"Yeah," I say through clenched teeth, coming close enough to his orbit that if he attacked, I'd be fucked. Luckily, he doesn't even reach for his gun. So, I keep talking, "As long as we're getting paid, right?"

The man chuckles. "That's what I'm saying! Hey, are you going to join us for a round at Stella's when your shift is over?"

I give him a non-committal shrug and veer toward the house. "Sure, sure. I guess we should finish our patrol in the meantime."

"Oh shit, you're right—" The man looks at his wristwatch and then takes off toward the west end of the property. "Cover things here for me. I should have finished my patrol ten minutes ago."

As the bastard retreats, I grate out, "Sure fucking thing..."

For the moment, there's no one else around to witness me standing in the middle of the lawn, watching the house. I wonder which window is Frey's?

Probably the one with frilly pink curtains that I can spy on the second level. I inhale sharply at the thought of her, and before I know it, I'm tearing across the lawn, heading for the back door. In my peripheral vision, I spy a few more guards patrolling the outer perimeter. These fucking idiots don't even question my approach.

So much for all the buildup. In the end, I walk right through the back door like I own this fucking place. I enter through a rear hallway that looks like something out of a damn museum. I knew the Heywoods were loaded, but nothing drives that nail home like seeing the pristine floor that I track mud all over on my way to a curved, opulent staircase leading to the upper level.

With every step I climb, I start creating a plan of action. I'll hunt her down. Corner another guard if I have to—beat the shit out of him for answers. Already, my hands are curling into fists, ready for violence as I spy someone lingering nearby.

One look at her, and all the fight leaves my body. I sway, forced to acknowledge the effect she alone has on me—this slender little princess, bathed in sunlight from a nearby window, framed in a white doorway, her expression filled with pain.

The relief at seeing her with my own eyes is instant. Before I can welcome the feeling, I notice how jumpy she is. She's looking over her shoulder and peering down the hall as if expecting a monster to pop out of the shadows. Little does she know that I *am* that monster. The sound of my footsteps must frighten her, because before I know it, she's running into the nearest room.

I follow her, easily keeping pace as she tries to close the door in my face.

"C-Can I help you?" she asks, as her breath catches.

"I didn't mean to scare you," I say as I step forward. She tenses up when I speak and scrutinizes my outfit. She's spending a bit too much time inspecting my muscle beneath this too-small uniform. Damn, I really enjoy her eyes on me. I can't help the smirk that overtakes my face.

"I would like to be alone," she croaks, inching toward the window. "I'm sure my father will be okay if—"

I can't wait any longer and surge inside, closing the door behind me, triggering the lock.

"I'll scream," she chokes out, bolting toward her nightstand. Fingers shaking, she wrenches open a drawer. She seems to hesitate for a moment before she makes up her mind and brandishes an old letter opener clutched in her hand as she turns back to me. My princess has a feisty streak.

"You don't want to hurt me, princess," I warn.

She pauses as if she's analyzing my voice and my use of her nickname. I don't have much time, and while this is entertaining, I've been away from her for too long.

I remove my glasses and take another step toward her. "And," I add, advancing closer. "I think the only company you really need, is me."

The next second, she's lunging toward me. "Daze!"

SEVEN

FREY

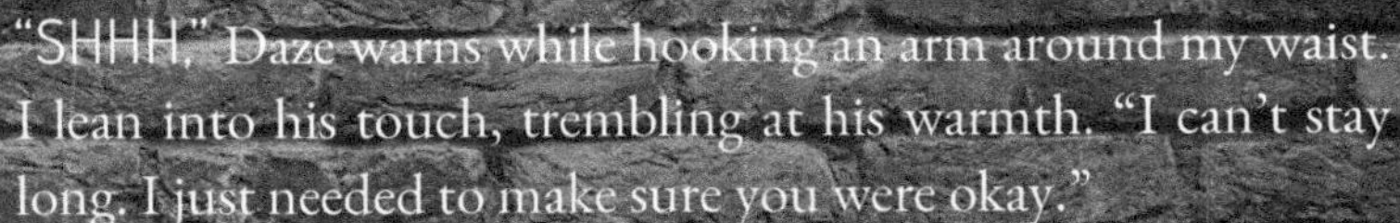

"SHHH," Daze warns while hooking an arm around my waist. I lean into his touch, trembling at his warmth. "I can't stay long. I just needed to make sure you were okay."

"That *I'm* okay?" I crane my neck to inspect him better and wince at the sight of his left eye. It's still swollen and bruised. So is his forehead. When I attempt to brush my finger along a particularly nasty gash, he winces. "What about you? If you don't have a concussion, I'm the Queen of England. Gosh, you need a hospital—"

"I'm not the only one."

Uh-oh. His tone is gritted. Angry. Gently, he bats my hand away and turns his attention to my face. Alarm rips through me as his expression shifts. I try to cover my left eye with my hand, but it's too late. Gone in a flash is his trademark playful grin. His eyes narrow to slits as he gingerly runs his thumb across my cheek with a gentleness that takes my breath away.

His voice, however, is anything but. "That son of a bitch. He hit you."

Silas—but the memory of his blow isn't what makes my blood run cold. It's the look on Daze's face. I've known he was dangerous, capable of violence.

I've seen firsthand just how brutal he could be.

But the full extent of the rage he conceals has never been on stark display until now. His teeth are bared, eyes a blazing silver. He looks like he could kill Silas with her bare hands.

And relish every drop of blood spilled.

"Daze... Stop." Fear rises within me, but surprisingly it isn't because of the memory of Silas' punch. Eager for a distraction, I take his large hand in mine and squeeze until he looks at me. "It's nothing," I stammer, stroking his palm, but he's already turning on his heel, shrugging me off.

"That motherfucker," he growls, curling his hands into fists. "I'll kill him. I'll gut him like a fucking—"

"You won't," I blurt, horrified. I cross over to the door and press my back against it, blocking him. "Promise me."

"Promise you?" He whips around. My cheeks catch fire as I imagine what he's probably thinking—how easy it would be to move me out of his way. For whatever reason, he doesn't try to. Instead, he narrows his eyes. "You have no idea what he's just started because of you. Do you?"

"Started..." I blink, thrown off by the venom in his tone. "What are you talking about? Though maybe I'm the one who should be angry? Silas said... Daze, how exactly do you know my father?"

"Damn it." He sighs and approaches me, his head lowered. I brace for him to push me aside, but he doesn't, instead reaching out. The way he touches me is just as reverent as how my father used to hold his Bible during teachings, before the spotlight made him a stranger. Like the thing beneath his fingertips had the entire universe inside it, and one wrong move could wreck it irreparably.

Of course, Daze—someone I've known for barely a week— doesn't feel that way about me. That doesn't stop my brain from making the comparison. Especially when his eyelids lower, making the gray of his eyes gleam like silver. He's so beautiful like this, that it's easy to believe anything he says next. Even...

"I was worried about you." He uses his thumb to brush a piece of hair from my face, smoothing it behind my ear. At the same time, he frowns as if surprised by the words leaving his mouth. "I was. So fucking worried. For even touching you, he's already a dead man, but if he did anything more than that, I'll—"

"I'm okay," I rasp, though it's a lie. I think he needs to hear it almost as much as I need to say it. *I'm okay.* I can survive one little beating the way he's survived several so far. Seeing him in person, alive and kicking, must be the jolt I needed to steel my resolve again. Silas can go to hell, but I won't let him take any satisfaction in using me as a toy to wreak more havoc.

Speaking of which—Silas couldn't cause half the chaos that having Father walk in and finding Daze here would.

"You shouldn't be here," I croak. "If my father sees you—"

"Trust me," he says with a crooked smile. "I know how to blend in. One of the bastards on your so-called security detail asked me if I was joining them for happy hour after this shift. They don't suspect a fucking thing. Even if they noticed... I needed to see you."

My belly quakes as his voice dips toward that low, unsettling baritone. The one that made it impossible to sleep at night. Whenever I closed my eyes, my brain would replay that scene from his gym. The couch. The bathroom. His bed.

I think that no matter what happens, I'll spend the rest of my life dwelling on those moments, for better or worse.

"You needed to see me. Badly enough to risk another head injury?" I ask, fighting to sound stern. I fail. My breath hitches, and I can't stop myself from leaning into his touch as he strokes along my jawline.

"Yep. So, you can stop stalling and tell me everything that bastard did to you."

I stiffen, hating the first thing that comes to mind—Silas' warning.

"He threatened to hurt you," I confess. "He said that you worked with my father before. He insinuated that you lied to me—"

"Fuck him." It's unnerving watching his expression change, shifting from worried to furious all in an instant.

At the same time, a heartless monster wouldn't look at me like he does. He cradles my cheek against his palm, his lips pursed in concern. "He won't ever touch you again," he swears in a guttural tone. "Never. You don't have to be afraid of him—"

"I'm not afraid of *him*," I insist, inching out of his reach.

He watches me go with his hand still outstretched, touching nothing.

"I'm afraid of you. The way you talk about violence like that. It's disturbing."

"Disturbing." His expression falls flat, and suddenly he seems miles away. A different person from the caring man he was just a second ago. "Maybe you missed the memo, Frances, but I'm not some perfect choir boy like what you're used to. Don't expect me to apologize for giving a shit if someone puts their hands on you. Fuck—" He grits his teeth and shrugs. "I came here to see that you're okay, and I did. If you want me to go—"

"No." As he takes a step forward, I draw in a breath and reach for his arm.

"Daze, Wait." Now that he's here... Maybe it's selfish, but I don't want him to leave. Not yet.

With a wary glance behind me, I do have to at least acknowledge the obvious.

"How do you know that someone won't walk in? In fact—" I break off as a set of heavy footsteps echo somewhere in the distance. Only when I'm sure they're gone do I whisper, "We probably have about five seconds before someone notices that I'm carrying on a full conversation supposedly with myself."

The anger leaves his gaze, and suddenly he's playful again, approaching me with that characteristic swagger. "That's where you come in," he says in a gruff murmur. "You could do something that might eternally damn your good-girl soul —learn how to lie."

I choke out a laugh, even as I bristle at the taunt. "Little old me? I think I preferred when you tried to teach me how to fight."

"Ah." He bares his teeth in a feral grin. "That's the feisty little Freylie I know. I can teach you how to do a lot more than that. Right after you tell me one thing... What else did he say to you?"

Silas.

"He said you wanted to ransom me," I blurt out, watching him carefully for a reaction.

"Bullshit!" His eyes widen, his nostrils flaring with rage, and I instantly regret saying anything. "What else did he say?"

For a split-second, I consider coming clean, bringing up the supposed secrets that Silas hinted he was keeping—but my latest trip down memory lane has taught me at least one lesson—there's no point in living in the past. All it does is bring pain.

"Nothing," I say.

Daze raises an eyebrow, unconvinced.

"Nothing I care to recall anyway. But if you came all the way to badger me with questions, maybe I should scream for my father's guards to rescue me from boredom."

"Is that a threat?" He wants it to be. His eyes sparkle with renewed excitement. Suddenly, Silas and his corrosive energy seem a world away. "Oh, you can play the reluctant princess martyr later," he suggests, lowering his mouth to my ear. "I'll tell you why I came here. But first, I need... I just need you. Innocent fucking Frey to make me forget the shit I need to do—what I *will* do to make things right. I can spare you the details. Lie to your face if you want me to. Just give me five minutes that I don't have to spend watching my fucking back. Can you do that?"

It's a crazy, illogical ask, but he makes it seem plausible. I run my fingers over his lower jaw, tracing every curve and chiseled jawbone. He leans into my touch, his eyes half-closed.

"Is this really worth it?" I ask him, even as my body reacts to his nearness in a way that screams *yes*, it is. Every second stolen with him feels well worth the price.

"You tell me." His hand ghosts between my legs, finding the hem of my skirt.

My breath feathers as he tickles my inner thigh.

"Though you just got discharged from the hospital," he admits, pulling away. "You need rest—"

"I'm fine," I say, grabbing his hand, returning it to its previous position. "The doctors think, at worse, I have a mild concussion. Nothing serious, and no need to avoid any strenuous activity. They just wanted me to rest. And I can."

Later. Much, much later.

Daze angles his head to inspect me from head to toe. "Don't tell me you've already started to practice your lying, Freylie... Though you are dressed the part of a sweet little innocent. I must admit, I think I prefer you in this getup," he says with a guttural chuckle while tugging on the hem of the modest skirt Father made me wear home. "The perfect church girl —" He fingers my starched collar next, and my heart flutters at how his eyelids flutter. Especially when he murmurs, "I wonder what you'd look like on your knees."

My cheeks flame, but I don't rush to scold him for the lewd suggestion. Maybe I'm still delirious from my ordeal, or perhaps dealing with Father and Colton has left me more shaken than I want to admit. The things that used to make me hesitate before, now seem tempting.

Daze grunts in surprise as I sink to the floor before him. I'm praying that no one below can hear the quiet thud and question it. Looking up at the man in front of me, though, I can't muster up too much concern.

He is so beautiful. And, for the time being, anyway, he's all mine. My fingers shake as I reach for the front of his slacks.

He beats me to it, unzipping the fly and letting the material slide down his hips.

"Beautiful," he tells me in an undertone. "But if all we have is a few minutes before someone comes knocking, I want to make sure you get your fair share."

He pulls me to my feet and guides me back to the wall nearest the window. His lips skim over mine as he grips my hips in both hands. I shiver as he gathers up my skirt in a fist and hooks the thumb of his other hand beneath the gusset of my panties.

"I can't stop thinking about this," he grunts, stroking me with the tips of his fingers. "How fucking good you feel. The sounds you make…"

And I'm just as guilty for dwelling on him. My mouth waters at the memory of the last time I slept in his arms. At least until Silas came—it was heaven. Drunk on the thought, I find myself breathing out, "We could make them again."

"Damn right, we will. But first… Fuck, *please* tell me you are on birth control." The intensity in his tone suggests my answer is more important than I can grasp. Those steel eyes bore into mine, searching for an answer.

"Um, yes. I'm on the shot to control my periods," I manage to reply before he lunges and captures my mouth in a searing kiss.

"Thank fuck, I need to feel you with nothing between us." The way he says it makes me weak in the knees, and I nearly miss his next declaration. "I'm clean, and after Sammy, I've always worn a condom. I know it's a lot to ask, but..."

Clean. He isn't talking about physically. A million old warnings from my high school's sex education class hit me at full force. Pregnancy. STDs. Do I really want to take those risks with him?

Once I meet his gaze and feel my heart jump eagerly, I have my answer.

"I trust you," I whisper back. "I do."

"Baby..." The look he gives me as he caresses my cheek gently is indescribable, like those three words mean more to him than I know. Before I can question him, he blinks as if a sudden thought just came to him. Then he nuzzles against my throat, and I lose all train of thought.

"Now that that's taken care of, I'm going to make those pretty lips give me more than a few sweet sounds—but there's a catch. We have to take one little precaution," he whispers into my ear. "Be a good girl and open your mouth for me."

I do, confused. "What are you..."

He steps back and snatches something from my bed. I blink in confusion as I make it out—an old stuffed rabbit from years ago.

"I hope Mr. Bunny doesn't mind sacrificing himself for a greater purpose," Daze whispers, stroking one of the bunny's ears in a way that makes my heart race. "Now open."

I obey. Still, I don't understand what he intends to do with it until he brings the plushy to my mouth.

"Good girl," he praises as I bite down on the surprisingly soft toy. "I don't want you to make a sound. Now... Bend over."

A gasp catches in my throat, smothered by the material between my teeth. He makes that simple command sound so darn dangerous. Not a demeaning act, but the catalyst to something incredible. My body is already gearing up for it, and I feel an ache begin to build between my legs. Suddenly the air in here is stifling, and the distant voices of people speaking downstairs feel a world away.

It's slightly terrifying how easily he can do this—make me forget everything. Who I am. Who he is. Even where we are doesn't matter as long as I feel him settle against me, navigating my body as if every last inch of it was made for him.

He takes my hips in his hands, steering me toward him. When I brace my hands over the end of the mattress, he steadies my waist, keeping my weight balanced on my heels rather than forward. As a result, the bed barely twitches.

I bite down as his hands roam over my butt, cupping a globe against one palm in a way that makes my face heat. I can't stop myself from arching toward him, eager to feel his fingers lower. Higher. Everywhere.

"Greedy," he grates out in a barely audible murmur. "Get ready for me. Spread your legs."

He takes his time, heightening the heart-stopping tension in the air. I can hear footsteps traveling somewhere in the house.

Humming. Catherine's? Whoever it is, they seem blissfully unaware of what's happening just out of sight.

And for some reason, knowing that doesn't entirely terrify me like it should. I'm panting as Daze runs his fingers beneath my skirt and skims over my panties. The poor stuffed animal in my mouth is mangled around a groan I can't smother.

My reaction triggers a low rumble in his throat that he bites off. Then he uses both hands to drag my panties down my legs. A heartbeat later, I feel him pressing against me, eager to thrust in.

How I don't scream when he finally enters me, I have no idea. I just know I'll never be able to look at this poor stuffed bunny again without blushing. I swear I bite it in half as I clench my jaw around another groan.

With my body gripping him like a glove, he drops the cocky act. Grunting with pleasure, he rocks into me, somehow managing to seem restrained enough to thrust in deep while barely making a sound. My position is mainly for show, considering he shoulders most of my weight, snatching me into him over and over again.

My vision begins to blur. When he uses his thumb to press against that elusive bundle of nerves, I lose my grip on the bunny, and it falls to the floor. Suddenly, those wandering footsteps pause. Return, inching closer, but I'm too far gone to process the potential implications.

All I can do is reach back, clawing at his forearm as he bucks into me. Harder. Faster. Then, without warning, he stops.

"Frances?"

That voice seems to come from another universe. Kind. Sweet. *Catherine?*

"Frances, are you okay in there?" The doorknob turns with a telltale click as the lock engages. Belatedly, the current danger reaches my brain.

Oh no...

"Say you're okay," Daze bites out against the nape of my neck as I bolt back to awareness. He may have stopped moving, but I can still feel him, feel every ridge, feel his warmth. "Say you're taking a nap—"

"I'm fine," I call out.

The insanity of the situation hits me as my voice echoes off the walls. Daze is still inside this very room—inside me—and only a thin wooden door conceals that fact from the outside world.

"Are you sure, honey?" The doorknob jangles again. "Do you need some painkillers? Is it your head?"

"I'm just..." Before I can finish my thought, Daze nibbles my neck. "...tired," I choke out. "I—"

Daze finally moves—but not to withdraw. He grinds himself into me, sending bolts of electricity up and down my spine. *Good Lord.* I have to bite my tongue just to stay silent.

Right when Catherine tries the door yet again.

"You sound a little faint, honey. Don't forget that the doctor wanted us to monitor you for a concussion. Maybe I should come in—"

"N-No! I'm fine," I say. "B-But, you know what? I could use some soup if you don't mind."

Daze chuckles in my ear, almost drowning out Catherine's reply.

"Of course!" Hurried footsteps trail off toward the staircase, and I nearly collapse with relief. Thankfully Daze doesn't relinquish his grip on my hips—even as he swivels his, forcing me to press my palm against my mouth and bite down on the flesh in lieu of Mr. Bunny.

"That was some damn good lying, Freylie," he tells me. "I didn't think you had it in you."

"What if she came in?" I counter.

"You'd like that, wouldn't you?" he taunts with another wicked bark of laughter. "She'd see who you really are, my naughty rogue angel."

"You're...a bastard," I bite back, struggling to match his low tone. I know I'm blushing, but I relish his dirty compliment.

"Not a bastard." He leans in, nuzzling the back of my neck with what feels like an open mouth. His breath is scorching, punctuating every word he grates out next. "That's not what I need you to call me right now. I want you to say my name. In your sexy little whisper. Give it to me. Now."

He slams into me so hard I can't smother a pathetic, squeaking sound my palm barely muffles.

"Tell me..." He runs his lips along my quivering throat, bringing his ear as close to my mouth as he can. "Say it."

"Daze." My voice breaks, but somehow, I'm rushing to voice it again. "Daze—"

"That's it," he murmurs, still flexing his hips. "Just like that."

He folds himself over me, risking our tentative balance. I'm awash in his scent, locked within a cocoon of safe warmth. The sensation of his lips on my earlobe is the final spark that tips me over the edge. "Fuck," he rasps, lunging into me. "You feel so damn good..."

My knees buckle and give out, pitching me forward. The bed squeals just once, way too loud, but by then, my toes are curling, and I'm catapulting to cloud nine. Pleasure hits white-hot. Utter bliss. I'm not even sure if I make any noise as I throw my head back against his chest and feel his release flood into me.

"Not bad for it being your first time keeping a dirty little secret," Daze whispers into my ear as he catches his breath. At the same time, he reaches for a pink box of tissues on my nightstand. After using one to clean between my legs, he pulls my panties back up and smooths my skirt into place. His fingers linger, imparting a gentle, soothing caress as if in apology for his prior actions. "If I didn't know any better, I'd think you were used to having naughty strangers in your bedroom, Freylie." He has the nerve to wink at me while tossing the used tissue in the wastebasket by the door.

I form a fist and playfully smack his chest, but nowhere near hard enough to hurt—or make a sound. "Bastard."

"Cursing, too?" he mockingly tosses back. "Naughty girl. If I had the time, I'd see you were punished."

"How so?" I ask, cocking my head back to see his face.

A dangerous smile plays over his lips. He steps closer to tower over me, and a peek downward reveals that his pants are still down around his ankles. "Wouldn't you like to know? First, I'd find out what other toys you have in this room," he says, letting his lips come alarmingly close to mine. "Especially the small, pretty, *durable* kind. Then I'd find out how many ways you can scream my name…"

"Frances! I'll bring your soup up in five minutes," Catherine calls from downstairs.

"Saved by the bell," Daze says, stepping back. "But if I were you, I wouldn't eat that soup until you know who you can trust. In fact, I can think of something better than lunch." He bends to pull his pants up, but in the process, he removes something from the seemingly spacious pockets. Two things, actually; a pair of sunglasses like the ones he wore and a square of black material—a shirt, I realize as he unfurls it. "Freedom."

"You want me to leave with you," I say, taking a step back. Of course, he wouldn't risk sneaking in just for a quickie. His aim was always this—break me out.

And I should be running into his arms, desperate to leave. Silas threatened me, presumably with my father's permission. He has me under lock and key with no obvious way out.

But...

I can't deny that there is one small silver lining. I'm back where Hale spent his last moments. If no one else will tell me the truth, maybe he did in his own way before he died. I can't waste that chance. I need to get inside his bedroom, at least. Just once.

Licking my lips, I try to find the best way to verbalize this insane request. In all honesty? There isn't one. So, I settle for pleading. "Daze..."

"No." His eyes go cold, honed like lasers. I cringe from the harsh inspection. No one would guess that just seconds ago, he'd looked at me like... Like he'd do anything for me. "You're not staying here. Are you fucking crazy?" I recognize the low cadence of his voice. "Do you think that Silas moved without the go-ahead from Daddy Dearest? You're not that stupid, Frey."

"I'm not," I say thickly. "Just hear me out. If I can find something that Hale left behind, then maybe..."

"Maybe what?" Daze snaps back. "You won't wind up dead next?"

I flinch. "That's a cryptic warning."

His frown wavers, softening for a heartbeat. "Cryptic and the best damn advice you need at the moment," he warns. "If you won't let me get you out of here, you need to be on guard. I mean it. If anything happened to you…"

He doesn't seem to realize that statement could also apply to him. I didn't forget what Silas hinted about regarding him, and I don't know why a part of me hesitates to ask him outright now. It could be pure selfishness—for the past few minutes, he's made me forget everything beyond this room. I'm not in a hurry to plunge back into that chaos.

Not yet.

"Speaking of guard… How will you get out of here?" I ask. Honestly, I have no idea how he even got in, given the number of men on the property. If there is anything Daze Keaton doesn't seem to shy away from, though, it's a challenge.

"How else?" He winks, but there's no real humor in the expression. He looks pained. I'd assume it was his head hurting him, but I'm not that naïve. In this instance, I'm the only source of his hurt. "Through the front door. It probably won't be smart to stick around any longer. I should go. The guys are probably wondering where I am."

"The guys?" I whip around to the window. I can make out the shadowy shape of a guard traipsing around the pool and my heart skips at the thought of him spotting Daze on his way out.

"Yeah, it's okay—" Daze strokes my chin until I turn back to him. His wry smirk conveys that he isn't afraid in the slightest. "I called in some old friends to help me find you. You met one of them. I believe Lex gave you a note when you were in the hospital."

"Lex?" I wonder aloud, trying to remember the name of the orderly who delivered my dinner last night. "I don't remember a Lex. I think his name was Jet."

"Yes. Jet is Lex's cage name," Daze confirms, chuckling. "We all went by them. Mine was, well... Daze. Unimaginative, but considering how my opponents wound up knocked on their ass, barely able to remember their own name, it fit well enough."

"Oh." I gulp at the mention of his past. "How many friends did you call in?" I'm more curious than ever to get a little peek into his world. There is so much I don't know about him.

And I crave—no need—to know everything I can.

"I called in Damien, also known as Mayhem in the ring," he adds. "A crazy son of a bitch, but he brought a couple other ex-fighters with him. Lex and Kane, an ex-Marine, who goes by Hellion. I'd love to fill you in more, princess, but I better go before your stepmom comes knocking again." He flashes a teasing smile, but I can sense the worry he's trying to hide in how he never stops stroking my cheek. Touching me. These frantic caresses betray what he has enough tact not to voice—he doesn't want to leave me here.

My shoulders slump as he finally pulls away to button his pants. Before he can finish zipping up his fly, I can't resist running my hands over his chest, helping to smooth his uniform. His heartbeat rages beneath my palm, and I linger for as long as I can, counting the seconds to the slow, steady rhythm.

When I gather the nerve, I finally ask, "You'll come back?"

He runs his hands along my head, arranging my hair into a low bun. I smile at the gesture and gently bat his hands away to secure his creation with a hair tie stolen from my wrist.

"You bet your ass I will." A darkness clouds his expression, and I can't tell what he's thinking. "When I do, you be ready to leave. One day. That should be enough for you to do whatever Nancy Drew shit you need to. One."

"I'll be okay," I insist. Do I really believe that, though? I toy with the idea of telling him what Silas let slip. But if I did tell him the full truth, would he really leave without a fight?

Probably not.

EIGHT

DAZE

FUCKING, Frey. It's cruel the hold she has over me with one goddamn look. She has that innocent fucking gleam in her eye now. The one that makes my heart stammer like mad. The pouty, haunting expression has me cupping her chin to coax her to meet my gaze despite every brain cell I have urging me to leave.

"Promise me," I demand in a harsh whisper, leaning in to press my lips to her forehead. "Promise me you'll... You know what these people are capable of now. Be careful."

She nods, unintentionally bringing her mouth within range of mine—and I gladly take advantage by swooping in for a kiss that has her gasping. I use my tongue to savor that little sound and draw out a ragged moan she can't suppress. It's just a kiss. In theory, the sex should excite me more. I should be aching to be inside her again. One hungry taste of her quivering lips shouldn't be enough to have me dizzy, with fucking fireworks going off in my skull. When I pull back, it's mainly to preserve my own sanity.

With Damien and his boys waiting, I can't delay any longer. Fuck. The thought of leaving her still stings like a motherfucker.

"You should go," she says, running a trembling finger along her swollen bottom lip. "I promise I'll be safe."

"I'll hold you to that, Freylie." I turn and force myself to step away from her. With my hand on the doorknob, I can't resist and look back one last time, fighting the urge to throw her over my damn shoulder and drag her out of this fucking house. God, I can't believe I'm letting her stay here. I have to trust that now that her eyes are open, so to speak, she'll be careful.

Pulling the door open, I scan the hallway before crossing the threshold. After I've taken a few paces, I sense Frey trailing behind, her steps soft and delicate. She must be feeling the same reluctance to part as I am. I can't resist sneaking another glance her way as I descend the stairs.

She has her head held high, and despite her hair threatening to fall out of its neat little bun, she's the picture of grace. The kind of perfect woman I have no business in hell fucking with.

Turning back, I head for the foyer, ready to take my shot at leaving through the front door.

"Oh!" Frey's little gasp makes me freeze, and I look over to find her at the base of the staircase, her wide eyes fixed on a nearby doorway. "C-Catherine."

"Oh Frances, you didn't have to come down!" a woman trills from beyond my line of sight.

Shit! I duck into a nearby parlor room as a set of hurried footsteps come this way. Judging from the lack of screaming, I've gone unnoticed for now.

"That's okay. I'm feeling much better," Frey replies, her voice steady. God, my princess sure is getting better at her lying.

"That's good," Catherine chirps, unconcerned that Frey's forced laugh sounds like she just bit into a lemon. "You can keep me company. Your father requested pot roast for dinner, and I know it's one of your favorites. Feel up to helping?" she continues.

"Yes! We should head into the kitchen," Frey calls out, no doubt her way of cueing me to exit.

I could observe her all night, but I better get out of here. After checking that the coast is clear, I slip into the foyer and then march right out of the front fucking door. The guard posted nearby just nods at me. Fucking moron. Heywood would be pissed to know how much of a joke his "security" team has turned out to be. In fact, seeing them in action has me more determined than ever to get Frey out of this hellhole.

After clearing the front walkway, I round a row of tall hedges near the back fence and spot Kane and Lex waiting right where I left them. They're facing away, and it takes me a moment to see what has their attention. Damien, of course. That crazy motherfucker. Bold as you fucking please, he's behind a guard with both hands wrapped around the poor bastard's neck. The man struggles, clawing at Damien's face as he stumbles on his feet, pushing Damien against the perimeter wall. With a hollow laugh, the crazy son of a bitch just tightens his grasp on his throat until the guard goes limp. As if he's a sack of trash, Damien drops him to the ground.

"Fuck, Damien. I was gone for what? Thirty minutes? What the hell happened?" I demand, gesturing to the unconscious guard. "I thought we were clear—keep it subtle."

"Subtle ain't my style." Damien rolls his neck and smirks. "I told you we were doing this my way." He laughs. "Believe me when I say that Lex and Kane had to talk me out of smashing these fucker's heads in. A little cat nap won't hurt him. That's the least of your worries."

With their entertainment over, Kane and Lex turn around. They sport matching grins when they see me. Here it comes...

"Looks like someone had a good time," Kane insinuates.

"Oh, I think it was more than 'good'," Lex adds.

"Where is your girl?" Damien demands, eyes narrowed. "I thought you planned on getting her out of this place?"

I swallow hard. "Frey needed more time to try and unravel a few mysteries."

"You mean you're letting her stay?" Kane looks more surprised than I feel that I let her have her way.

"What can I say? She was really persuasive," I add with a chuckle.

Lex tries to cover his laughing response with his hand, "I bet she was."

"Consider our debt squared for now," Damien says. "If you need us, we'll stick around the city for a few more days. You have my number."

"I appreciate the assist. I'm making my own crew, and we are going to take this damn city back. If you're interested, there's a place for you here," I offer.

The three trade indecipherable glances before Damien shrugs and meets my gaze head-on. "Let us know the specifics and we can go from there. I, for one, don't mind sticking around a little longer," he says with lethal intent gleaming in his eyes. Lex and Kane nod in agreement. I guess I'm not the only one searching for my place.

"Thanks," I reply. Relieved is far from what I feel as I watch them go. I just hope—maybe I'll even go so far as to pray— that Frey has more bravery in that slender body than what those innocent little eyes convey.

If her father is even half the monster I know him to be, she'll need all of that, and then some.

FREY

IN THE KITCHEN, I take over cutting up vegetables, barely tethered to the present. All I can think about is Daze. Did he make it out okay? God, I hope so...

Eventually, Catherine attempts to shift the conversation to something about the weather. Maybe it's the aftermath of what happened with Daze affecting my judgment, but I can't seem to keep my mouth shut. In my head, I planned to use tact and cunning to find out more about Hale.

When push comes to shove, I just blurt out what I'm desperate to know. "You were there that night," I say, as Catherine moves to carry a dish to the sink. "With Hale when he..."

Crash! Catherine stumbles back from the counter as a plate smashes to pieces at her feet. "Damn it!" She stoops to gather up the jagged shards, but when I join her, she doesn't look at me. She stares at the floor instead. Her hands shake so badly that she cuts herself on a broken piece of porcelain. Hissing, she pops the bleeding digit into her mouth and then sighs.

"I'm sorry," I blurt, crouching to assist her. "I just saw his room, and I was wondering... I was wondering if there might be any of his things left and—"

"I don't like to remember that night, Frances," she says finally, her voice soft. "Please don't bring it up again."

It's a logical request—I know that. Still, I feel like a dog who caught a whiff of a bone. Daze was wrong—I can find out the truth for myself. I have to try.

"I was there too," I point out. "I just... I just need to clarify some things, please. Things that I'm not sure if I'm remembering correctly or if I'm just torturing myself—"

She shakes her head, her eyes wide. "Frances—"

"Please," I insist. "Just tell me what you remember. It's important."

"Oh, alright..." She runs the fingers of her uninjured hand through her coifed brown curls. "I remember that your father had been working late that night. We weren't expecting Hale to show up at all. He'd been so distant before then. I was hopeful that maybe he'd decided to work things out between him and Michael. We'd prayed so long for that."

"I remember," I say thickly. I'd rushed over with that very hope in mind. By that point, Hale had been gone for days without a word—though now I know that he'd spoken to someone in the months leading up to his death. Daze. "When I came over..."

I found him in his old room.

"Yes." Catherine smiles weakly. "The strange part is that it seemed to be going well, all things considered, between those two. They were even having a debate over Bible stories, and—"

"Who was?"

"Hale and your father," Catherine says. "Michael came home early. I'm not sure why, but they had a discussion in his office, just the two of them. Hale stormed out. I thought he left, at least until..."

"I didn't know that," I croak.

Father never told me.

"I think it still bothers him," Catherine admits. "To be the last one to see him alive. Sometimes I can tell he's distracted. Angry. I mean—upset," she adds quickly. "It was a shock to everyone what happened. As for Hale's room, I'm sorry, honey. Your father had his things packed up and donated."

"Oh." I feel like I've been kicked in the stomach. Still, something she said sticks out to me. "You said they were talking about Bible stories?" Frankly, it sounds like wishful thinking at best.

Catherine, however, doesn't seem to be lying. "Yes," she nods solemnly while gathering up the last shards of the plate. Rising to her feet, she tosses them in the trash can and then washes off her bloody hand in the sink. "I took it as a good sign. At least they were talking about something other than their differences for once."

"Yeah," I say, hoping my skepticism isn't apparent. By that point, Hale had turned his back on Salvation and Covenant. Father relies on Bible verses and scripture during his lectures to both his children and the congregation, but I doubt Hale would stick around to listen.

"Do you remember which one?" I ask halfheartedly. Maybe she just misinterpreted something? Or... Maybe I'm gambling my own safety and sanity on a pointless whim.

"I think so." Catherine inclines her head, her brows furrowed. Then she nods. "It was one about Paul and his companion. I forget his name, what was it? I can't remember, but they seemed to be having a heated discussion. You know how your father can be. Now, if you'll excuse me, I really should get these potatoes in the oven. Michael gets so grumpy if his meals aren't ready on the dot."

"Thank you," I say, though internally, I'm more confused than ever. Hale spoke to my father about the prophet Paul before he died? It doesn't make sense with what I already know. Still, I force a smile and help Catherine finish the meal.

By the time we set the table, it's dark out. Catherine flits around the dining room nervously, rearranging the plates and silverware while fretting about hoping the food stays warm. When Father finally arrives, she nearly trips over her feet in her rush to get him settled.

He doesn't seem grateful for her efforts to have the meal ready at his preference. Whatever discussion he had with the commissioner appears to have left him brooding. His brows are drawn as he takes his place at the head of the table. While

Catherine scurries to pour him a glass of wine, he clears his throat. "You seem to be in good spirits, Frances," he says.

It takes everything I have to maintain my fake smile. "Yes," I say, folding my hands in front of my place setting.

I can't ignore the anxiety building in my stomach as his eyes pass over me. Does he happen to know about his unusual "guard" who so boldly entered the house? God, I hope not. Thankfully, he seems as calm as always, observing his kingdom with the composure of an old king.

How I used to envy that look. His ability to be so detached from the rest of the world. Even from us. As a child, I thought it was a good thing—a sign of how truly at peace he was within himself. Now? I'm not so sure.

His cool demeanor makes it harder to question his motives without an emotional response—like, why arrange for Silas to take me? Why work with that monster at all? And why didn't he tell me that he spoke to Hale right before he died? The thought gnaws at me even as we say a prayer and begin to eat.

With every forced bite of salad, I see Hale's face, demanding and bitter. He won't let me go until I get my own answers.

So, for now, I just wait, watching as Catherine and Father painfully pick their way through aimless, polite conversation. Finally, he turns his attention to me.

"How are you feeling, Frances?"

"Fine," I lie.

He purses his lips, his gaze unreadable. Then he sets his fork aside and steeples his fingers, eyeing me from above the point they make.

"The police are still insisting on asking you some questions regarding the incident," he says. "They've been persistent, but I will make them wait as we discussed. We've arranged for a press conference early next week where we will announce a new initiative to combat crime. They can speak to you then."

"Oh?" I ask, my throat dry.

"The details will be made clear soon enough," Father says cryptically.

"I could always go tonight," I suggest. "I feel a lot better."

"No. You should rest." He picks up his fork again, and I exhale, relieved. Suddenly, he inclines his head. "There is one more thing I wanted to talk to you about," he adds in a tone that makes the hair on the back of my neck stand on end.

"Y-Yes?"

"I think it's time that you return to the fold. I know that, given the intricacies of my campaign, I've been too busy to run the day-to-day operations of the congregation. That changes now. For your welfare, I will make an exception. Tomorrow, you will accompany us to the morning sermon, where I will address the flock."

"An exception?"

He sits tall, his gaze alight in that steely, cold way that always warned he was about to undertake a chilling sermon. Something more serious than the normal day-to-day study. When that icy gleam snuck into his eye, it meant he was about to tackle a lesson with far more importance. Armageddon, repentance, or the ghastly differences between heaven and hell.

"I know you've needed time after your brother passed," he says. "But in giving you that time, I believe I have neglected both your safety and your soul. For that, I doubt I will ever forgive myself, but while it is too late for Hale, I can still save you."

He slams his hand onto the table for emphasis, making Catherine and I jump. I'm not used to the heat in his voice. He rarely sounds this passionate. Only amid his most fiery sermons have I seen him come close to this level of intensity.

"Save me how?"

He sits back, folding his hands beneath the table. "You will meet with me regularly for intensive study. It is time you remember your duty, Frances, and the higher calling we all have been selected for. No more wallowing in darkness. Do you understand?"

I'm not sure if I do. This isn't the first time he's threatened a more "intensive" style of worship. Hale and I had been presented more than once to be sent to the religious enclave where Father was trained in his spiritual beliefs.

But those moments had always been in anger, triggered by some transgression on the part of Hale or me. This time feels different, and I think my time with Daze has helped me to read between the lines in a way I normally wouldn't.

This isn't a request.

"When do we start?" I manage to croak.

His lips contort into an expression I don't recognize—something far too lifeless to be a smile.

"Tonight. Leave us—" He cocks his head toward Catherine, who quietly scurries from the room. Then he stands and follows her to the sliding doors that separate this room from the main hall of the house. One by one, he slides them shut, and my heartbeat races with every thudding sound they make.

"Rise, Frances," he commands with his back still to me.

I stagger from my chair and stand awkwardly beside the table. In the past, whenever he took me aside for private study, we would meet in his office and sit across from his desk while going through various scripture line by line.

This moment feels different. For one, I don't see his trusty, worn copy of the Bible anywhere.

Unease builds until I can't keep silent any longer. "What's wrong?"

"You," he says in a tone that raises goosebumps along my skin.

"W-What—"

"You are lost, Frances. As your father, it is my duty to guide you in more ways than one. I won't let you go down the same path your brother did."

He doesn't turn around, and I can't see exactly what he's doing from this angle. Praying? No... He reaches for his waistband, and all the air escapes my lungs at once.

"Father?"

For a terrifying moment, all I can do is watch him unwind the strip of black leather from his belt loops. He does so slowly. Carefully. Once the length of the belt is free, he extends it with an experimental flex of his wrist. A hissing noise reverberates as it strikes the floor. Then he pivots, so that I can clearly see him looping the length around his right fist. With his eyes on mine, he nods downward.

"Kneel, girl."

I swallow hard. The walls of the dining room seem to press in from all sides. "Father, I—"

"Do not be afraid," he says. His voice reverberates throughout the room, resonating in my bones. "I'm doing this out of love and necessity, Frances. *He who spares the rod hates his son, but he who loves him is diligent to discipline him.* Now kneel."

This isn't happening. Everything about this moment, right down to Father himself, feels too surreal to be reality. I've never seen that gleam in his eyes. They seem to burn, bathed in the glow of the chandelier above.

"Frances." He takes a step toward me, and my knees buckle.

One by one, I force them to bend, lowering myself to the floor. The fear lancing down my spine puts this moment in stark contrast to the eager way I kneeled before Daze only hours ago. I'm holding my breath as my skirt settles around me. I've never noticed how clean this house is before. There isn't a speck of dust anywhere. It's perfect, with nothing alluding to the darkness that might dwell inside it.

A darkness I've been blind to until now.

"I've been too lax with you, girl." Before me, a shadow stretches over the floor, thin and wispy. It bites through the air with a hiss, and then—

"Repentance," Father growls in a voice I don't recognize.

At the same moment, pain sears across my upper back, and I can't silence a cry. My mind struggles to put the pieces together to explain the cause behind the stinging agony I feel as I fall forward. His belt? He hit me with it.

"On your knees," he commands in a tone I don't recognize.

"F-Father?" Eyes wide, I turn to see a stranger looming above, his expression feral.

"It is the only way to find salvation, Frances," he growls. "Do you understand? Say it."

I'm too stunned to arrange my words properly. That second's worth of hesitation earns me a punishment in the form of another stinging blow. This time I can feel the leather bite through the material of my shirt, leaving an aching welt behind. That mark will last for days.

So will the next blow.

I jolt forward, biting back a gasp.

"Obey your father, girl. Say it. Repent for your disobedient, insolent behavior. I held my tongue when you lied to me again and again. Still, I held out hope." His voice rises in pitch, bordering a shout, but it never loses that polished cadence. He might as well be giving a sermon. Not attacking his own daughter. "Repent!"

Another blow ignites the flesh between my shoulder blades. God, it hurts. My eyes water. I can't choke back a cry. "F-Father—"

"Say it!"

"I... I repent," I bite out.

"Then endure your punishment with grace," Father commands, as I hear his belt whistle through the air.

A stinging lash sears the flesh along my spine, but I chew on my lower lip rather than cry out. I wish I had Daze's strength. His bravery in the face of pain and an ability to stare even death in the face without flinching.

I'm shaking now, and there is no disguising it. I don't feel brave in the slightest. I feel weaker than ever, helpless to my fate.

But even as I shudder in agony, some rebellious part of me warns that I'm not pathetic. I'm on the right track. Something I've done has triggered this change in him, and I need to stay the course and keep going.

I need to find answers, no matter who or what gets in my way.

DAZE

AFTER ONE OTHER DETOUR, I make it to the bar by sundown and go in through the back. I can't deny the unease I feel run down my spine. Chris was my old man's righthand before shit hit the fan. By the time I came to power, he'd already been out of the game for years. Regardless, I'm sure I can trust him. Ben? Him, I trust with my life.

Still... I'm partly surprised when I creep down the back hallway and find Ben and Chris trading shots at the counter, no Silas in sight. Ignore the fact that Silas is at large, and it could be a fuzzy, family reunion of sorts.

"Ah, look. The man of the hour returns!" Ben raises his glass to me in a mock salute. "I just got done telling Chris here that you needed a break in between running for your life and all to go screw your little church girl. I hope you enjoyed yourself."

"Very fucking funny," I snap. Though given the risk he's taken by joining my side, Ben has the right to make more than a few jokes at my expense.

Chris, on the other hand, just laughs. "You know you can count on me, Day. We were talking about how things were with your old man. Back before..." He clears his throat. "I still refer to that time as my good old days."

"Marcus was one crazy son of a bitch," Ben muses after another shot. "You didn't inherit his brains, Day, but you sure as hell got his balls."

"If you ask me, I'd rather not get anything from the man. Brains. Balls. He can keep it all."

"Don't be like that, Day," Ben starts.

"Marcus was the best son of a bitch to run the Saints," Chris pitches in. "He had his problems, sure. But he was a damn good strategist. If he were here, he'd suggest we smoke Silas out. Draw him into the open—"

"Then I guess it's a good thing he isn't here then," I bark. Fuck. I know this isn't the time for petty daddy issues bullshit. Doesn't make it easier to stomach any mention of that bastard without wanting to punch the fucking wall. I form a fist but stop myself at the last minute.

I'm not like him. Won't ever be—because I actually give a damn about my son. I may not be a perfect dad, but Sammy won't ever have to clean up my mistakes. I'll handle my own shit and face the consequences head-on. Everything I do will be for his benefit, not mine.

"Considering that Marcus is in the ground right now, I don't think he'll be much help when it comes to strategizing," I say. "We use our instincts. Rely on the resources we have."

"I think Daze has a point," Ben cuts in, flattening his hand against the bar. "We should aim for stealth. Going at things balls-to-the-wall is one thing if you have an army at your back. Alone, we need to think strategically. Be calculating."

"Because if there's one thing Marcus Keaton never was, it was fucking cautious," I say bitterly. When you smashed through everything, it wasn't hard to have the illusion of being strategic. The bastard went at the world like a hammer, holding nothing back. Business. Booze. Women. He attacked anything in his path the same way—with violence and brutality.

If he met a girl like Frey, he'd use her for only what he could get out of her. Sex. Money. Power. She said Silas mentioned a ransom. Hell, that would be exactly what my old man would be after. Then he'd toss her aside without a backward glance.

Maybe that's the *real* reason I let her wind me around her pretty little finger and skip away without putting up a damn fight. She pleaded. Begged. I couldn't take her choice away. Not then, at least.

"Look, I know now isn't the time for a walk down memory lane, Day, but maybe you should try to be more like your old man in this instance," Chris suggests. "When Marcus ran the Saints, we never had shit with anyone."

"Yeah, because he was so fucking good at pretending to lead, he forgot to actually follow through with the 'leading' part,"

I hiss before I can stop myself. It's been five years. I should be well past the daddy issues by now. But fuck... Hearing him praised like some sort of king stings like nothing else. To Ben's and Chris' credit, it's not like they know the full truth.

They have no idea as to the hell that bastard left us in.

"I need some air," I snap, heading for the door.

"Alright, but stay here," Ben calls out. "We're just nailing down the specifics. I'll come talk it over once you've chilled out. Maybe take a cold shower."

"There's a spare apartment upstairs. You'll see the stairs by the back door," Chris adds as I spin around and head back the way I came.

Sure enough, I make my way above the bar and find one of the two apartments unlocked. Inside, I collapse on a battered couch and try to think. Absently, I reach into my pocket and pull out something I picked up on the way here —a small switchblade. With a polished wooden handle and compact size, it's the perfect weapon for a corrupted little princess.

I made the mistake of leaving her unguarded once. Won't happen twice. In the meantime, Ben and Chris can take their talk of strategy and shove it up their asses. What I really want to do is hunt Silas down like the sick animal he is and put a bullet in his skull.

Frey's sweet little lies didn't satisfy my itch for revenge, go figure. If anything, the sight of her face bruised and pale merely fed the hunger building within me for blood. Silas'.

Heywood's. Anyone who gets in my way can suffer the same damn fate.

But then I'd just be following in my old man's shoes, wouldn't I?

Marcus Keaton made a reputation out of playing the big man, but if there was one thing he taught me, it's that some of the most revered men aren't shit behind the scenes. It's just a role they perform. The general belief is that attaining power is the hard part and walking away from it is as easy as turning your back and hitting the door.

That's bullshit. When you want power badly enough, gaining it is easy. You can justify any and every damn task necessary to make it happen—whether it's stealing, murder, or something far worse. You'd sell your soul for a crown if you had to. *Really* had to.

You'd even make a deal with the devil.

Walking away is to admit that it all meant nothing. That the power was just a façade—a mask to hide your fucked-up life behind. Sure, you might be a piece of shit deadbeat, but look —you had authority, even if you sowed only bloodshed and chaos in your wake. You were king.

And everyone stupid enough to love you got mowed down in the crossfire.

My old man made that mistake. I grew up watching him strut and preen like the biggest peacock on the block because he ran the Saints. What a good man, they all said. A good man, a good father, and a good provider—it's sad how easy that word gets thrown around when all a man has to do is climb the ranks of a criminal outfit. It didn't matter that he spent more time on a bike, riding with his boys, than he did at home. It didn't matter that coke whores and side bitches knew more about him than his own damn wife did. It didn't matter that the members of the Saints have better memories of the bastard than I do.

The world always equates power with success, and that's that.

The funny thing is, I didn't understand what it felt like until I'd achieved it for myself—power. The all-consuming high that comes with being on top. A feeling that you can do no wrong and the entire world rests at your feet. I felt invincible. Unstoppable. Like a goddamn king.

And while I wore that banner of president, no one dared to say what a shitty father I was. Or how badly I'd failed Renna. Or how much of a screwup I'd always been. It wasn't until I walked away that those truths about who I'd always been popped up in conversations.

Power doesn't change a man—the world around him changes. It kisses his ass and blows smoke in his face, and the shitty parts of him get overlooked and glossed over. Damn, I can't lie and say I don't miss it a little.

But I never wanted that mantle back. Not for one damn second. I'd rather live seeing shit clearly than in a bubble. I'd rather be known as a fuck up than be too blind to see what people really think.

The real addictive thing about power, though, is that the benefits are just secondary. What truly matters is that armor. The ability to be untouchable and put everyone you care about behind that protective barrier. No one fucks with the king, if his reign is brutal enough. If he's ruthless enough.

If he defends his kingdom cruelly enough.

And, unfortunately for me, I need that, but not for myself. When I go over my motives for returning to the fold, all I see are three faces—two have always mattered to me, but the third is new. Pretty green eyes, perfect blond hair, and innocent face. She'll get eaten alive in this world without someone looking out for her.

Maybe it's stupid to care, but I want it to be me.

Even if it might get me killed in the process.

"Earth to Daze!" A fist slams into my shoulder, snapping me from the internal monologue. Ben stands over me, an eyebrow raised. I hate when he does that shit—catch me off guard.

I draw myself into a sitting position, feet braced on the floor. It's dark. I can barely make out Ben's face in the dim glow of an overhead light.

"Can I help you?" I ask, fighting back a yawn. The knife is still in my hand, and Ben raises an eyebrow at the sight of it. I can tell what he's thinking. *Have you calmed the fuck down?*

"Nice toy," he says instead. "Don't think it'll do much against Silas, though."

"Good. Because it's not for me." I flip the compact weapon into the air, catch it by the handle, and then hit the concealed switch to retract the blade entirely. "It's for Frey."

"Ah. At least you're thinking with your head. The one in your skull, anyway," Ben says sarcastically. "A weapon will do her good. Then maybe you won't be so distracted, worrying about her."

"I don't have any choice *but* to," I reply, looking up. On top of finding a safe place for us, there are a million other things to stress over—like getting Frey out of that fucking house whether she likes it or not.

"You should really get that head looked at," he says with a nod my way. "Where is your girlfriend, by the way?" He makes a show of looking around. "I figured I'd find you two humping like rabbits—"

"Very funny," I snap. "I couldn't get her out this time." And I'm still regretting letting her stay in that fucking house. I don't know what I was thinking. Scratch that—I wasn't thinking. Looking at her, and those wide green eyes... I couldn't say shit against her.

"Ah, no wonder you're so pissy. Well, while you were busy throwing a tantrum, I've been doing some recon," Ben says, crossing his arms.

"Yeah?" I shift to face him directly. "You have my attention."

"I think I found a potential hideout that's safer than the gym or some shitty one-bedroom flat—" He eyes the apartment disapprovingly. "Obtaining it will be tricky, though. For the time being, Chris will let us crash here, but we need to find our own place and fast."

"What did you have in mind?"

"Well, that's where the 'tricky' comes in," Ben admits, pursing his lips. "We're gonna have to steal it."

I can't tell if he's joking or not. Then again, Ben always did have a shitty sense of humor.

"I get that you're excited about getting back into the game and taking on Silas, Ben, but let's not get ahead of ourselves," I say. "The whole point is to not get killed *before* we can take the bastard out."

"I know that," Ben snaps. He runs his thumb along his chin, his brows furrowing. "But isn't the point to also make sure we can field an entire crew and find a good location that's easy to defend and won't be the first damn place Silas decides to hit up when he realizes you're still in town? Just hear me out."

"Okay then." I prop my chin on my fist and raise an eyebrow. "Who are we stealing this so-called hideout from?"

He smiles in that crazy ass way he used to back in his heyday. When he earned his top spot in the Saints through sheer pig-headed willpower.

"We're going to steal a warehouse with a perfect vantage point of the city, stocked with more than enough supplies to arm a few men, and it comes with the bonus that when Silas hears you've taken it for yourself, he'll be quaking in his boots. Do this, and everyone in town will know you mean business."

"And yet, you've been dancing around the issue of who exactly we're stealing from," I point out.

"Well, that's the fun part," he says. "This perfect fortress? We're going to steal it from the Cortez Cartel."

Ah, so that *was* his attempt at a shitty joke.

"You've lost your fucking mind."

"Hear me out—" He holds up a finger, his gaze serious. "You want to make a statement, right? Prove to everyone that you mean business. Nothing says that more than coming out swinging and reclaiming some old territory even Silas has left alone."

"Taking on the cartel is definitely a statement," I admit. "So is dying in the middle of such a stupid fucking idea."

"Ah, but there's the secret part that makes my plan fool-proof," Ben says with a sly grin. "We aren't going to die. We're going to reclaim that territory, and we're going to do it without risking our neck any more than you already have by basically declaring war on the Saints."

"I'm listening. How?"

"We use strategy," Ben says evasively. "Leave it to me. I'll make the arrangements. In the meantime, you should think more about who you might want to recruit into your new outfit. You can't do shit alone."

"I'm already on it," I say, thinking about my offer to Damien, Lex, and Kane. Walking away from the Saints left me few allies to call upon. But quality over quantity, right? "I made some connections in lockup. I'll see who might be up for the challenge."

That's not all. I need to see Frey. I can't shake this itch—a sensation gnawing at the back of my mind that something's wrong. She's in danger.

And starting some offshoot of the Saints isn't the only task on my list needing to be addressed. The next important item is to get her out of that house and away from Michael Heywood.

"I know that look," Ben says ominously. "Seems like I'm not the only one coming up with dangerous schemes. Just keep one thing in mind, Day. Sammy. He needs you now more than ever, and while getting killed by the cartel isn't ideal, having your ass thrown in prison isn't either."

He has a point, not that I plan on either outcome happening any time soon.

"I'll be a good boy, Benny."

"Good. Go see Chris. After you apologize for being a dick, maybe he can give you first aid or some shit."

"Fine," I call back, rising to my feet. "You both can wear sexy nurse uniforms if you want. I'm game."

"Smart ass," Ben snaps, but when he looks my way, he isn't laughing. "I want you to promise me something, Day. You'll *think* things through from now on. No more reckless bullshit. Got it? You don't want to be compared to your dad. Fine. Acting like you actually give a damn might be a good place to start."

I deserved that jab. Doesn't make it sting any less, though. "You know me, Ben," I reply with a mock salute. "Scouts' honor."

I keep my word—until dawn, anyway. Chris has his ear to the ground—according to him, Silas has gone quiet. No bands of his goons hunting for me. Nothing from Heywood's end either.

It's *too* damn quiet. I don't trust it.

The second Chris turns in for the night, I head out, alternating between checking my cell for any updates from Damien and keeping an eye out for any of Silas' boys.

In the end, I'm not shocked by where I ended up. Surprise-surprise. They've switched up security around the Heywood mansion, and I know better than to try the same trick twice. Still, Frey has another fucking thing coming if she thinks I'll let her stay there another day. Fuck no. Lucky for me, there's more than one way to break into Heywood's inner sanctum. Yeah, I turn my sights to another target ripe for potential infiltration. Frey herself mentioned it—the church.

I know of the place, though I've never been. A modest brick building in the heart of the city, it certainly doesn't look like much in the glow of dawn. Definitely not the seat of power of the man quickly becoming the top politician in the city, favored to win his next election.

I've seen cage-fighting arenas with more spunk—though few had the same amount of security posted on the premises.

Heywood's left nothing to chance, putting on a damn good show after his daughter's supposed "kidnapping." He has at least ten men on the ground from what I can determine, and even more, are no doubt inside. There are a few police officers, but most of the guard appears to be private security—an unusual escalation in protection even for a man rising the political ladder. Almost as if keeping criminals away isn't Heywood's only aim.

He wants to keep someone in.

I dwell on the prospect of breaking in for only a second before I send a text to Damien—*I need intel. Salvation church. Gimme all you got.*

A reply comes seconds later. Apparently, I'm not the only one who couldn't sleep. *Done.*

As I formulate a plan, I have to ask myself the question I know that Ben would ask if he were here—Is one woman really worth putting my neck on the line for?

When I picture those green eyes, an answer comes to mind that unsettles me more than anything else—yes.

FREY

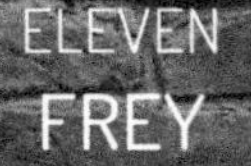

I FIND it unsettling how abruptly the world can change overnight—and then return to normal with equal speed. There is no big, monumental declaration of a shift in the status quo, either. No neon sign to mark the glaring differences. If anything, the transition is seamless. It's as if everyone just blinks and forgets to process that something horrific has happened. They go on as before, smiling and cheerfully serving breakfast without so much as a frown.

"Did you sleep alright?" Catherine asks while setting the table with a stack of steaming pancakes and a dish of eggs. "I heard you go to bed late."

I flinch at the statement. Did she hear the lash of a belt striking my skin, also? Looking at her face, I can't tell. She's the picture of perfection—bright-eyed and well rested, already wearing a beautiful blue dress for this morning's sermon.

There are cracks in her façade, though. Whenever I stare at her, her eyes veer away to focus on the wall behind me. A wall, coincidentally devoid of any pictures of Hale. There used to be several, but now only blank spaces remain as if they'd been taken down too hastily to replace.

"Are... Are you ready for the service?" Catherine asks while fiddling with a handful of silverware. She starts to set a knife down at the head of the table and fumbles, dropping it. With a cry, she lunges to fix the mess. Only once the setting is neatly arranged does she seem to remember I'm even here. "Your father knows it might be stressful, but he'll keep any reporters at bay."

I'm sure he will. Just like I'm convinced that every bit of this morning has already been planned out and choreographed. We'll leave and arrive together as a family, no doubt to an array of cameras eager to get a glimpse of me after my supposed ordeal in the grasp of armed criminals.

The reality is I don't know who to fear more, Silas or my own father?

Or, someone whose cruelty could potentially outweigh them all...

Daze Keaton.

"You're not eating much," Catherine scolds once she's settled into the seat across from me. Father's place setting that she so carefully arranged is glaringly empty. She seems troubled by the absence. Her hands shake as she pours herself a cup of tea, though she never lets her cheerful expression waver. "I think your father must be skipping his meal today. Oh well, a few leftovers never killed anyone. Perhaps we could bring them by the outreach later? They've been busier there than ever after what happened. Visitors mostly, dropping off flowers and gifts for you—" She clears her throat and risks a glance over her shoulder like a child making sure her parents aren't in earshot. Then she leans toward me and whispers, "You know, for what happened. So many people came out to show their support for you, Frances. Colton even went out to thank them. He was so devastated when he heard the news. Michael, of course, thinks it's wasteful, but I think it's so nice."

"Wasteful," I echo, feeling my brows furrow. For some reason, that word choice triggers a memory. It was a bitterly cold day, but we had to stand outside for hours. My dress was a thick black wool that itched like hell. I was younger, staring at a plot of disturbed earth, piled high with flowers of all kinds and a few heartfelt cards. Father stood beside me, his hair blonder then, his gaze steely as ever.

"How wasteful," he said in disapproval.

He sneered at the mangled rose I'd held in my hand that some well-meaning usher had passed out as we left the church. Without explanation, he snatched it away and threw it carelessly onto the pile of sentiments. Then, in a booming voice that radiated throughout the entire cemetery, he launched into a biblical lesson on the perils of grief. Even back then, his philosophy could be politely summed up as —*keeping a stiff upper lip.* Some of our neighbors had whispered other words to describe his demeanor. Cold. Cruel. Like any devoted daughter, I'd written the naysayers off as bitter. They didn't understand him. Father loved us all in his own way.

Without the blind loyalty of youth clouding my judgment, I can finally admit the truth—I'd been lying to myself. I didn't want to see what those not under his spell so clearly had.

"Frances?" Catherine waves her hand in front of my face. "Are you okay?"

"Yes," I say, pushing my plate aside. "I just remembered something. He said the same thing at my mother's funeral. Her fake one, of course—not that anyone outside the family knew that. He scoffed at their crying faces and gifts. He called them wasteful." My voice sounds so stern. Am I angry? Yes. For one of the first times in my life, I don't rush to suppress negative emotion. I'm angry.

Catherine just stares at me, her eyes bug wide. It isn't fair to lay this on her. I know that. But Silas' words keep itching at me. *He's been willing to throw away more than one of you precious Heywoods...*

What had he meant by that?

"You're probably exhausted," Catherine says, nodding to herself. She grabs a serving dish of eggs. "You should eat—"

"I'm not hungry," I snap. So much for our charming charade. I told Daze I would be fine another day—it seems I lied without even realizing it. I'm not fine. Ignoring reality has been my tried-and-true method for surviving this long, but my patience is wearing out. Some things can't be overlooked. Like pain. My back is on fire, aggravated by the polished, high-back chair I'm sitting on. My left eye still aches every time I blink. I can't breathe without thinking about Hale and how much I failed him.

And I know that Daze will find some way to break in, even if he has to risk getting hurt again. All for me—but I'm too much of a coward to unravel the twisted mysteries staring me right in the face.

"I need to know what happened to Hale," I say in a voice I barely recognize as my own. "I need to know the truth—"

"Frances, please," Catherine pleads. She reaches for my hand, and I realize that her fingers are trembling. Worriedly, her eyes dart in the direction of the staircase. "I know you've been through an ordeal, but your father has been stressed with the election. It might be best not to risk upsetting him. I know! I can make you some tea. That might help calm you—"

"No!" I wrench my hand away, but I'm just as startled by the action as Catherine seems. "You were beside him at Hale's funeral, weren't you?" I ask. By then, I'd been so lost in grief that I barely remember that day. "Did he call the flowers wasteful, then?"

"No," Catherine replies, her eyes glistening. "He loved your brother, and so did I. It isn't nice to bring up such awful things. Even about your mother, may she rest in peace. I'm sure your father—"

"She's not dead." I start to push back from the table. It's too hot in here. I can't think. "That's the lie he's been telling for the last few years, but she's alive."

"No, sweetheart." Catherine shakes her head, a beautiful frown playing on her lips. It's like she practices in the mirror how to appear as such—the wholesome, sweet wife to Michael Heywood. "She's gone. You need to accept that—"

"No." I lurch to my feet, compelled to keep talking, blurting out one of our dirty family secrets. "She was an addict who got sick of him. Did he tell you that? One night, she packed up her bags without a backward glance. I saw her leave."

"You don't know what you're talking about!" Catherine's voice changes in pitch, hoarse and thready. No longer does she look charming and innocent. Her eyes are wide, her bottom lip caught between her teeth. She looks... Horrified. "She's dead, and I—Frances, please, sit down. Please! Before Michael hears you! *Please!*"

I obey, compelled by her cries.

"Good. Now, can we at least have a civilized breakfast?" She pounces for my plate and grabs a ladle of fresh eggs. "Let's eat. Here, have some more. There's plenty."

Despite her best efforts to forge cheerful chatter, I'm too tired to play along. We finish our meal in silence, just in time to greet the figure who appears in the doorway, dressed in a coal-black suit.

"Michael!" Catherine lurches to her feet, fighting to smooth the front of her skirt, but I don't move. "I didn't hear you come down. Oh, dear, the food is all cold. I'll warm up your plate."

She flits off, though Father pays her no notice. His gaze is squarely fixed on me, and I find myself watching him with the same intensity.

In the morning glow drifting in through the windows, Michael Heywood looks the same as always. His white hair is neatly coifed, smoothed back to enhance the intensity of his blue eyes—the same hue as Hale's. They were more alike in physical appearance than personality, sharing an identical smile, as well as the quiet, suppressed way they managed their anger. Hale had a peculiar manner when something was troubling him. His brows would furrow, and his mouth would quirk downward into an "almost" frown.

Our father differs from him there, though. There is no mistaking his rage—his eyes darken to a dangerous shade of navy reminiscent of a sky when storm clouds roll in. He radiates that silent fury in every inch of his body, and his voice echoes, low and gravelly.

Like it does now.

"Morning, Frances," he says. "I take it you're ready to leave with us this morning? We will be joined in our pew by the Abernathys. They wanted to visit last night, but I decided that you should rest. You will speak with them after the services, I'm sure. Lewis Abernathy's support is vital to my future plans for this city."

Colton's father? He's a prominent investor from what I know, and an ardent supporter of my father's—though he rarely shows such special favor publicly. While they have their own pew a few benches back from ours, they've never sat with us before. For the Abernathy family to join us means more than just a simple seating arrangement, I suspect. It's a significant shift in the church's hierarchy that I can't even begin to process.

"After the services?" I repeat.

Father watches me with an unreadable expression. "Yes. Colton wishes to discuss a matter with you in private."

Oh, God. My stomach flips as I consider disobeying entirely. Running away. Screaming. Doing anything to show that I can't be cowed so easily. Beneath the gauzy material of my starched, white blouse, I can feel at least seven welts aching across the length of my back. I could barely sleep, plagued by their discomfort.

Even so, I grit my teeth rather than let the pain show. Instead, I just nod. "Yes."

"You will conduct yourself properly, of course," Father continues. "All eyes will be on our family, watching for any sign of weakness." His gaze rakes me over from head to toe, inspecting every detail of my ensemble.

In addition to the blouse, the rest of my clothing is what Catherine suggested—no doubt with his input. A modest gray skirt and cream cardigan. Every ounce of material feels like shackles, tethering me to a personality I'm not sure I want to embody anymore. The perfect, obedient daughter who ignorantly stood on the sidelines as her brother dealt with something nefarious.

So nefarious it got him killed.

At the same time, I'm not like Daze, bold and self-confident. I can't take on the world with a brazen swagger and hope for the best. I have to endure in my own way, whatever that may be.

It might just consist of playing along like an obedient, good girl for the time being. So, I force a smile and stand up to join my father in the doorway as though nothing is wrong.

"I'm ready."

I feel his eyes on the back of my neck as Catherine scrambles from the kitchen, fighting to tear off her apron.

Minutes later, we leave, flanked by his security. I can't resist scanning the faces of the men nearest me. I don't see a familiar battered, blond head among them. Unease gnaws away at my newfound resolve. Could he have gotten caught?

Though, I think there would be some mention of it. My father wouldn't hesitate to parade another "criminal" through the streets in the name of justice. The real question, though, is why I even *want* to see him again. Why I can't ignore the hope fluttering in my chest as I scan the front lawn for any sign of him.

The best thing would be for him to have changed his mind about coming. Keep safe. I still wish he were here though, whispering encouraging words into my ear. His advice would be vile, of course, riddled with vulgarity. *Toughen up, Blondie,* he'd snipe. *Don't get sidetracked. Try to see things as Hale saw them.*

Only I'm more confused than ever. He went from hating my father to debating biblical stories with him the night he died. A part of me wants to write off the information as trivial—but I can't. There's something there—if only I could figure out what.

I'm almost relieved when we pull up before the Covenant building, escorted by a police car. The square, two-story establishment looks the same as it always has.

Safe and simple, adorned only by a neatly tended front lawn of potted flowers that highlight a sign displaying the message of the week. Today's is simple—*Honor thy father.*

That ominous feeling of unease building in my gut grows as I'm herded inside, forced to march past pews filled with parishioners who crane their necks for a glimpse of me. Catherine said there was an outflowing of support. For what? The innocent victim of an attack that might have been planned by the figure walking beside me?

I feel like a fish in a bowl, on display for the entire world.

"This way, Frances," Catherine says, nudging me toward the front pew my family has dominated for years. Already seated there are a stern-faced man and woman with golden hair—with fake smiles plastered on their beautiful faces. The Abernathys. Beside them sits Colton, his expression the picture of concern. At least until our eyes meet—something cold flits across his gaze, gone in a flash, but I'm unsettled by it, none-theless. *Is something wrong?*

By the time I've settled in the furthest possible spot from the others, I've pushed the fear to the back of my mind. Father keeps going, heading for the pulpit centered on the low stage at the front of the room. It's strange how much time I used to spend in this place, with its familiar white walls and burgundy carpet meant to evoke the spilled blood of Christ. Yet, I barely recognize it. The pews are dark wood, worn with age, but even in the weeks before my father entered politics, I can't ever remember them being so full of people. Most of the faces peering at me from around their open Bibles are that of strangers.

The recent news coverage has been a boon for Covenant's attendance, it seems, and though he isn't technically allowed to hold a leadership role while he campaigns, Father looks at home facing down his swelling congregation.

When he steps forward and hefts his leatherbound Bible before flipping it open, I feel myself tense. What words of wisdom will he share today? As the gist of his chosen sermon for the morning becomes clear, my blood runs cold.

It's the tale of Abraham, a pious devotee tasked by God with a duty meant to put his loyalty to the test—sacrifice his own son, Isaac, without question. My father portrays that tale beyond the obvious lesson about devotion, however. He frames it as a duty. When God calls upon one of his flock, not even blood should stand in the way. Not a son. Not a daughter. A true follower will uphold any duty bestowed upon them by God without question.

Each word resonates differently than the many other speeches I've sat through over the years. His voice rings out harsher than I remember. Colder. His eyes seem to skip over everyone else and linger on me.

"Faith is fearless, and to embrace piety is to be a soldier for the Lord, unrelenting and unrestrained by mortal concerns." He looks me dead in the eye as he speaks. "A true worshiper must hold nothing sacred over the will of God."

Sweat runs down the back of my neck, aggravating every welt it meets on the way. As father drones on, I get up and scurry to the back of the room, desperate for fresh air. To my shock, no one tries to stop me, and I find my way into the women's bathroom. Finally alone, I lean against the counter, panting for breath.

I'm being paranoid by reading into that sermon far more than I should. Right? That wasn't a message directed my way —no, a warning. Was Hale the one he thought stood in his way to some righteous goal?

Or my mother... Catherine didn't seem like she was parroting my father's lies for once when she responded to my outburst. No. She insisted on my mother's death as if she knew for sure she was gone—and that knowledge terrified her.

It terrifies *me*. I don't even recognize the shivering mess staring back from the mirror's surface. I look nothing like the bold woman who kissed Daze—and more—in the narrow bathroom of his apartment. Maybe I never was that person. I was always meant to be frightened, meek Frey, who watches from the sidelines, too afraid to stand up for herself.

Suddenly, the door opens, and I struggle to compose myself. Did Catherine come to check on me? I look over, expecting to find her smiling face, eager to shepherd me back to the main room and under Father's purview. Instead, I spot a figure who, at first glance, doesn't fit the mold of the average female parishioner. They're too tall, for one, and possess ample muscles that strain the white dress shirt and slacks they wear instead of a dress. Wait...

I gape as the figure presses a finger to his lips while closing the door behind him. He grabs the large trash can positioned nearby and places it in the doorway, blocking the entrance in case someone tries to come in.

Rather than inspire fear, my body goes limp with relief at the sight of those familiar limbs. Voice a choked whisper, I croak, "I didn't think you'd come—" Though I'm selfishly glad he did. Still, I can't resist adding, "There are guards posted all over."

"I know." That smile vanishes every fear I have. It flits over a familiar mouth and illuminates the gray eyes I've come to recognize. They—and the blond hair neatly combed to obscure the bruises on his face—are the only parts of this figure that belong to the gruff, wild Daze. Otherwise, the man wearing a crisp church outfit with starched slacks could be a stranger, eager to listen in on a typical morning sermon.

"Breaking into my house is one thing," I whisper, fighting to sound stern. "But if Father sees you—"

"We have about ten minutes before he wraps up that charming speech of his," Daze says, evading my question. In two steps, he closes the distance between us, pressing me in against the nearest wall. "So, I hope you've said your good-byes, princess."

"Ah—" I barely manage to choke off a cry as my back twinges. Thankfully, Daze seems too busy inhaling my scent to notice. I wiggle closer to him, shifting so that my hip takes the pressure instead.

Then I copy him, breathing in deeply. He smells good—different from his usual musk. I think he put on cologne, which I doubt he uses regularly. It's merely part of his ruse to blend in. Just to get to me?

"What if someone sees you?" I ask, though I don't sound as worried by that as I should.

Having him near me acts like kryptonite to the niggling self-doubts. I can think clearly again. One unsettling speech shouldn't be enough to rattle me so easily. I need to refocus.

I attempt to do so while holding Daze's gaze, seeing myself reflected in those piercing eyes. With every passing second, I note changes in him that weren't there even the other day. He isn't smiling for one. The lack of the trademark expression makes him look older. Colder.

"Something's wrong," he says.

"Huh?" I fight to make my expression blank. Desperate for a distraction, I run my hands along his forearms. It's easier that way to sense the tension rippling in his muscles, ready to explode at a moment's notice.

"What happened? You don't seem very happy to see me," he adds, reaching up to flick a wayward strand of hair from my face. Then he holds onto that lone curl, twisting it around his fingers. "In fact, you look fucking terrified. Don't lie to me. He did something to you. Said something. More than that fire and brimstone shit he was spewing out there." His eyes narrow, and I feel his hand inch toward my lower back. "You winced before. When I touched you here—"

"No." I try to bat him off. "I'm fine."

"Little liar," Daze snarls. His upper lip curls back from his teeth, and I'm suddenly aware of how much larger he is than me. How much stronger. Yet, his touch is persistent along my waist, unnervingly gentle. His voice, however, is a chilling contrast as he bites out, "Turn around."

I stiffen. Catherine had spent the morning in such blissful ignorance that I'd almost convinced myself that I was just *that* good at hiding my true emotions. Apparently not. With one look, Daze has seen right through me, and I don't know whether to be terrified he can read me so well or...

Relieved. At least it means that I'm not crazy—that the unease and constant prickling dread I feel isn't all in my head. Something is horribly wrong, even if I can't definitively say what.

But I'm not stupid enough to reveal everything to Daze, either. He's taken enough beatings as it is.

"I don't want to do this now. Please." I force a smile and step into him, painfully aware of every noise emanating from the hall. I can only pray that no one has to pee before the end of the service. "Nothing's wrong with me," I lie in a way that I think is convincing. At least until my voice breaks. Thinking fast, I change tact. Lying is his game. Playing pretend is mine. "And even if there were... I don't want to care. Just make me forget. Please, Daze. That's all I want. It's what I need. I *need* to forget."

His eyes narrow to slits, and I brace for him to spin me around and rip my shirt off anyway. Instead, he presses his thumb against the corner of my mouth as if testing the validity of my last statement. "Fine then. We'll dance around that subject for now if you want, but you aren't that good of an actress, Freylie. I'll find out the truth later, once I get you to my place."

Oh no. I grit my teeth at the reminder of his unofficial timeline.

"Daze, wait—" I place my hand on his chest, but he draws me into him, palming my waist. He boldly plunges a thumb beneath my blouse and my breath feathers. I can barely choke out, "Daze, stop—"

"Done waiting," he rasps. "You had your day. Now you're all mine." A devastating smile spreads over his lips, but his eyes remain dark. Way too serious for games. "You gave me your word, Freylie. You're coming with me."

"You think I can skip out in the middle of the service? You're joking, right?" I force out a laugh, though deep down, I know he means every word. His desperation to leave is apparent in how his fingers grip me possessively, conveying the strength coiled in each digit.

"Like hell I am. Pretend I don't know you're hurting. Keep your secrets if you want—" He nods toward my shoulder. "But do you really think I'll let you stay in that fucking house a second longer? You may put your faith in prayer, but I don't. Silas has already come after you once, and we both know that your brother didn't accidentally overdose. You're coming with me. No discussion. We can leave out the back with no one the wiser."

"Daze..." An unfamiliar warmth spreads through me, and I feel dizzy. "Are you proposing to kidnap me again?"

He raises an eyebrow. "Why not? Your old man has already gambled your welfare at least once for a publicity stunt. This time, you won't risk a beating by a fucking psychopath. And don't think I didn't realize that fucked-up sermon was directed at you."

I wince at the reminder. Maybe it's the heated passion in his voice, but I can't deny that his plan sounds convincing. Tempting. A part of me wants to throw caution to the wind and risk sneaking away now, right from under Father's nose and the watchful eyes of his security.

But...

"I can't," I say, hating how weak I sound compared to him. My voice is just a thready whisper, but I fight to make it sound stronger. "I need more time. There's something about Hale's death no one is telling me."

And maybe my mother's supposed fake funeral should be added to the list.

I can't stop picturing Catherine from this morning. The look on her face...

"I know it's stupid," I say in response to Daze's enraged growl. "But I need to figure out what. Maybe then I can finally get him justice. I just need to do *something*."

Or at least get to the bottom of what Hale had been trying to tell me. He wasn't crazy—and Catherine got so jumpy when the topic of that night came up for a reason. Something more than trauma and grief. There was fear in her eyes, too, I'm sure of it.

"I need to do this while I'm close to them and still in the house. I owe Hale that much. Please—"

"You don't owe him your life," Daze counters, boring his gaze into mine.

"I know that. I'm doing this for me. And... I need you to trust me, the way I trust you. Remember? You still haven't told me how you knew my father—the *real* reason. Should I demand to hear it before I can even think of leaving with you?"

He has the decency to look away. "Fine then," he snaps after a painful few seconds of silence. "I'll give you another day, maybe two. After that, you're coming with me, even if I have to carry you out of that fucking house with your daddy watching."

"As romantic as that sounds, I think you should worry about yourself first—" I prod his forehead. Despite how well he's cleaned up, a neatly coifed hairstyle can't completely hide the bruises. I wish I had a first-aid kit or something to treat him with. A wet paper towel will have to do. With a sigh, I grab one from the dispenser, run it beneath the faucet, and then dab at the nastiest mark along his temple. "You have Sammy to think about," I tell him. "Besides, you can do something for me instead of trying to scale the walls of my house."

He cocks his head just enough to still maintain contact with my hand. "What?"

I can't shake the feeling that he's right. I'm in danger, and no longer can I willfully pretend I'm not. There is only one solution, and yet... I can barely get the words out.

Tilting my head back to meet his gaze, I take a steadying breath. "I... I want you to get me a weapon."

His eyebrows go up, but I don't think he's half as startled by the request as I am. Before I can even process the logistics of such an insane ask, another demand slips out of my mouth. "*And* I want you to teach me how to use it."

"I think I'm starting to rub off on you." He doesn't seem too troubled by that prospect, however. He purses his lips, seemingly mulling over the request, and a thrill shoots down my spine. I'm not used to this—being heard.

"What kind of weapon?" He grabs my wrist, tracing a path down to my fingers. He takes his time, smoothing over each one as if gauging which method of violence they'd be best suited for. "Maybe a switchblade. Something small you can conceal at all times. Frankly, princess, I don't know if I'd trust you with a gun."

"You actually think you could get me one?" I don't know if I'm horrified by the idea or merely intrigued about what he really does when he isn't cage fighting or dragging women off bridges. Something involving a need for an intimate knowledge of weapons and how to find them, anyway.

"Already on it," he continues, still stroking my hand. Then he reaches into his pocket and presses something firm to my palm. In awe, I realize I'm holding a sleek, compact switchblade. As I watch, Daze presses a silver button on the side that sends a pointed blade extending from one end.

"Great minds think alike," he says with a grin. Then he sets the knife on the counter. "But we'll start with basic defense, first." He steps in, maneuvering me in front of him with my back against his chest. I close my eyes against the resulting sting—his nearness is worth any agony. "Let's say I'm some asshole that's snuck up behind you and gone for your throat —" He releases my hand in favor of palming my neck instead, gently enough that I can still breathe. "Besides screaming, what do you do?"

I raise my hands and mime digging my nails into him. "Try to get him off."

"Wrong." He leans forward, forcing me to feel the contours of his much larger body against mine. In theory, the answer to his question seems obvious. I wouldn't stand a chance if my attacker was even half his size.

"Don't think like that," Daze scolds into my ear as if reading my mind. "When someone has you from behind, the first thing you do is go limp. Make yourself deadweight."

I raise an eyebrow skeptically, eyeing the still-closed door. Despite my ever-present fear that someone might barge in at any moment, I'm dizzy off the warmth of his breath on my neck. The way he feels. How he smells, with his usual musk mingled with sweeter cologne. The mixture makes my mouth water and my tongue grow damp. I almost miss what he says next.

"Focus, princess. When grabbed, you go limp. Do it."

"Okay…" I obey, letting myself slump into his grasp.

"That will throw off your attacker," Daze explains, loosening his grip as he speaks. "He'll expect you to fight, and he'll instinctively relax when you don't. The second he does, you grab his forearm with both hands and focus all your weight to the floor."

I rock forward on the balls of my feet while grabbing at his hand. The force alone is enough to break his grasp and let me wiggle away.

"Good," he says, wrenching me toward him again. "Do it faster."

After five more attempts, he finally seems satisfied enough to move on to the next step of this impromptu lesson.

"We don't have a lot of time left, but there is one thing you need to know. The most important thing."

"What?" I ask when he trails off.

He spins me to face him, but I'm not prepared for the heat I find in his gaze. "That I'll always have your back. Always."

"I said that I trust you, but how can I?" I'm not being spiteful for the hell of it. Even now, it feels like he's still withholding a piece of himself from me, even as he promises me everything.

"You want me to prove it?" He moves in to brush his lips over mine. "Fine. With every second that you stay with these bastards, I want you to think of this—"

His hand is whisper-soft, ghosting down to my inner thigh. He teases me with just the tip of a finger at first, but I can't silence a whimper. It's insane how confident another person can navigate your own body in ways you could never dream.

With barely any contact, he has me jolting on the tips of my toes, lacing my fingers around his neck.

"I want you to imagine me inside you," he breathes against my throat. "Just like this... I want you to close your eyes and hear my voice. You got that?"

He stills, crooking that beckoning finger.

"Y-Yes," I bite out.

"Good." His lips brush my earlobe, his voice dangerously soft. "I want you to remember me saying this—you are mine, Frey. All of this."

He sounds too serious. My belly quakes at the prospect, and I'm tempted to ask him, "Why? You barely know me—"

"Because I always know what I want." He nudges my panties aside and eases a finger inside me. My eyelids flutter, and I lean back, relying on the sink for support.

"And I'm not afraid to claim it. Do you hear me, Freylie? This pretty little pussy is mine," Daze grates out, stroking me in a slow, ruthless rhythm. "This little cry you make when I touch you...here—"

He crooks that finger, and my breath catches. It's sinful how good he feels. I've barely adjusted to the sensation when he flexes his thumb, teasing the bundle of nerves that makes me cry out.

"And I want you to remember how this feels," he says, his voice hoarse. "Tell me."

I can barely get the words out. "It feels...good," I manage to croak. "So good—"

"But not good enough," he declares. "I want you to imagine me fucking you like this, against the wall, with your pretty little skirt a fucking mess and your nice bun undone. And your eyes so damn wide. Can you do that?"

My cheeks heat at the innuendo, but I can't deny the power that image has over me. He makes something so seemingly degrading sound...incredible. My heart rate skyrockets at the thought of him bringing such an image to life. "Yes..."

"Good girl." He touches me in earnest, griding his palm into me, while stroking me with his finger at the same time. I have to bite my lip to keep quiet. I can't stop my hips from arching and my nails from snagging at his skin. "Damn," he hisses through his teeth, stepping into me while his mouth finds mine.

This kiss is nothing like the others we've shared. It's rough. Brutal. Biting. He sucks at my lower lip. Then nips, making me jump. I return the favor, and the sound he makes...

It has my toes curling. I smooth my hands over his shoulders, sensing the coiling muscle beneath. His heartbeat races against me, undermining the suave, calm persona he always embodies. The truth seems to be that I affect him just as much as he affects me.

"I think I'm having difficulty imagining exactly what you wanted me to," I admit against his mouth. He rears back, an eyebrow raised.

"Oh?"

"Yes. I think you might have to demonstrate it in detail for me."

"Can do."

Before I can even blink, his hands are delving beneath my skirt and hooking around the waistband of my panties. One harsh yank triggers a horrific ripping sound, and then they vanish—not that Daze seems to mind the destruction. He hooks his hand beneath one of my knees, yanking it up to his waist. Then he wrenches open his fly with one hand.

I watch him in awe, feeling my cheeks flame. "I think I like you in this good boy church getup," I tell him thickly. "It makes you look almost wholesome."

He growls out a laugh that might be loud enough to draw notice—not that he seems to care. I doubt that even if my father waltzed in on us right now, he'd have the decency to stop. He looks at me like I'm the only thing that matters in the entire universe. Not even his safety comes close.

"Looks can be deceiving, Freylie," he murmurs, diving in to run his tongue along my bottom lip. I shiver at his taste—musky and sweet. "I think it's time you learned that."

He takes his thumb and runs it between my legs, barely touching the aching flesh. If he had his way, I bet he'd tease me like this until my breaking point, using this power over me to make me do and say whatever he wanted. At the moment, though, time is too short, and he doesn't seem willing to deny himself another second.

He enters me so slowly I can track his every reaction. The way he hisses out in relief at the feel of me. The way his eyes threaten to roll in the back of his head simply because of how much pleasure he gains merely by this act. Then he bites his lower lip as a feral hunger sets in. When his vision clears and homes in on mine, I know only to brace myself.

His next thrust makes my teeth clatter together. A moan revs in my throat as he draws back and rocks into me again. The second I adjust to the invasion, he changes tact, swiveling his hips to go harder. Deeper.

It's so, so good. All thought—and fears—go right out of my head. The fact that we're in a church bathroom ceases to matter. I forget that I can't moan the way I want to. I forget that every grunt that rips from him as he rocks into me merely increases our chances of being discovered.

None of that matters.

Helpless, I rake my fingers through his hair, digging my nails in as he begins to slam into me in earnest. Fiery pleasure ignites in my belly, spreading throughout my body until it builds into an all-consuming inferno.

"Fuck," Daze grates before seizing a tender bit of flesh on my shoulder between his teeth. He bites down hard enough to border on pain as his thrusts lose their polished cadence. He's reckless. Wild.

I do my best to arch into him, letting my body demand more until I'm shuddering with the need to finally cross over the point of no return.

"You're about to come," Daze says, giving a name to the desperate, aching sensation building within me. "Fuck. I can feel you. Come for me. Just like that, sweet girl. Give me all you've got."

I close my eyes and let his grated command work its magic over my body. I can feel my body clamping down over him, gripping so tightly he groans like someone in the throes of grievous torture.

"Not yet," he bites out, though I think he's speaking more to himself than to me. With renewed focus, he takes my other knee in hand and yanks.

This angle gives him more leverage, and he uses every last bit of it to his advantage. Without warning, he pivots, and I'm further back on the counter, with my back against the mirror.

"That's more like it," he praises as a startled cry rips from my throat. "No one's here to see you now, little princess. Stop holding back and fuck me like you want to come."

I grasp out with one hand, curling it around the rim of the counter beneath me. Using that grip for leverage, I rock my hips into him while pulling his face down to mine. I take him up on his challenge and use the kiss to turn the tables.

I lose all traces of the polite, perfect manners that have been drilled into me my entire life. I take what I want—using my teeth to pry his mouth open and hook my tongue around his.

He growls in shock and angles his hips to retaliate. From that position, he strokes a part of me that makes my vision go white. I have to gasp for air, and before my lungs can fully fill, he reaches between us and grinds his thumb against my clit.

He's too good at this. I can only submit to the pleasure and hang on for the ride. Contrary to his taunt, he can't seem to stave off the release his body desperately seeks indefinitely. With a hoarse, guttural shout, he slams into me one last time.

The grating friction triggers my body's release, and I can't even savor the fact that he beat me to the punch. My toes curl as I ride each slow, heady wave of ecstasy. At one point, it feels like it will never end. I'll just exist like this for an eternity, locked in mind-numbing pleasure with him.

Eventually, my breathing steadies, though, and I slowly come back down to earth with Daze panting against my ear.

"Was that a good enough demonstration, Freylie?" he asks between breaths. "Think you can remember that?"

I can only muster up a breathless sigh in response.

"Good." He runs his fingers along my bound hair and presses his forehead to mine. I greedily breathe him in, savoring this nearness. In total, we've probably been here less than twenty minutes, but it feels like something has changed between us, even in that short amount of time.

His eyes tell me he feels the same way, even if neither of us dares to voice what it is.

"I think your fellow parishioners might start to wonder where you are." Suddenly, he pulls back, nuzzling against my neck until the last possible second. "I should go before they come looking..."

He should. That doesn't make it any easier to nod in agreement.

"You should leave first," he adds, helping me to my feet. With a start, I realize my panties are in two torn halves on the floor, savaged beyond repair.

"Wait—" Daze snatches a handful of paper towels from a nearby dispenser. He wets them beneath the faucet and then crouches, cleaning me up with a care that mimics how I fussed over him. "There," he says, obscuring his handiwork as I rush to smooth my skirt into place. "You look perfect. *Virginal,* some might say—"

"Very funny!" I ruffle his hair as he rises to his feet.

"Here, don't forget this," he murmurs as he reaches for the blade he left on the counter. He places it in my right hand before curling my fingers around the weapon.

He kisses me hard one last time. Then he murmurs, "Clear the hallway for me if you can so I can exit before some lady gets a lot more than she bargained for."

"Oh? I think you'd like that," I taunt, throwing the words he'd murmured in my bedroom back in his face as I slip the knife into the pocket of my skirt. "They'd see who you really are. My dirty rogue angel."

He laughs while I continue to adjust my appearance. After tossing my torn panties in the trash, I can't resist lingering near him for another second. One more. He doesn't resist, letting me reach for his hand and run my finger along his palm.

When I finally exit the bathroom, it feels like I'm going through a portal to another dimension. One in which the world seems colder and grayer, and there isn't the wild, chaotic energy that Daze exudes without even trying. In its place is just fear and unease that builds until it feels like I'll explode.

It takes everything I have not to turn back. Instead, I make sure the hall is clear before I return to my seat beside Catherine just as Father finishes up with his service to polite applause. Sitting down only reinforces the fact that I'm not wearing anything else beneath the thin material of my skirt. I know my cheeks are on fire as Catherine leans over and whispers in my ear. "You were gone a while. I was just about to go in after you. Are you alright?"

"Of course. I'm wonderful." I even muster up a polite smile. Within seconds, I've fallen back into my perfect, charming daughter charade. When the congregation finally breaks to mingle and pay their respects, I survive only a handful of forced greetings and introductions before I can't take it anymore.

I bolt, sensing one of Father's men hot on my heels before I even enter the lobby. "I just need fresh air," I tell him as I scurry toward the main doors, but the reality is that I'm praying to catch a glimpse of Daze retreating down the block. Maybe I'll be brave enough to chase after him—damn the consequences.

Or, better yet, one last glance at him can give me the strength I need to keep going.

Instead, the front lawn is devoid of anyone but a few lingering reporters who strain to get a photo. I haven't decided which is a worse foe to face—them or the people inside the church—when someone climbs over a metal barrier keeping them at bay, despite the guard's warning.

"I'm unarmed," he says, raising his empty hands. He comes close enough to touch me, but no further. "I just want to ask her a few questions if that's okay. She doesn't have to respond if she doesn't want to. I can give you my press credentials if you want."

Withdrawing a pen from behind his ear with one hand, he fishes out a notebook from his pocket with the other. He's young, with tousled brown hair and dark eyes that gleam behind the frames of his glasses.

"Frances Heywood, if I'm not mistaken?" he asks, turning to me. "My name is Jamie Colland with the Daily Reporter. I just wanted to ask you a few questions about—"

"She has no comment," a guard snaps before I can voice a word for myself. He storms to my location, stepping in front of me. "Miss, perhaps we should step back inside—"

"That's strange," the reporter says, craning his neck to hold my gaze, "because one might think you'd have something to say regarding the rumors about the organization your family runs and that you have attached your name to, Ms. Heywood."

I stop short. The accusatory note in his voice startles me into responding. "What are you talking about?"

A potential answer comes to mind. Could he be referring to Hale and his doubts about Salvation?

His sharp brown eyes give nothing away. "I'm talking about the spate of disappearances being reported throughout the city in the past year and a half," he says. "There's been at least a dozen that I know of, most of them homeless or former addicts with few family ties to the local area. One thing they do have in common, though? They've all been through the doors of Salvation and roped into one of your 'employment outreach' programs. Do you have any comment on that?"

"That's enough." The guard grips my arm and manually steers me toward the front entrance of the church. "I think Mr. Heywood would be interested to know that you and your employer believe it's okay to harass innocent civilians," he calls back.

"I don't intend to harass you, Ms. Heywood," the man says, though he keeps his distance. "I merely want to get to the bottom of what's happening to some of the most vulnerable citizens of our city. If you share the same interest, I ask that you give me a call." He fishes a business card from his pocket and offers it to me.

"This way, Ms. Heywood." The guard maneuvers me inside before I can protest, and I look back in time to witness the reporter setting the card on top of the church's welcome sign.

"Give me a call at any time, Ms. Heywood," he shouts, his voice muffled by the glass doors slamming shut. "All I want is to get to the truth of what's happening. I believe your family might hold the answer."

His words ring ominously as I'm steered back inside the main room of the church. Hale was worried about something involving Salvation—something so bad that it drove a wedge between him and the rest of my family and may have even gotten him killed. Something so bad that he felt compelled to team up with a man like Daze to find answers.

Do those missing people have anything to do with his concerns? Westpoint City isn't the most idyllic place in the world—after all, my father has based his entire campaign on reducing a rash of increased crime. But multiple disappearances within a year, all of them able to be traced back to one place?

It sounds too convenient to be a coincidence.

Still, I try to keep my concern from showing on my face as I rejoin Catherine and my father, who are addressing a handful of parishioners. The closer I come, the harder it gets to maintain my carefree expression.

"Frances," Father says, gesturing to the man across from him. "Colton has expressed interest in joining us for dinner tonight. What do you think?"

I keep smiling. I didn't even realize that Colton and his parents were standing nearby. "That sounds great."

It doesn't. A dinner is just one more distraction threatening to get in my way of finding answers before Daze's timeline. Do I really think he'll drag me out of my house in front of everyone if he feels the need to?

Yes. I think he might.

"Good, it's settled then. I'm sure you have plenty to catch up on. Catherine and I will be in the car." To my surprise, Father retreats, leaving behind at least two guards who lurk nearby while Colton grabs my hand and guides me to the back of the church.

"You look good," he says, glancing over the slight bruise on my forehead. "I didn't sleep at all last night, worrying about what could have happened."

He sounds earnest, but I can't shake a paranoid sense that he doesn't appear anywhere near worried enough. Almost as if he's going through the motions, feigning shock at an event that he was well aware of in advance.

I try to shrug off the suspicion.

"I'm fine, but I'm a little tired. I really should be heading back—"

"Wait." He tightens his grip on my hand, and I have to suppress the urge to wrench my fingers away. "You'll be there tonight, won't you?"

"Tonight?" I jump at the chance to weasel out of the event without rousing my father's ire. "Oh, I hope so, though I'm still really tired. I'll let you know if we need to reschedule—"

"Then I'll tell you now, what I expect so that you're prepared regardless," he says. "I've already mentioned it to your father, and we've come to an agreement that now is the right time. I know you've been distracted after what happened with your brother, but you can't spend the rest of your life, grieving for him, Frances. I'm sure you realize that now."

I don't know how to respond. "What do you mean?"

"I think it's time we take our relationship to the next step. Tonight, I plan to formally announce my intent to pledge my devotion to you, Frances."

My mind goes blank. All I can do is blink. "What?"

"I'm going to propose," Colton insists, enunciating every word. "And your father has assured me that you will accept."

"Assured you?" Anger rips through me, and I can't control it. I wrench my hand away and step back, too horrified to keep up with my calm, happy charade. "What are you even talking about? He can't promise you anything! I decide who I want to marry and when. We barely even know each other."

"Enough!" With a wary glance at anyone who might have overheard, Colton steps forward, bringing his lips near my ear. "I've put up with your attitude long enough, but no longer. I even stood aside while you embarrassed me the way you have. Do you truly think we're all really that stupid? That we don't know about *him*?"

I feel the color drain away from my face. "Who... Who are you talking about?"

Darkness clouds his expression. "You know exactly who I'm talking about. We've turned a blind eye in the name of forgiveness, but that ends now. You are mine, Frances, ordained for me by God. Don't make the mistake of assuming that forgiveness always triumphs over righteous duty."

He wrenches me closer, his gaze boring into mine.

"When I propose to you tonight, you *will* accept. You will go back to the way things were. You will volunteer with your head held high in the Lord's service, and you will stay by my side the way a wife should. Do you understand me?"

It's eerie how much he sounds like my father. He even has his cadence down, as if he studied just how to mimic him in the mirror. "You aren't the Shepherd," I tell him, fighting to keep my voice steady. "And you don't control me, Colton. Let me go—" I try to pull my arm away.

"Not yet, I don't," he says, tightening his grip. "But I will. Far sooner than you think. It's inevitable, Frances. You belong with me. It won't be long before you see that." He leans in, forcing a kiss against my cheek.

"Stop!" I push him off and nearly succeed in getting away. His hand latches onto my forearm before I can take a step, drawing a gasp from my lips.

"Don't you ever walk away from me," he snarls, wrenching me to face him. "You will marry me. Your father will walk you down the aisle. And on our wedding night…" He exhales raggedly, his nostrils flaring. I barely recognize him, and tension gathers at the base of my spine as he curls one of his hands into a fist. Would he really hit me? Here?

I can't stop myself from scanning the room, but the guards are absent, presumably posted out in the lobby. There's no one to witness anything he might do—and I doubt it was by coincidence. No. He and Father conspired to arrange this little meeting.

As a warning.

I swallow hard and aim to sound calm. "Colton…"

"And on our wedding night," he continues over me, his face reddening. "I'll see just how much damage you let that criminal swine do to you. Your father used his influence to have the nurses perform an exam while you were unconscious. I know he soiled you. Seduced you. God, you even reek of corruption."

I go still, unable to keep my face blank. Daze's knife is in the pocket of my skirt. Drawing it now would certainly ruin my father's chances of charming more money out of Lewis Abernathy, but I consider it. Then I force my hand flat against my hip and lick my lips to find traction to speak, "I don't…"

"When I am your husband, you will repent for your sins," he warns, his breath hot on my face. My resolve breaks, and I slide my hand into my pocket, gripping the switchblade. As my thumb finds the button to trigger the blade, Colton hisses, "I'm sure your father can teach me all about dealing with an unruly wife. See you tonight."

He releases me abruptly and storms away, his head held high. Something in his posture sticks out to me. Maybe it's the confident tilt of his head. In any case, I'm so shaken I feel my knees buckle in response, and I have to catch myself against a nearby pew.

He wasn't referring to Catherine with that last statement.

He was referring to my mother.

TWELVE
DAZE

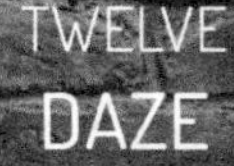

I DON'T DWELL on shit. Not like the way Ben does or Chris, pining away for the glory days and living with one foot always in the past. I don't second-guess myself, either. In a world where a bullet could end your life any minute, there's no fucking time to hesitate.

But I'm hesitating now. Every ounce of me wants to turn back, strolling into that church and throwing Frey over my shoulder if I have to. She thinks she's brave for looking into what happened to her brother. She is. But bravery doesn't always outweigh stupidity, and she's too naïve to sense the undercurrent of bullshit brewing that I can. Something big is about to go down.

And if I don't get her out soon, she'll be destroyed in the aftermath.

But before I can even think about getting her away from Heywood, I need to solve the tiny problem of finding a place to hole up and defend.

When I return to the bar. Ben is there, leaning against the counter, his arms crossed, gaze questioning. "You look like you just got punched in the stomach," he says. "Don't tell me you ran into Silas again, already?"

"No," I say—though that's another thing to worry about. Why hasn't he come by to rub my nose in the mess he's created? If I wanted to be smug about it, I'd claim the bastard was too chicken shit to face me, but that's not it. Whatever trouble I sense on the horizon, Silas is no doubt behind it.

"I've been thinking about this plan of yours," I add. "It still sounds crazy as hell, but we don't exactly have other options."

"I had a feeling you'd say that," Ben says with a smile. "That's why I went ahead and made the arrangements while you were out. As I said before, it isn't anything too risky. It's just going to take...balls."

"Something tells me you aren't talking in the literal sense."

With a wink, Ben grabs his jacket from a table in the corner and heads for the door. "I'll explain on the way there. This is going to work, Day, and if it doesn't? Well, it's not like we'll have much time to dwell on that with bullets in our skulls, right?"

I don't laugh at the joke.

As things stand, taking a bullet is well worth the risk if it means getting Frey out of that house a second sooner. Dwelling on the past can't help shit, but my mind keeps replaying those last minutes with her over and over. Fuck, I can still taste her on the tip of my tongue.

I can't shake the feeling that, if I don't act soon, that might be the last of her I'll ever have.

This far north, the cartel isn't anywhere near as powerful as they are in other sectors. Their foothold extends to just a few neighborhoods, and their distribution is pitiful. That doesn't mean that they don't have influential backers elsewhere who wouldn't hesitate to swoop in to protect their interests in the event that someone else tried to take them out.

They also control some of the most illicit and lucrative aspects of the underground vice trade. The shit the Saints used to turn their noses up at in the name of honor. I know that Silas rubs shoulders with them every now and again.

And I know that, despite his public image as the perfect leader, they had my old man's balls in a vice.

While risky, driving them from Westpoint could serve as a better message than anything else I could pull off in the meantime. It's worth a shot.

Or so I thought until I hear the details of Ben's crazy ass plan.

"You want me to stroll in there alone and tell them to leave?" We're positioned in an alley near the cartel hideout on the outskirts of the city. Ben wasn't lying when he claimed it would make for a good base. It's situated on a hill with a clear view of all oncoming roads. With boarded-up windows and plenty of real estate, it obscures how many men might be inside it, making it a challenge to attack from any direction.

But that goes for the cartel lackeys holed up inside. Given that Ben suggested we come alone, we aren't exactly in a position to knock on the front door, let alone try and take the place.

"Don't make it sound like that," Ben snaps. "I'm not saying you skip in there and ask for tea. You go in on your terms as the leader of the new arm of the Saints and offer to cut a deal."

"Silas rubs shoulders with these traffickers, and now you want me to do the same shit? Have you lost your fucking mind?"

"You need men, right? Unless you want to go recruiting Saints' members from under Silas' nose, you gotta start fresh. You offer to cut a deal of protection. They join our crew or get the fuck out of dodge. I think they'll take the former option. You forget that your name comes with a reputation, Day—"

"Because of fucking *Marcus*?" I hiss out the name. "I know you and Chris wanted to suck his dick, but that bastard wasn't all he pretended to be. Trust me on that."

"What the hell has gotten into you?" Ben asks, placing a hand on my shoulder. "The other night, I wrote off your little bitch fest as you being worried about your girlfriend. If there's something more you want to say, then fucking say it."

"It's nothing," I grunt, shrugging him off. "Just get to the point."

"Well, for your information, I wasn't talking about your dad's reputation. You aren't exactly known as the candy man around here. I bet if you go in there with enough swagger, you could have them join your crew. It's all about confidence."

"Confidence. Then why the fuck aren't you barging in there and sweet-talking them your damn self?"

"Because I'm not you," Ben says seriously. "Now, enough bitching. You want to put Silas in his place? This is where you start. Go in there and show them who's boss."

In all likelihood, I'll just wind up dead. My intuition is telling me to drop this stupid plan and turn back. Come up with something else.

I've barely gone a step when I get a mental image of a face—hers. Then Sam's. That kid deserves more than scraps for a legacy. Kicking Silas' ass to hell and back is only one motive for regaining my status—and not even the main one driving me.

It's them. I can't stand back again and let them be used as pawns against me, and the only way to protect them is to prove to this city who truly deserves to run it.

And that man isn't Silas or Michael Heywood.

THIRTEEN

FREY

IS THERE an end to my father's list of potential victims?

First, my mother.

Then Hale...

Am I next?

I keep telling myself that I can handle this. Compared to the risk of failing Hale once again, all these dangers are nothing. There was a moment when I almost believed that reassurance.

Now that I'm stuck in this mess, I don't see a way out without the walls closing in on me from all sides. There are other enemies in my midst besides my father. Catherine is hiding something, and I've never seen Colton like that before. Cold. Ruthless. Determined. It's like he's morphing into a version of my father's worst attributes, only without the suave charm. The memory of his expression sends a chill down my spine, and I can't help clutching Daze's knife. It's hard to even stomach the idea of enduring the dinner tonight. Pretending. Suffering.

My only distraction is a small, seemingly insignificant object that consumes my focus as I sit on my old bed and twist it between my fingers. I stole it on the way out of the church without my father's guards seeing me, or so I hope.

Jamie Colland is printed on the front—the reporter from earlier—but a handwritten message has been scrawled onto the back above the address of what I assume is an office building—*We need to talk. Come to the church after nightfall if you can. I'll be waiting.*

I ponder the strange request as his earlier questions still ring in my mind. Why have people gone missing who are supposedly tied to Salvation's outreach program? What could that mean? A year and a half ago is roughly around the time that Hale started to distance himself.

That can't be a coincidence.

But if Catherine was telling the truth, Hale wasn't arguing with my father about anything related to Salvation the night he died. They were debating Bible stories.

More confused than ever, I fish my personal leatherbound Bible from my nightstand and open it, flipping through the pages until I reach the stories pertaining to Paul. On the surface, nothing relevant sticks out. Just the stories of Paul spreading the gospel, and Paul meeting with other prophets. Then the tale of Paul and his companion Silas in jail...

Wait. My finger traces that name over and over as my blood runs cold. *Silas.* Catherine had interpreted the name as belonging to the scripture, but the reality is far more nefarious than that.

They weren't having a friendly religious debate that night. My father and Hale were arguing about Silas.

I feel like such an idiot for not realizing sooner. Tears spring to my eyes, and I struggle to breathe in and out without shouting. Screaming.

Silas himself mentioned my father, but it doesn't sink in until now just how closely linked they might be—more than just to create a crime-fighting cover for a political campaign. They're involved in something so bad Hale died over it. Something bad enough that a reporter is asking about missing people. And something so bad that I can't risk staying here another day. That sermon wasn't my father rationalizing his treatment of Hale. It was about me.

"Frances?" A knock on my door makes me jump, and I barely manage to shove the business card under my pillow before the door opens, revealing a smiling Catherine. "Are you okay in there? I was hoping you might help me with dinner. I'm making baked chicken and mashed potatoes—"

"Sure," I croak, but before she turns away, I lurch to my feet. "Wait. There's something I need to ask you, and I need an honest answer. Please."

"What?" She smiles at me, but her lips tremble around the edges. A panicked hopelessness sneaks into her gaze—like that of a deer caught in the glow of oncoming headlights. "If you're worried about tonight, don't be. I've made sure that everything will be perfect. I even made that special cheesecake you like. All you have to do is just try to enjoy the moment. Things will get easier then, I promise."

"No, it's not that." I suck in a steadying breath, and soldier on. "I want to know what really happened the night Hale died. The truth."

She frowns and takes a step back into the hall. "I told you. He and your father were in his office and—"

"They weren't having a friendly debate," I interject. "They were arguing about someone named Silas. Weren't they?"

A flush spreads over her cheeks. Fervently, she shakes her head. "I don't think so—"

"There is something you aren't telling me, and not just about Hale, either," I press, approaching her. I take one of her hands and try to impress upon her that same uncanny, probing stare that Daze utilizes on me. The one that makes me spill the secrets I wasn't even aware of holding. "What was it? Did you hear them shouting? Fighting? Tell me!"

"I heard..." Her nose wrinkles, and suddenly her eyes go wide with terror. "Please, Frances. Just leave it alone. There's no use in dwelling on the past now. It won't do either of us any good! Just drop it, please."

Her pleading tone tugs at something inside me. Sympathy, I think. Deep down, I recognize the panic in her voice. It's the same hopeless way I felt on the bridge, staring into the abyss.

Like the swirl of emotions inside me was so endless, there wasn't any possible way out.

At least until a rude, abrasive stranger made me look at things from a different perspective. Despair doesn't have to be debilitating. In fact, you can use it as fuel to power your determination.

"Tell me the truth, Catherine," I say, tightening my grip on her hand. Her trembling fingers feel so fragile, liable to snap if I grasp too hard. "If not for my sake, then for Hale's. Do you think he'd want you to lie? To just leave his life in the past as if he didn't matter. Hell—"

"Frances! Your language," Catherine gasps.

I ignore her. "You've tried to erase him from our lives! There isn't a picture of him left in the house! Don't you see how cruel that is? He was nice to you. Don't turn your back on him now."

"I heard... They were shouting," she whispers. "It wasn't like their usual fights. It was violent. Angry. Then Michael—" She breaks off, turning away. "I left something on the stove. I should really get moving."

"He said something to him, didn't he? Father. What? Tell me, Catherine."

She looks back slowly, her eyes glistening with unshed tears. The reaction makes her seem so much younger. It's hard to remember that she's only a few years older than Hale. Despite the age gap, she strived to meet the demands of her role as Michael Heywood's wife and Covenant's co-steward.

Now I see her as the fearful woman she truly is, no different from me.

"He'll kill me if I say anything," she whispers. "I mean it, Frances. I've never seen him so angry, and when I learned what happened after, I was gutted. I went to school with Hale, did you know that? I cared for him, really, I did, but Michael... I know he didn't mean it. I know he didn't. But..."

"Say it."

"He threatened to kill him," she says hoarsely. "He said if he didn't prove his loyalty to the family, then the family would have no further use for him. He said that his mission was far too important to jeopardize for anyone. You know how important this election is to him," she insists. "He was just overcome by the stress, that's all. What happened to Hale wasn't his fault. It wasn't."

I can tell from her tone that she isn't trying to convince me, but herself.

"Thank you," I say, releasing her.

She wiggles away from me and practically races into the hall. "Dinner will be at seven," she calls back. "Your father wanted you to wear the blue dress. It's in your closet."

As she goes, I watch numbly, unable to do anything else. That creeping, crawling, uneasy sensation returns, and I have the urge to wrap my arms around myself just to feel sane. Catherine's words keep echoing inside my head—though I think a part of me has known the truth all along.

I just didn't want to admit it.

My father played a role in Hale's death. He might have even killed him. For what? Because Hale had the bravery to question him.

In any case, I can't stay here a second longer. A fragile plan comes to mind, but deep down, I know it's foolish. Reckless. A lot like Daze, I think. If he were here, I know what he'd tell me to do. Slow down. Breathe. Grab anything important that I might need.

In a mad dash, I race around my room, trying to picture what I might need on the outside. Not the Bible, or a collection of porcelain dolls, or any of the old knickknacks I left in here before moving to my apartment. When I finally slow to a stop in the middle of the room, it sinks in just how little I have left to show after twenty-three years spent in and out of this house. There is nothing worth taking from this room, at least.

But what about others?

A nagging suspicion won't let me rest until I creep across the hall and into my father's study. It's been months since Hale died, and if there was anything to find in here, I'm sure it's long gone.

Still, I run my fingers along the sturdy wood and hunt for any trace of him. I don't even find a speck of dust. There's nothing on the floor either, and no glaring sign detailing exactly what happened to Hale stuck to the wall. There is just the same quiet, slightly imposing space I spent most of my childhood in.

There is one room I haven't ventured into just yet. All this time, I've let cowardice hold me back. Fear. No more.

Squaring my shoulders, I enter the hall again and head for the bedroom not far from mine. The door is closed, and when I push it open, I hold my breath, unsure of what I'll find. When I finally peek past the doorway, my chest deflates, and I feel tears threaten to fall before I can think to hold them back.

The place isn't the same as the night I found him here. Most of his stuff had already been moved out, and only the heavy furniture remained, including a fancy leather chaise that was our mother's favorite. It's funny that he always accused me of missing her and ignoring the glaring reality of how she left— but he held onto more mementos of hers than I ever did.

That chair is gone now, and the room has been swept clean as though Hale never existed. All that remains is an empty bed, a naked end table, and a window shrouded in plain curtains.

I'm sure Father didn't take the time to properly store his things. No, he had them thrown out, most likely to the dump, where I'll never be able to recover them.

In these past few weeks, I have been so used to grieving that anger feels like an electric shock to my system. I grit my teeth in the face of it, curling my hands into fists. It's one thing for him to move on with his life, but to erase Hale's memory is another.

Any remaining hesitation I may have held about leaving vanishes, and I head for the door. I'm not exactly sure what makes me turn around and approach the closet instead. It's not like I'll find anything in here. Sure enough, Hale's clothes, old guitar, and other mementos are long gone. Only a lone cardboard box remains, tucked away and forgotten.

I stoop to open it without expecting to find much—and I don't. Just papers and his old leatherbound Bible, the twin to the one in my room. I was wrong. Father didn't clean this room out personally. I'm sure Catherine did, squirreling away the few parts of Hale she'd deemed worth keeping. His old Sunday school assignments, and childhood photos. His copies of the early Salvation pamphlets and the journals he used to carry when he studiously took notes on Father's every sermon, wanting to be like him someday.

I skim over them, feeling as though a knife stabs into me with every scribbled word. He was so different in those days. Lost in nostalgia, I lose track of time, and glancing over one notebook soon becomes ten. It appears that Catherine saved them all, even the more recent ones. He dated the entries as he got older, documenting right up until two years ago. Then something changed.

His notes stopped centering on Father's sermons and switched to another topic entirely—*Salvation*. He was obsessed, repeatedly sketching the building inside and out, and labeling all entrances and exits. He also noted the names of everyone who volunteered there under Covenant's banner, including me.

Then, roughly eighteen months ago, something shifted. His writing became disjointed and sloppy. His topics varied wildly and seem more like frantic notations in some mad scientist's journal. He wrote down numbers, names, and dates with seemingly no rhyme or reason.

But he drew symbols, including more detailed renditions of the Saints' patch logo. He even drew a face with messy blond hair and piercing eyes that I recognize even etched in ball-point pen. Daze. Beside his face was an arrow Hale had drawn and written "connection?"

My heart lurches at the word choice, but I keep reading.

He sketched other faces, but none of them I can recognize. Men. Women. They vary in ages from young to old; in total, there are roughly eight. On the final page, Hale scribbled a potential reason for why he'd been so fascinated by them.

Missing, he wrote, alongside a series of dates. *Employment program. Work-study. Location?*

Absently, I turn the page only to find nothing written on the other side. But there, in the binding, barely noticeable, is a rugged tuft of paper. Other sheets have been torn out.

By Hale?

I start to close the notebook, only to make out an indenta-tion that catches the light—something he must have written on one of those last pages, hard enough that he'd scraped the words into the material of the cover beneath. All I can make out clearly is one word. A name? Jamie Colland. The reporter.

It feels too chilling to be a coincidence. Carefully, I take the journal back into my room and dig out an old purse from my closet. Inside it, I also add a few pairs of underwear, a pen from my nightstand drawer, and the reporter's card. After that, I leave it under my bed just as Catherine calls from below.

"Frances. Your father is on his way. You should get ready for dinner, and then I could use some help setting the table."

I shout back, "Coming!" I try to remember how to project some semblance of calm. To play it safe, I obey her suggestion to wear the blue dress, and I barely recognize myself in the mirror when I'm done. This girl doesn't even resemble the old Frances from before that day at the bridge. She looks so much older. So tired, with bloodshot green eyes and scraggly blond hair that barely covers the bruises on her face.

I certainly don't look strong enough to take on anything sturdier than a wet paper bag, let alone my father and whatever nefarious actions he's been up to.

But I don't have any other choice but to try. For strength, I grasp Daze's knife, tucked in my pocket. Thank goodness for dresses with pockets. God, it's like I can feel his bravado seeping out of the metal and into my hand.

With a sigh, I head downstairs and join Catherine in the kitchen. She's smiling like always, chattering away about the morning and how nice a sermon it was, and how pretty it is outside. One might think our conversation from earlier had never happened.

While she's unaffected, however, I've made up my mind since we spoke—Jamie Colland is my only shot at getting more information regarding my brother. I need to meet him, no matter what.

I try to tell myself that using Catherine in my attempt to escape isn't wrong—even though it goes against years of teaching. As long as I keep her in the dark, she can't be blamed for anything I do in the long run. Holding onto that logic, I gather up the nerve to put my fragile plan into motion.

"I'm sorry if I seem distracted lately," I say, while helping her fish the good porcelain plates from the china cabinet in the dining room. "There's just been a lot going on all at once. And now things with Colton…"

She beams. "He told you about that, didn't he? Isn't it wonderful! I've always wanted a daughter to help plan her wedding. I know I'm not your mother, but I would love it if you let me help."

I force a smile so fake my jaw hurts. "Of course. But, in light of everything, I think I need to clear my head. I should pray for a while before dinner. I won't be long. I just need to compose myself to face everything properly."

Catherine's cheerful grin falters. "Oh, I'm sure Michael won't mind if you're a few minutes late—"

"I don't think I can focus here," I add in a rush. "Not with everything that happened. I need a clear space where I can connect with my thoughts and immerse myself in prayer. Do you think I could go to the church for a little while? I could take some guards, and I won't be long. Then I can get myself in the right headspace and face this new journey as I should, with a full heart and an open mind."

"Well…"

"You can ask my father if you want," I add, hoping I sound convincing. "I'm sure he wouldn't want me to be as distracted as I've been. Not with something so important at stake. I know that my relationship with Colton is very important to him."

"I... I guess it won't be too much trouble, as long as you take the guards," Catherine says finally. "I'll call your father to let him know you'll be gone, but I think he'll be pleased to know that you're accepting things with a positive mindset."

She smiles and flits off while I try to disguise how much I'm panicking internally. Before I know it, Catherine has already assembled the cadre of guards who will accompany me.

There are three of them, each one tall and imposing. Some of my resolve fractures in the face of them. How can I possibly evade one of them, let alone three?

"Your father would like you back within an hour," Catherine explains, confirming that she called him for permission. "He said he's proud of you for remembering your place in this family and that you have his blessing."

The words sound harmless enough, but I can't help but hear a threat tucked within them. By the time I leave the house and pile into the family's second sedan, I'm not sure if I can go through with anything. Not Colton. Not a desperate escape. Not making sense of Hale's scattered thoughts and notes.

I don't know if I can even keep my own sanity by the time this night is over.

I'm spiraling, so lost in my thoughts that the driver has to tell me twice that we've arrived before I finally climb out and enter the church.

It's empty this time of night, and I'm allowed inside only because of my father's status. One of his bodyguards has a key that lets us into the main room, and I woodenly take my seat in our usual pew, staring through the semi-darkness and trying to compose my thoughts.

I can't play the role of the fragile doll forever. Sooner or later, I have to decide for myself the kind of person I want to be. Someone who isn't like my father or Hale.

I have to be me.

FOURTEEN

DAZE

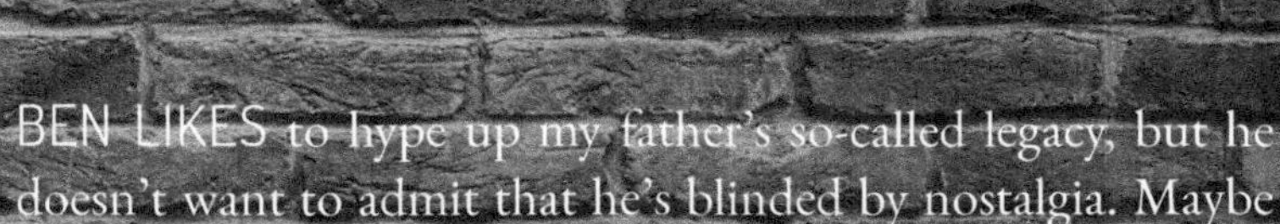

BEN LIKES to hype up my father's so-called legacy, but he doesn't want to admit that he's blinded by nostalgia. Maybe some pride.

I don't share the same delusions of grandeur when it comes to my old man.

Every kid has that realization—the day you truly see through the bullshit web of lies your parents and the rest of the world have spun around you your entire life. Santa doesn't exist, the Easter Bunny isn't real, and your old man doesn't have the typical nine-to-five job that legally puts food on the table. You realize that he isn't the perfect hero the rest of the world sees him as either.

He's just a man—one with more damn flaws than he can count, and he's just as fucked up as everyone else. Maybe more. Behind closed doors, he gives out more punches than candies, and he uses fear to get his way instead of love.

But you can't tell anyone on the outside the truth. They just give you a skeptical eye and shrug. "Your father was a damn good man," they'll say. "I don't know why you can't see that."

But they never saw the real bastard, and they've never met the real me. The real Daze Keaton who doesn't give a fuck about honoring tradition or upholding the lies of whoever came before me. My only concerns can be counted on one hand— and two of them are people well outside of my control.

That doesn't erase the fact that I had to pretend for the sake of everyone else. For so damn long, I pretended that leading the Saints was the only time I felt happy. That I could do a better job than the old man and keep my soul intact doing it.

It was a lie.

Stepping into his shoes made me understand my father in a way I never had. He wasn't a mindless, drunken idiot all the time. Once he had big ideas and a picture of the future where he could garner some small shred of respect—it was all he wanted. But respect comes with a hefty price tag, and the only way to get it is by violence. Anger. By dipping your toes in shit that used to make your stomach turn, and by ignoring the very people who you claim to love.

Some honorable men can be happy working a typical blue-collar job and die within the system that will always keep them just below the poverty line. There's no shame in that.

Some men crave more in order to sleep at night. They comfort themselves with the lie that they can achieve greatness through bloodshed while keeping their sanity intact. They aren't evil, they tell themselves—no, they're just desperate. Typical, fucking desperate.

Those are the kind of men who truly run the cartel and other criminal outfits in the city. You understand that, and you can rule them all, but it's a fine line to toe.

Ben had a point when he said that in theory, I could waltz right in and charm these stupid fucks out of their own hiding place.

Intimidation isn't the winning tactic, though. The truth is— holding up a mirror and making them face what they truly are, dirt and all.

That's enough to bring any real man to his knees. That's what my old man excelled at, when all was said and done. Not any heroic, leadership shit, but plain intimidation. Brutal honesty. He was good at turning it on someone with the precision of a gun, but the catch was he couldn't ever do the same with himself.

Years later, I'm telling myself all the right things as I approach the cartel hideout with my hands in the air like a fucking pussy. That I can walk away at any time. That things won't spiral out of control. That I can still be a good person while undertaking the mantle of leader again. A decent father for Sammy, and a man worthy of Frey. Yeah...

All lies, though I don't let myself admit that. Not yet.

I just keep walking.

Up close, the place is even more appealing than Ben led on. There are plenty of potential hiding spots for a sniper, and when a man opens the battered metal door that serves as the entrance, I'm sure he's seen me coming from a mile away.

"What the hell do you want?"

"To talk," I say. "You can save the bullshit threats. I know whose territory this is."

"Oh?" The man laughs, but there's no warmth in the sound. "Then you should know that the best thing to do is turn around and walk away, pretty boy. Because we know exactly who you are, Daze Keaton."

That's a minor hiccup I'm sure even Ben didn't expect. They could know who I am by my cheerful reputation like Ben suggested—or Silas could have put them on alert, and his relationship with the cartel could be closer than I thought. In any case, it's too late to back down now.

I keep walking.

"If you know who I am, then you know that petty threats don't mean shit to me. I want to speak to whoever's in charge. Now."

Another bit of laughter comes from behind the door before it slams shut. Not an ideal reaction, but I don't budge. Sweat runs down the back of my fucking neck as I remain out in the open like a sitting duck. From where I'm standing now, this plan feels stupider than ever.

But sometimes reckless stupidity is what it takes to catch your opponent off guard. They have no choice but to give in.

Finally, the door opens again, revealing a different man with cropped dark hair and narrowed eyes. He looks me over and then nods his head, beckoning me inside. The gesture might be taken as a good sign, if he didn't have a gun displayed on his hip.

Fuck Ben. He didn't mention weapons during his little reconnaissance spiel. Still, I keep walking, entering the main floor of the building. The interior isn't any more appealing than the outside. There are at least ten men spread throughout, with even more probably lurking out of view. The place is sparsely furnished, with only a handful of metal tables lining the bare walls and a few flickering artificial bulbs providing most of the sparse lighting. Should we take it over? It's definitely a fixer-upper.

But I know how the cartel operates, and I'm sure that the real firepower—and merchandise—is somewhere out of view.

"You want to talk, so talk," the man who let me in demands, crossing his arms. He must be the so-called leader I asked for. I don't recognize him, and apart from the identity of the cartel as a whole, I don't know any individual members by name anyway. This bastard, however, looks confident enough. He has his head cocked, a smirk playing over his mouth, but I don't sense that cocky swagger Silas likes to show off. He's smart. I can work with that.

To Ben's credit, his idea sounded good in theory, but I wouldn't be the "leader" if I didn't put my own twist on his asinine task. So, I improvise.

"I want to make a deal. One better than whatever piece of shit arrangement you have with your current boss."

The man laughs. "I can't tell if you're crazy or just an idiot," he says. "But I'll humor you. What can one man with no crew and not even a pot to piss in offer?"

"I can offer you a hell of a lot more than the table scraps fed to you by both your masters—safety. From the hell someone like Michael Heywood can unleash on the city once he gets into power."

"Oh? And how do you plan on doing that? I heard you talked a big game, but damn. I didn't realize you were actually that fucking delusional."

"Easy," I say, ignoring the insult. "You join me, and when we take over the city, you won't get scraps. You'll get a slice of the pie."

"And let me guess. Your terms are that we lick your boots and hold onto that bullshit promise when Silas uses his real power to crush you and anyone dumb enough to stand by your side by the end of the week? Our scraps may not be much, but they're tasty enough. I don't think we can survive off an imaginary pie, but I appreciate the sentiment."

"It's not bullshit," I say with more confidence than I actually feel. "I won't just take over the city by the end of the week. I'll go a step further and drive Silas out for good. Do you want to know why? Because I have something he doesn't. You can scoff now and continue to cling to his coattails, or you get in on the ground floor and stop watching from the sidelines."

"You have yet to tell us the details of your genius plan," the man says. "So, I suggest you get around to it, or get the fuck out."

"We take down Michael Heywood," I say. "Or if you want to be poetic about it, we cut off the head of the snake."

He looks me over. "You think you can just snap your fingers and take out the city's darling preacher man? I don't know if you're as crazy as they say or just fucking stupid."

"Call me prudent," I counter. "Because you and I both know that Heywood is playing nice now. Once he's in power, even his love affair with your master, Silas, won't keep him from cutting loose ends."

"Is that so?"

"Well, the man killed his own son and had his daughter kidnapped and beaten all to score political points, so you tell me."

To his credit, the bastard keeps his expression blank. "Bullshit."

"You think he isn't capable of that?" I counter. "Then go skip along and keep licking Silas' ass. He'll toss you a few scraps to pacify you and your little outfit. Until he doesn't need you any longer. Then you'll find yourself gutted while Heywood parades your corpses around to placate the masses."

The man scoffs, but he doesn't draw his gun and demand I get the fuck out. He's listening. Good.

"Hear this. You'll only have one shot to cut ties on your own terms before you all wind up in body bags. Silas can't risk a bloodbath, not now, with Heywood betting his chances on keeping the crime rates low. You'll have him by the balls. There's no better time to cut out on your own."

"Only to kiss your ass instead?" The man crosses his arms. "What's in it for us? You talk a good talk, but I know your reputation, Daze Keaton. Crazy as shit, but not quite as crazy as your old man. Word on the street is that when it came down to it, you couldn't cut it. Silas had to take over before you had them all knitting teddy bears and holding hands and shit. Let's say we take you up on this suicide mission. What's your plan for dealing with Heywood, anyway? Hold hands and pray for peace?"

"No," I snap, though the bastard has a point. It's an outcome I've been dancing around, but without Frey here to listen, nothing is stopping me from voicing the truth. Fuckers like Michael Heywood and Silas can only be dealt with one way. Even the most optimistic bastard could see that.

But that doesn't mean I'm in a hurry to admit as much.

"Use your imagination," I say. "But enough gossiping. You in or out?"

"And if I'm out? What's to stop my boys and me from sending your head to Silas on a silver platter?" He looks down at his gun for emphasis.

"Do it. I'm sure he'll tie a pretty bow around your inevitable body bag when he's done with you. Might even remember your name."

The threat could be a bluff, but I wouldn't put it past them—yet another reason Ben's plan was dumb as shit to start with. Though, to his credit, there is one thing Ben does better than anyone, and it was his main asset back in the glory days of the Saints. No one can read a room better, and now that I've seen them for myself, I have to admit he might have been right about Silas' loose coalition. A bunch of low-level bastards with no real skin in the game. Only a coward would stick his nose up at the chance to become relevant in Westpoint's criminal underbelly.

So which type of man am I dealing with now?

"Do what you want, but my offer remains the same. You join me, you no longer have to subsist on Silas' scraps. You'll have a seat at the head of the table. Or you can be a good little boy and stay in your place. Your choice."

I start to leave.

"Wait. You talk sense for a pretty boy, but let's see if you have the balls to back it up. Your idea sounds nice and all, but there's still the issue of your reputation, Daze. You can kick ass from what I've heard, but you've always drawn the line at getting blood on those soft little hands. I heard what you pulled off at that sloppy fight Silas set up, but it's one thing to defend yourself. You want us on your side? You do a little job for me."

"What do you have in mind?"

"You seem to think Silas is the only one whose 'ass' I have to 'lick,' but you forget. We belong to the cartel, and they aren't easy to walk away from. There's an enforcer who lives in the city and reports back to the boss. You want us? You take him out, but it won't be easy. You'll need to make a show of it. Something big enough that the cartel will think twice about sending their men here to regain control. To be honest, *Daze*, I don't think you have it in you. Though, we hear a lot of rumors in this part of town. I guess the apple didn't fall too far from the tree—"

"What the fuck is that supposed to mean?" I snap. His men inch closer, uneasy at how my voice raises. Fuck it. I can't help the anger I feel coursing through my veins. Hearing Chris and Ben hype up the dead bastard was one thing. Having some random motherfucker throw the truth in my face?

Hell no.

"No offense meant," the man says, raising his hands in a gesture of surrender. "It's just that if you're anything like him, then I know we're in good hands. I heard that as long as the pay was right, he'd take any contract. Men. Women. Kids—"

"You shut the fuck up," I snarl, curling my hand into a fist.

The bastard cocks his head. "Or what?"

Or...

Nothing. Marcus and his fuck-ups are in the past, but I still have to handle the present. "You want to make a deal? Fine. Give me a name, and consider it done."

The man raises an eyebrow. "Has the pretty boy gotten off his moral high horse?"

"You want the job done? Then give me the fucking details."

It's not like I have much of a choice.

But I'm not Marcus, either. I won't crawl into the gutter just to keep my image intact.

FIFTEEN

FREY

IN KEEPING WITH MY WORD, I pray in my family's usual pew for a half hour. Head bowed, hands clasped over my lap, I'm the picture of piety. Daze would whisper some blush-inducing innuendos, were he here, and I cling to that mental image for as long as possible. Reality, however, can only be ignored for so long. The darkness and unyielding quiet serve as an odd backdrop to the wealth of new revelations I haven't had the time to deal with until now.

As the significance of everything sinks in, I really do wind up praying. For composure. For the ability to keep my mind clear and free of fear. For strength, bravery, and all those elusive traits that Hale seemed to possess in spades over me. I pray for Daze and his safety, given his penchant for accumulating head wounds.

Then I pray for myself and my own soul.

If I go through with my plan tonight, I might add a few more sins to my already growing list—but so be it.

Eventually, my meditative peace is broken when someone steps forward, their voice booming in the empty room. "We should get back, miss. Your father has arrived at the house."

Which means that Colton won't be far behind, ready to spring his proposal on me with no chance to refuse.

"Okay." I stand and head for the door with the guard leading the way. Near the threshold of the entrance, I hesitate.

"I should use the bathroom before we leave. I'll be just a minute." Before the man can protest, I turn and retreat down the hall. Once inside the restroom, I barricade the door just as Daze had and try to think.

There are too many guards to outrun on my own. Even if I made it out of the building, I couldn't evade them easily. I need some way of drawing their attention off me. A distraction—

As if in answer to my prayers, a piercing sound shatters the quiet, blaring incessantly. The fire alarm? A horrible fear paralyzes me. What if it's another explosion like what happened at Salvation?

"Ms. Heywood!" I hear footsteps rushing down the hall, presumably the guard. "We need to go!"

I start for the door. "I'm coming..." A peculiar smell itches my nostrils, and I stop cold. Smoke. No matter the cause, this is as good a distraction as any. Scrambling for the door, I wrench it open and tear into the hallway.

The dim lighting doesn't betray much, but the air is thick with heavy smoke emanating from the back of the church.

The offices? Coincidentally, those are the only other sections of the church with an emergency exit out of view of the entrance.

There's no time for doubt. I race in that direction and pray that the door to the back wing isn't locked. Thank God, it isn't, but the smoke grows thicker with every step I take. Coughing, I press my arm to my nose and attempt to breathe through my coat sleeve.

My eyes burn. As I grapple toward my father's office, I finally spy a glimpse of bright orange through the open door. Fire.

"Ms. Heywood!"

Footsteps pierce the darkness, but I run toward the end of the hall. The emergency exit is there, but when I throw myself against it...

It doesn't budge.

Oh no. I push and shove until my arm aches. Then I kick it. Ram my shoulder against it. With every passing second, the smoke grows thicker, and all I can hear is the crackling from the flames.

"Miss! Where are you?"

Suddenly, the door gives way with a metallic squeal, and I stumble out into the fresh air—and run right into the figure standing here. Before I can react, they press a hand against my mouth.

"Don't speak," they say into my ear. "I don't want to hurt you."

Before I can panic, they pull me into an alley so dark I can barely see directly in front of me. There, they let me go, and I spin to face them, desperate to make out their features. I can only discern dark eyes and a vaguely familiar face, but a name doesn't come to mind.

"Who are you?"

"Someone curious to know why Michael Heywood's daughter would run out of a burning building and away from her contingent of armed guards."

"You're the reporter," I say, recognizing his voice. "What are you doing here? Did you set the fire?"

"No. I've been hanging around hoping that you got my note," he says. "Then I saw the smoke and heard you pounding on the door. That's an emergency exit. It should have opened easily, but it was stuck or something. If I weren't here to help, I doubt you would have opened it yourself."

"Stuck?" I back away. "What does that even mean?"

He shrugs. "You tell me. It seems someone might not want us to talk. Though I think our conversation can wait until we get somewhere safer, don't you think?" The distant wail of sirens gives his suggestion more urgency.

"Come on. I know a safe place. This way." He heads off deeper into the alley, but I don't move.

With a wary glance over my shoulder, I note figures moving in the distance. Is being under my father's thumb worse than venturing into the unknown with a stranger? I look back at him, undecided. "Why should I trust you?"

"You could take your chances with the guards back there," he says. "But you were running from them for a reason, weren't you? All you'll have to fear from me is a bad cup of coffee and probing questions, but we need to move now. Are you coming, or not?"

I take a step toward him, trying to ignore the voice in my head warning me against it. I still have Daze's knife, after all. I tell myself that I'm brave enough to use it. Though, for all I know, this man could have a gun or worse.

I should go somewhere on my own. Find Daze. Pray that Father doesn't catch me...

"I can sense you might need some convincing to come with me," the man says. "Normally. I don't beg to question a source, but I'll make an exception in this case. Come with me, and I'll tell you the truth about your brother's death."

"Hale died of a heart attack," I say, parroting my father's public explanation.

The man laughs and slows enough for my hesitant steps to bring me closer to him. Cocking his head, he eyes me from over his shoulder, just as a piercing fire siren roars to life, seemingly just blocks away.

"A fitting lie, I have to admit," he says. "But I have my hands on a deleted autopsy report that says otherwise. Hale died, by all appearances, high as a kite—but that's just another cover-up. I know for a fact that he couldn't haven't gotten his hands on the drug found in his system. Not alone."

It's a detail I had never even considered before. "How?"

"Because up until recently, it was in police custody as evidence from a drug bust seized over a year ago."

He pauses, letting the words sink in. Then he nods toward the mouth of the alley. "Want to learn more? Then come with me."

I don't move an inch. "How do I know you're telling the truth? It could be a rumor."

"Because I have the paperwork, and I'm willing to show it to you. Now let's get out of here before those guards of yours actually do their job and come find us."

He extends his hand. "I'd ask you to trust me, but to be honest, you shouldn't. Not until I've shown you what I have, but, frankly, I think this is your only shot."

I hate the part of me whispering that he's right.

As his hand hangs in the air between us, I sigh.

Then I step forward, nodding for him to lead the way.

SIXTEEN

DAZE

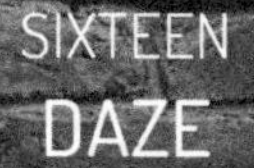

"DAZE."

I look over to find Ben standing near the entrance of Chris' spare apartment. From his frown, I can tell he's been there for a while, watching me. And, judging from the pitying look on his face, he noticed the absence of a certain blond.

But first things first.

"Did you find him?" I ask.

Ben nods. "Found someone by that name anyway, but I think your new friends gave you the wrong intel. This man isn't *just* the liaison to the cartel boss Rodrigo Cortez—he's the man's fucking cousin. I don't think his death will go unnoticed—not that I agree with you turning into a contract killer."

"Don't have a choice." I try to ignore the way I know he's looking at me. Disgusted. Disappointed. Same old same old. "There always had to be a catch, or those rat bastards would have done it themselves. Besides…" I can't help but smile bitterly at the thought. "When it comes to taking on contracts, I've learned from the best."

"Is this about your old man again?" Ben asks, leaning against the doorway. "You've been touchy about him ever since you came back. I thought it was jealousy at first, or some shit. Then I remembered that you aren't the jealous sort. That's Silas' shtick. So, tell me what's really going on."

I turn my back to him and stare out of the window nearby. A shitty set of blinds cuts the view of the city beyond it into equal rectangular pieces. Much like the pieces of the Saints my old man left for me to hold together, all by my damn self. "You remember when I first took over?" I ask without looking back. "After Marcus up and died?"

"Yeah," Ben says. "And Jesus, Day. It wasn't like the man *chose* to have a heart attack—"

"I never told you," I say over him. "But things weren't as perfect as he let you all believe. The books were a fucking mess. We owed thousands to the cartel alone. Gambling debts."

He whistles. "Damn. Day, why didn't you say anything?"

I laugh and eye him from over my shoulder. He genuinely seems shocked—but I wasn't. I'd known for years by then that my old man wasn't shit. "Do you want to know how he got us in so deep so fast? Cage fighting matches. The kind that Silas runs now. He'd bet on the fighter he knew would win and pocket the winnings. They were fixed. Every last one."

"Wait a second…" Ben strokes his chin, fighting to process the information. "You used to fight in the ring back then. Don't tell me—"

"Yep. I was his prize patsy," I admit, scowling at the memory. "I used to throw fights on command. Win them. Lose. Take a beating. Whatever he fucking wanted. Until one day, I got sick of his shit and went against his bet. I didn't throw the match like he asked me to. I fought like hell instead—and a good thing, too, because the other fighter was tough as shit. His name was Damien, though he went by Mayhem in those days—"

"Mayhem." Ben frowns and strokes his chin. "I heard of a guy by that name. A mercenary. Bounty hunter. The kind of bastard you don't want to cross—"

"I crossed him that night," I counter. "But I owned up to my shit and helped him pay off his debts. When Heywood had me arrested, I ran into him in lockup, and we had each other's backs. My old man, on the other hand? He wasn't so grateful. He probably lost thousands that day alone. I'm sure that worsened the hole he dug for himself."

"Fuck." Ben must move to the couch because I hear the cushions squeal. "Why the hell didn't you say anything?

"And ruin his perfect image?" I shrug. "I gave that man enough of my life. He could keep his secrets, but I won't let his lies define me. Not anymore. I won't leave a mess of lies for my son to clean up, either. Samuel can make his own way. His own name. He won't ever be tied to some bullshit legacy."

Lyra may not understand now, but she will. Already, Sammy's thriving without me. The happiest fucking kid on the planet. I tell myself that every damn day. I have to.

"Damn... No wonder you've been so pissy lately," Ben says after a few minutes of silence, presumably once he's finished processing what I've said. "And now, with what happened last night, no wonder—"

"What happened last night?" I whirl around to find Ben sitting with his head cocked.

"Oh shit." His eyes widen. "You haven't heard."

I don't like his tone. "Heard what?"

"One of the reasons I came over here was to talk about this —" He stands and tosses something toward me that I hadn't realized was in his hand until then—a newspaper. Plastered all over the front page is a photo of a familiar building beneath the headline.

FIRE AT COVENANT CHURCH. ARSON SUSPECTED.

"Fuck!"

"Yeah," Ben says with a grimace. "That's where your little girlfriend likes to pray, isn't it? You should know that, according to the police, she's missing."

"What?" I picture her, dressed like a church girl, ripe for any bastard to abuse or worse. How the fuck could I leave her there?

"They didn't write it in that paper, but I've done some digging. This disappearance wasn't planned by her daddy, however. You know anything about it?"

"The fuck I do. Who the hell else could it be? Silas?"

"No. He wouldn't be this subtle." Ben starts to pace, wringing his hands together. "But, to be honest, I don't know who else has the balls. Maybe the cartel? This could all be one fucking setup."

"No... If it was any rival gang, they'd leave a mark. They'd want to take credit."

"Your little girlfriend never ceases to be full of surprises, that's for damn sure. Where are you going?"

I'm already heading for the door. "To find her. There has to be something you missed. She wouldn't take off alone."

Or maybe she did. She'd grown tired of waiting for me and ran off with another punk who promised her answers.

The sick part? Were it true, I couldn't even blame her. "Damn it, Frey..."

"You aren't going anywhere," Ben says, hot on my heels. "You have to deal with this shit for the cartel first. Or do you enjoy hiding in a hole in the wall, waiting for Silas to strike you down whenever he feels like it? Listen to me, Daze—" He grabs my arm, wrenching me to face him. "We gotta keep a level head here."

"So now you think we should carry out the hit after all? Didn't you just point out that the target is the fucking cousin of the cartel boss?"

"A minor detail," he says, waving his hand. "The point is, we don't have any other options, Day. This was your idea to strike out on your own, remember? Getting men and a proper base won't happen out of nowhere. Look—" He places a hand on my shoulder. "We need to lay the groundwork, or you might as well head over to the Saints right now and turn yourself in."

I rock on my heels, knowing that he's right. "I can't just leave her out there."

"I know. Which is why you'll go handle the cartel, and I'll do my best to track her down. Hopefully, by the time I do, we'll have an actual hideout to work out of, and we can set our sights on Michael Heywood. But you need to keep a clear head, understood? You wanted to be the boss, remember? Well, you have an errand to take care of. So, I suggest you get to it."

"I'll give you from now until I've done that fucking errand," I snarl, shrugging him off. "Then I'm going after her, regardless of what you think."

"Don't forget that I've stuck my neck out for you, too," Ben says. "If anyone wants to see this through without winding up in a body bag, it's me. Besides, if you don't think I'm up to the task, why don't you ask that crazy-ass friend of yours to do something useful."

He has a point.

"Fine. You find Frey. I'll have Damien track down Cortez—"

"Wait a second, you don't mean you plan on going after the bastard alone? I meant you should do some intel. Get some weapons. Maybe recruit some backup, at least. Not go barging in to assassinate a cartel leader without thinking it through first!"

"Too late for that," I counter with a grim smile. Then I head for the stairs, sensing him behind me. "Besides, as you said, I wanted to be the boss. I've got this."

"Can I ask what your grand plan is?"

I laugh. "I think it's better if you don't know."

Not because I don't trust him.

If Ben knew how I planned to go about this shit, he'd give me another concussion just to stop me.

"YOU COULD HAVE GOTTEN some sleep, at least. I promise, I won't bite." The voice comes from the far end of a narrow living room in an apartment somewhere on the outskirts of the city.

For all intents and purposes, it's an upgrade from my father's home. I'm not under lock and key. Theoretically, I can leave whenever I want. Yet, a persistent cold sweat glues my blouse to my body, and I can barely keep my breathing steady.

"Where did you get this?" I'm referring to a set of screenshots displayed on an electronic tablet. There's a dozen or so, and each one looks like it was taken by a cell phone in a hurry. Every shot is a different section of what must be a larger document. The text is hard to read in places, but after scouring each one multiple times, I've gotten the gist of what they spell out.

That doesn't mean I believe it, though. In some ways, it's impossible to. And yet, all of the missing pieces regarding Hale's death finally seem to slot in place.

The sad part is that they point to only one conclusion...

"Coffee?" My companion steps forward, two steaming mugs in hand. Seeing the object on my lap, he frowns. "Don't tell me you stayed up all night reading that?"

I don't answer right away. I just flip through the same twelve images as Jamie inches closer and sets the coffee on a small end table beside me. After sipping from his mug, he sighs and sits on the couch next to me.

"I got them directly from the coroner," he explains, reiterating what he told me last night when he first showed me the device. "Before all trace of the report was purged from his files, that is. Those photos are the only proof it ever existed, and I doubt they'd be enough to stand up in a trial or anything."

"A trial," I echo in a faint whisper. "A murder trial."

Because according to the coroner, Hale's death hadn't been a heart attack, or even a normal overdose. He'd been killed. I'd suspected as much—no, I think I'd always been sure of it— but having my worst fears confirmed outright still hurts like hell. My eyes are so sore from crying that they ache whenever I blink. I'm sure they're bloodshot, too, explaining the pitying way Jamie reaches out to pat my hand.

"I know this is a lot to take in," he says. "I'm sorry."

"Why were you even investigating his death?" I ask, pulling my hand away.

"I wasn't," he says. "Not at first. May I?"

He reaches for the tablet, and I give it to him. He swipes until he finds a page that he holds up for me to see.

"I was investigating this—the street name is Black Heroin. Unimaginative, I know, but trust me. That stuff is nastier than the name implies. It's a highly potent, extremely lethal concentration of the drug, trafficked only by a particular cartel. It's rare, and only recently did it start showing up in Westpoint City—but, suspiciously, just in apparent overdose cases. Each one of those deaths? They can be linked directly to your father's Salvation community outreach program."

I try to process that accusation without reacting like some panicked little girl. Rather than deny the allegation outright, I swallow hard. "How can you be sure of that?"

"Hold on... Here." He angles the tablet toward him and fishes for another file. This one is just a typed list of names and dates.

"I got tipped off by a friend in the vice division that they were finding bodies, all people with few relatives or ties to the city. Men. Women. Under overpasses. In alleyways. Typical places where the homeless congregate, but these seemingly poor, destitute people all had Black Heroin in their system— not the usual street-grade stuff they typically find in vagrants. To give you an idea of how odd that is—the Cortez Cartel is the only one known to deal in that kind of drug, and it isn't cheap. A single gram can go for a thousand on the black market, and it's usually cut with something weaker when distributed for recreational use. It's not the kind of stuff some poor nobody can get their hands on easily, that's for damn sure."

"What?" Overwhelmed, I place my head in my hands, rubbing my temples. "Are you saying that my brother was working with the cartel?"

"No. I think it's far more complicated than that. I think his murder is connected to the same people disposing of those poor victims like garbage every other week. They've been careful up until now, ensuring that no one death is suspicious enough to trigger a full investigation. They've all been filed as accidental. It's only when you go looking for the right clues that you can even begin to piece them together."

He makes it sound so logical, but I don't follow. "What are you saying? My father gives out heroin with his free clothes and employment packages?"

To his credit, Jamie doesn't laugh. "Something like that. Black heroin is extremely potent as a murder weapon. The dose is small enough to not seem like an overdose at first glance, unlike the cheaper, street-grade stuff. The only problem? Black Heroin isn't trafficked in Westpoint City, however, a shipment was caught in the port roughly a year ago. Supposedly the supply has been under lock and key in the police evidence room since then. Do you see what that means?"

I'm starting to, but I can't bring myself to say it out loud.

Jamie doesn't appear to have the same hang up, "Either a gang in Westpoint City has gotten their hands on the most premium, sought-after drug on the market and decided not to traffic it, or… They have a mole in the police department who can supply them with enough doses to take out their enemies and make it seem like an accident. All while keeping their hands clean and preventing the finger from being pointed at any local outfit. After all, every drug has a signature. A calling card, so to speak, that can be traced directly to the main supplier. Now, can you tell me which gang would be powerful enough—and desperate enough—to carry out murders without wanting to take credit for them? You want my opinion?" He sets the tablet aside and crosses his arms, his expression thoughtful.

"I think you'd only take those risks if you had something to protect. These murders weren't done for clout or for the hell of it. They were purposefully carried out, and extra care was taken to have them swept under the radar, especially in a time when crime has been running rampant. The Saints, the cartel, and the other gangs aren't usually that damn humble. Not unless someone bigger is calling the shots. Someone big enough to have a mole planted in the heart of the Westpoint PD who can help themselves to a drug that can't be traced to any entity."

I squirm, coming to the same conclusion he already has. "Do you think my father is involved?"

"I don't think that. I know it for a fact."

I sit forward, unable to disguise my shock. "How?"

"Because I know how to follow the money. Nothing in this city comes cheap. If you want something done, you have to grease the right palms—" He holds up his hand for emphasis. "For the past year, every month, a prominent investigator in the Westpoint PD has been receiving a substantial sum of money in a brand-new, unreported account. Those payments correspond with the earliest known Black Heroin deaths. A coincidence?"

"I don't understand. What does that have to do with my father?"

"I'm getting to that," he says. "But first... How do I know that I can trust you? Not to be frank, Ms. Heywood, but what's to stop you from waltzing up to your father and telling him everything. Then I wind up on the hit list. I need assurances that you aren't as naïve as you've pretended to be."

I bite my bottom lip, weighing the potential options. There aren't that many. He's right. I could run home and tell my father—but this man doesn't strike me as the naïve type, either. If he had doubts, he wouldn't have casually spilled every detail of his hard-hitting story to a stranger, no matter who she was. Which means that he's either been lying this whole time, or...

"There's something you've left out," I tell him, meeting his gaze squarely.

He nods, impressed. "Now you're catching on."

Of course, he wouldn't tell me everything. He's held back whatever key piece of information he believes makes my father the lynchpin of this whole crazy scheme.

It's funny. I asked Daze to teach me how to fight when I should have asked him to show me how to bluff. How to talk my way out of any situation and convince my target that I'm on their side. Without his instruction, I'll have to make things up as I go along.

To his credit, he's given me a fairly good blueprint to follow. *Lie.*

"Let's say that everything you've told me is true," I begin, clearing my throat. "Why talk to me? For all you know, my father keeps me in the dark. I have no idea what he's up to or what Salvation has to do with any of it."

"Maybe," he says. "But I know that you've been around someone who does. One might deem him a key player in this whole mess."

An uneasy feeling washes over me. "Who?"

"Daze Keaton, former president of the Westpoint Saints. He isn't known for his undying love for your father, so the fact that you stayed with him for several days must mean that he told you a thing or two that piqued your interest."

I lurch to my feet. "How do you know that?" A horrifying possibility comes to mind. "Were you stalking me?"

"Stalking makes it sound so dirty, don't you think? Let's just say I've had my eye on Daze Keaton and his associates for a while. You can thank your brother for that."

"Hale?" I sway, pressing a hand to my chest as agonizing pain rips through my heart. I feel like I've been punched.

"Please. Have a seat." He nods to the couch. Only when I've collapsed onto it does he continue, "What do you know about him, your brother?"

I choose my words carefully. "To hear my father tell it, he was the troubled black sheep of the family."

"But what do *you* think?"

"I don't know," I admit. "I'm starting to realize that there is a whole side to him that I didn't understand, and he didn't trust me enough to tell me what he was afraid of."

"But he did tell someone," the man says. "Several someones, in fact. You want to know how I got my intel on where to look and for what? I'll give you three guesses."

I frown as only one option comes to mind. Should I be so surprised? "Hale?"

"Bingo. Believe me, I was skeptical when the son of the city's most prominent and pious politician sends a cryptic message to my email alleging a scheme involving the criminal under-belly's most powerful players. I didn't believe him at first. To be honest, I thought he was fucking nuts."

He wasn't the only one. "What changed your mind?"

Darkness falls over his expression. "I followed the money. Though, I will admit that I didn't think you played any role in it, not at first. Hale made it seem like you were just an innocent bystander—"

"He talked about me with you?"

"But then," the man continues as if I'd never spoken. "I saw the news and noticed how you looked at me the other day when I mentioned who I was. You know something. Hale gave me most of the puzzle pieces, but some are still missing, and I can't even think of going forward with this story until I have the full picture. Hopefully, we can help each other."

It's my turn to be skeptical. "How do I know that I can trust you?"

"Because I know the answer to the question you're dying to ask. I insinuated that Hale had been murdered, but you didn't even bat an eyelash. You suspected something, I'm sure, but you don't know the whole picture. If you did, I don't think you'd be willing to let your father parade you around the city for a photo op. I heard he has a big press conference this morning—" He makes a show of eyeing his wristwatch. "I think you're going to miss it."

"So, what is the full picture?" I'm ready for him to just talk in circles and give more cryptic warnings, but his expression changes as he sits forward, stroking his chin.

"I'm not a lawyer, so pardon me if I get this wrong, but they say the three things you need to solve a murder are, motive, means, and opportunity. When it comes to who would want to get rid of Hale, I can think of one glaring motive—keeping him quiet. As far as means and opportunity, I think we both know who fits those two criteria."

"Okay. Keep talking," I demand, playing along.

"Hale shared a lot of what he knew with me, but he kept other details close to the vest. It's only recently that I've been able to figure out some of those tidbits for myself, but I know one thing. As a journalist with standards to uphold, I've been restrained from going public with anything concrete until I have all my bases covered. Hale, on the other hand, was impatient, and I know for a fact that he was planning on confronting your father with what he knew. Not long after that, he winds up dead from the same drug that killed the very people he'd been investigating. Tell me you can see the connection there."

I can't see anything as my eyes well with fresh tears, but I blink them back, fighting for composure. "You still haven't said how my father is involved or why exactly Salvation is connected to those deaths," I point out.

"Come on, Frances. May I call you Frances? In any case, now that I've met you, you don't strike me as the quiet, obedient type. At least not fully. Think."

I take a page out of Daze's playbook and devise a solution he might have were he here. "You think my father made a deal to use Salvation somehow. He trades some of the homeless people to the gangs who run the city. But for what and why?"

"Now we're getting somewhere," Jamie says. "The answers to those questions are important, but the main one is what does Michael Heywood stand to gain? And how far was he willing to go to achieve that goal? That's one of the biggest missing pieces of this puzzle, and I think you can help me fill in the gaps."

"How?"

"I need you to get close to your father and find out who his real contact is—and I'm not talking about Silas Rotteridge or any other criminal punk in the city. This has to be something far bigger. I need a name. A real boogeyman to point to."

"Why do you think I can find that out when Hale couldn't?"

He sits back, eyeing me from head to toe. "Honestly? I'm not sure you can, but I can't go public with this story without a clear connection. I need to find it and fast. The second your father is elected, it might be too late to do anything to stop what's already set in place."

"What does that mean?" For the life of me, I can't come up with an explanation. At least, not one grim enough to explain his worried expression.

"Look, trustworthiness isn't something a lot of reporters these days are known for, but I'm willing to go out on a limb to prove to you that I can make this story public and get justice for your brother. To do that, I'm going to need your help. Time is running out. I have just three days before my editor pulls the plug on this story and sends me to some backwater town to cover PTA meetings."

"How will I even know what to look for?" I doubt Father would have his evil manifesto lying around for me to find.

"To be fair, I don't really know. But I'll give you whatever I can to help you figure that out, starting with everything Hale gave me. It's all on there." He nods to the tablet and returns it to me. "Every email. Every note, and every clue that I've pieced together. Maybe you can see something in it all that I missed. In any case, I think he'd want you to have it."

I consider mentioning the notebooks of his I have, but who knows if there's anything useful in them at all?

"You're welcome to stay here for as long as you want," Jamie adds, rising to his feet, "but I have to head out. These leads won't track down themselves. In the meantime, if you ever need to get ahold of me, use the number on my business card. Ring once. Then hang up and ring again, and I'll pick up right away. Otherwise, I'll come to you if I learn anything of interest."

"Why can't I just come back here?"

He winks and heads for the door. "Because this isn't my apartment. The real owners won't be back for at least another night, given their flight schedule, but I suggest you find a new place to lie low if you don't intend to go home just yet. Though, I kind of hope you reconsider. I just need one piece of evidence to tie your father to potentially the biggest scandal to hit Westpoint City. You may be the only one who can find it, so please keep that in mind. I'll be in touch. Oh, and there is one more thing..."

He shoots me a probing glance from over his shoulder. "I don't know what your relationship is with Daze Keaton or what you know about his past, but if I were you, I'd learn everything I could. There's enough to give you a basic crash course on that tablet. If you learn anything, you know how to find me. See ya around."

He's gone before I've fully processed everything he said. The first part to sink in is that I'm an accomplice in a break-in. I bolt to my feet, prepared to leave—but surprisingly, another realization takes precedence over even the prospect of trespassing.

Hale wasn't crazy. He wasn't a defiant black sheep and didn't kill himself. Some of those things I'd already begun to suspect but having them confirmed outright hurts like hell. I can't deny that.

I sink to the floor and wind up staring blankly ahead, trying to see some way out of this chaos. The first thing I should do, of course, is leave this stolen apartment—then find Daze. After that...

My father is probably on the warpath, searching the city high and low for me. If I return, a belt lashing will be the least of my worries. He'll lock me away forever or marry me to Colton on the spot.

But do I owe it to Hale to at least try and uncover the truth, for him?

For now, I push everything from my mind but the most pressing concern—footsteps. They march down the hall, loud enough to be heard inside. Warily, I creep to the door. A glance out of the peephole makes my heart sink. I see at least three men in dark uniforms marching around the corner. Police? Or perhaps part of my father's private security team.

Shit. I tiptoe deeper into the apartment and try to come up with a plan. After spotting myself in a decorative mirror, I decide that my clothing is the first thing I should tackle—walking around in a designer coat and dress will definitely draw notice.

Down a narrow hallway, I find the first of two bedrooms. It alone might have betrayed that this place couldn't possibly be owned by the reporter—unless, of course, he preferred shades of pink and a closet stocked with feminine clothing. I find a pair of jeans and a gray sweater and leave my dress on a hanger as a gift for the woman who seems to be my size. I make sure to move Daze's knife from the dress pocket to the jeans. Then I grab a hooded jacket hanging on a hook near the front door. Hopefully, the change in attire will help me blend in.

Then I gather up my stuff and try to think. If I want to locate Daze as my next task, there is the question of where I'd find him? I doubt he'd stay at his apartment after Silas' attack.

Besides, Father will have his men looking for me, and I'm sure that's the first place they'll check. The thought of him makes me glance at a clock on the wall, numb with dread. It's just past ten a.m. Ironically, as Jamie pointed out, his press conference should be airing now.

I fumble around until I find a remote and flip through the television channels. As if through divine intervention of the cruelest kind, within three tries, my father's face fills the screen.

"...time to forge a battle against crime for the welfare of my family, and that of every family in this city. If elected, I will enact a joint crime-fighting task force able to strike at the heart of every major syndicate in and around our city. We will destroy this scourge," he declares, staring dead into the camera. I swear he's looking right at me. "We will win."

I turn the TV off and rake my hands through my hair, trying not to panic. A joint crime-fighting task force? It sounds...destructive.

If Daze catches wind of this, only God knows what he might do to find me. Go directly to my father's mansion and waltz inside?

I inhale and try to keep my breathing steady. I can't panic just yet. But where can I go?

With those strange men in the hallway, trespassing doesn't seem so bad at the moment, so I hunker down with a view of the door and strain my ears, waiting for them to leave. It's silent for a few excruciatingly long minutes. Then I think I hear a door slam somewhere below. Hopefully, they've exited the building for good, though why they were here in the first place? I don't even want to know.

In any case, lingering in a stranger's apartment won't do much good in the long run. I stand and gather my things again. The last thing I grab is the tablet the reporter left, and my heart pangs as I start to tuck it into my purse.

Jamie's last warning creeps into my mind before I can help it, and I find myself powering on the device and searching for a single name—Daze Keaton. Two files pop up. One is a rather colorful rap sheet dating back to when he must have been a teenager. Breaking and entering, larceny, petty theft, burglary, assault, assault, *assault*. I don't think I'm surprised, but it's still startling to see it all listed with concrete dates.

But that isn't the revelation that makes me shiver. No, that tidbit of information I discover in the second file, which consists of an old newspaper clipping. LOCAL WOMAN FOUND DEAD—FOUL PLAY SUSPECTED.

Authorities have identified a body found in an abandoned building on Cherry Lane as Carenna Rotteridge, twenty-two...

According to the article, only one suspect was questioned in relation to her death. A past boyfriend and the father of her only child, Daze Keaton of Westpoint City.

DAZE

THE MAN I've been sent to kill goes by the name Carlos Cortez. It didn't take long for Damien to track down his location. While not a native of the city, he lurks at the same haunts anyone born and raised in this shithole would—the largest casino in the heart of downtown. Barely past noon, he's already there, camped out at one of the slot machines, nursing a steady stream of vodka shots supplied by an exhausted waitress.

He doesn't seem inclined to leave anytime soon—not to mention that he's flanked by at least three beefy guards, from what I can see. Which brings up a very good question—how the hell am I supposed to fulfill my promise to those bastards in the warehouse, without getting myself arrested?

Any other day, I think it'd be easier to come up with a plan. Or to keep my head in the game, at least. As it stands, all I can focus on is *her*. Frey. She attracts more trouble than I fucking do, and I can only hope that Silas hasn't gotten his hands on her, using the fire as a distraction.

I should be out there looking for her right now. Fuck Silas and whatever grand plan I'd need to take him down. But then I remember Ben's advice. The bastard has a fucking point.

So, I clear my head and think up a course of action on the fly. Getting a gun and killing the bastard outright would probably be the easiest plan—but it's a coward's way out. Something a punk like Silas wouldn't hesitate to do.

Or Marcus. Ben doesn't know the extent of just how bad things got when my old man ran the Saints—or the shit that bastard made me do to cover his tracks. I played along for as long as I could, but in the end, his lies caught up to him. Rather than come clean to the people who worshiped him like some hero, he shot his veins up with dope and OD'd.

I could have let the truth regarding his legacy come out then. I didn't. Like a good boy, I cleaned up his mess and staged his death as a heart attack. Maybe this is part of why I never believed the story of Hale's death.

Despite what Ben and Chris seem to think, murder wasn't above Marcus, but I'm willing to draw the line there. After all, those bastards in the warehouse said they wanted me to "take him out." They didn't specify how exactly, and—like any ex-cage fighter who survived a close match—I'm willing to take advantage of that wiggle room.

With Frey out there alone, there isn't exactly time to get rid of a body anyway. There aren't many non-lethal options to choose from, either. So, fuck the rulebook. I start forward, fully intending to trust no one's advice but my own.

I barely make it within eyeshot of the bastard before his guards square up, eyeing me warily. "Stay back," one of them warns. "Keep it moving."

"Or I can keep it blunt with your boss here," I say, keeping my focus on the man in question. "Word on the street is that he has a very cushy position, but I think he might soon find it under threat."

The guard hisses and spits on the floor, but his boss barely takes his eyes off the machine he's playing. "Make this piece of shit fuck off," he commands.

One of the guards steps forward, cracking his knuckles. As reluctant as I am to risk another concussion, it seems I need to show these assholes that I mean business. That leaves only one course of action—demonstrate.

I open my stance, rocking onto my heels. When the asshole attempts a right hook, it's easy enough to dodge and counter with my own right. What's the saying—The bigger they are, the harder they fall? That sure applies to him. As soon as my fist connects, I feel the crunch of bone, and the behemoth is on his way to the ground. Lights out for that fucker. I quickly assess which douche is coming for round two. I don't have time for this shit—Frey and Sammy, not to mention the guys, are depending on me.

So, enough playing around. It's time to cut to the chase.

"You're here wasting your time playing with toys when the real money to be made is out there. If you have the balls to go after it, that is. Or is the cousin of Rodrigo Cortez really the shit-eating punk the rumors say you are?"

That gets a rise out of him.

"What the fuck do you want?"

"I want to make a deal, and trust me, you'll end up with far more than the pennies you can earn from one game of slots."

He lifts his head to eye me from over his shoulder. "Who the fuck are you?"

"Someone who can help you garner something more powerful than money."

He laughs. "Get the fuck out of here—"

I slam my hand down on the screen right in front of his face. One of his men moves to grab me, but the man nods just once to keep him at bay.

"I'm talking about power," I taunt. "Real currency that can buy you a lot more than cheap-ass designer clothing and a couple of armed goons. Or do you like taking orders from your cousin back home or Silas Rotteridge here in the city? I'm sure you caught wind of the Saints' puppet master's little press conference this morning?"

I sure as hell had. Ben texted me an article he'd summed up with just two words—We're fucked. With Heywood's victory all but assured, I have no doubt he'll turn the full force of the government toward snuffing out any and all competition.

I say as much to the cartel bastard, but he just scoffs.

"That's enough." One of the guards moves toward me, but his boss waves him off. The man spins to face me, his hands braced over his knees. "You talk a big game for a punk who's come from nowhere. Who the hell are you, anyway? Wait..." He sits forward, his eyes squinted. "I know you. You're that Saints asshole. The one that ran away with his tail between his legs. Dale or some shit. Isn't that your name?"

"My name is Daze," I counter, "and I think only one of us will wind up leaving the city with his tail between his legs. You—though it will be willingly, of course."

The man laughs. "Get a load of this motherfucker! Cocky as hell, that's for damn sure."

"Cocky enough to ensure you can walk away from this city with more than you ever bargained for. Unless you're content being the whipping boy of both the cartel and the Saints."

The man scoffs. "Oh really? And how's that?"

"You sit back and watch," I say. "And you let everyone else do the grunt work."

"So, let's hear it then, this grand plan of yours."

I wouldn't call it grand—mainly just one desperate fucking bluff.

But it's all I have, and I intend to sell it with everything I've got.

Should I fail...

Frey won't have just her brother's death to contend with.

"Your men join me, and we stop Heywood from forming his little task force," I begin. "That gives your powerful cousin more time to conduct his affairs without interference. I'm sure he'll be pleased with you for that. In the meantime, you leave now and let me handle shit here. You get all the credit for none of the work."

It's a fragile fucking plan in theory—but so is power in any form. As his beady eyes squint, I can tell the bastard is thinking it over, envisioning the imaginary praise for keeping his boss out of hot water.

He strokes his chin and sits back in his chair. "Sounds easy. Too fucking easy—"

"Or," I snap, squaring my stance as one of his guards shifts in my peripheral vision. "You sit back. Let Heywood take over and drive you and every other gang from the city. Of course, they'll need a few trophies to parade on the news. The cousin of a cartel leader would make for the perfect fucking patsy."

He wrinkles his nose and waves his hand, urging his guard closer. Shit. I form a fist and open my stance. I could take one of them at least—as long as they don't get itchy to use a gun. Right when I'm poised to lunge, Cortez looks me over. "Fetch a drink for my friend," he says, sending his man scurrying to comply. "We have much to discuss, Daze Keaton. Have a seat."

"I prefer to stand," I bite back, suppressing all traces of the relief I feel. If there's one thing I did learn from my father, it's never let anyone think they're on your level. It's harder for them to stab you in the back that way. If he could see me now, he'd be spinning in his fucking grave. Cutting a deal with the cartel instead of strutting around, faking power and influence I don't have?

Keatons work for no one, he'd hiss.

It's a good damn thing that I've left everything tied to him behind, then. The Saints. His debt. His baggage. As Ben said, I have my own fucking reputation to go off now.

It's time I used it to my advantage, no matter the risk.

So, meeting Cortez's gaze squarely, I keep talking.

FREY

WHILE DAZE MADE his gym seem like some hole in the wall, it's much more than that. I only have to take advantage of the Wi-Fi on Jamie's tablet and google his name for a wealth of information to come up regarding a prestigious family history of champion boxers, stretching back generations. His father, Marcus Keaton, was a local celebrity. His entire family has roots in the area that go even deeper than mine.

And when I finally find the place, he has the decency to not be there. I linger in the alleyway, but I jump at every flickering shadow, convinced it's Silas or one of my father's men ready to grab me. A low sound teases the air that some part of my brain vaguely recognizes. A motorcycle?

The thought triggers a paranoid fear—is the entire crew of Saints nearby ready to mow me down?

It would serve me right. Daze has better things to do than sit around waiting for me, apparently. I should take a page from his playbook and handle my own business, starting with digging into the information Hale left behind.

With the hood of my borrowed jacket pulled low over my face, I retrace my steps to the sleepier part of the city, where I find a local library. Thankfully, no one seems to pay me any attention, and I can seclude myself in a distant corner on the second floor to go through the tablet in earnest.

My fingers tremble as I comb through Hale's autopsy first. It makes me cold to think of him, lying on a table while a doctor clinically records every detail of his last moments. Still, I push the emotions aside and try to dig deeper into the information.

The reporter was right about the Black Heroin—the doctor who performed the autopsy noted the rarity of the drug in their toxicology report. Apart from that, nothing out of the ordinary sticks out. There were no signs of struggle. No bruises or defensive wounds on the body. Almost as if Hale really did just overdose...

But the more I pour over the other information stored on the tablet, the murkier the overall picture becomes.

Six months ago, Hale reached out with a list of names that he wanted the reporter to look into—the same ones, in fact, that the reporter mentioned that day at the church. All of them were accepted into Salvation's outreach program.

And all of them wound up dead months later.

It's harrowing to read my brother's increasingly frantic emails. He must have been so worried by whatever grim conspiracy he thought was underway. I wish he would have reached out to me. Said something.

Instead, I only have what he left behind to go off. Even with the reporter's notes, I can't make sense of it. While Salvation seems to be at the heart of the disappearances, one key motive is missing.

Why? What could my father or whoever else may be behind this nefarious scheme want with the poorest citizens of the city? It has to be something more than just indiscriminate murders or accidental deaths. Maybe Hale knew what, and that was the topic he confronted our father with the night he died?

If that's the case, he didn't share the reason with the reporter. I don't find anything useful in his notebook, either. Just the same seemingly random lists of names and dates.

As the hours tick by, paranoid thoughts begin to creep in. Like that, this is all one big conspiracy meant to distract me from a far more selfish motive for running away—I'm scared. I don't want to live whatever plan my father has devised for me, and maybe I'm grasping at straws to distract from that.

Or...

I don't want to think of him as anything other than the stern, intimidating presence that he already is. Could the man who raised me truly be capable of more than blind ambition and reckless violence?

I don't want to believe it, but I feel an ominous pinch in my gut warning me that sooner or later, I'll have to face the truth whether I'm ready or not.

Maybe sooner than later—a man's been watching me. I tried to ignore him at first, but every time my eyes stray in his direction—a table beside mine where he pores over an open book—he's staring straight at me. The expression on his face is pensive, like someone trying to solve a complicated puzzle. Perhaps why he recognizes a strange woman? It's only a matter of time before he connects the dots to the most recent news stories dominating the local channels.

Surreptitiously, I gather up my stuff and tiptoe toward the exit. From the corner of my eye, I see the man stand and start to do the same, heading in my direction. Crap! I mentally kick myself for even venturing into public in the first place. My heart pounds with dread as I break into a full sprint down the steps to the first floor. I'm convinced that any minute, my father and his men will appear out of nowhere, ready to drag me away. Or worse. Silas...

"Miss! Hey, wait!" The man catches up to me, placing a hand on my shoulder.

My mind goes blank. I don't even process reaching into my pocket and drawing a knife. I only know that when I swing it around, the man steps back, his hands raised in surrender. Wait... I doubt my father's bodyguards would do the same.

"Sorry to scare you," he stammers, his face beet red. "It's just that I noticed what you were writing earlier. Those addresses? I thought you might be in Klein's architecture class, too. It's fucking killing me, but you've gotta be smarter than I am if you've already caught onto the same topic I have. It took me weeks to pick up on it."

"On what?" I blurt while wrestling the knife back into my pocket.

"The pattern," he says, an eyebrow raised. "You know, the purchasing pattern. I wouldn't have caught on if I wasn't so obsessed with seventy's era design, but... It seems like you might have looked into it from a different angle."

A different angle?

"Looked into what?"

He eyes me oddly. Then he laughs and winks. "Ah, don't worry. I'd play coy with my topic too. Since I don't recognize you from my class, I'll let you in on a secret. Check into Higher Limit Construction. That might give you a bit more insight, though it all seems shady as hell. Hopefully, the FBI won't break down my door before the deadline for the paper anyway. See ya around!"

He heads off, sporting a very convincing backpack slung over one shoulder. When he doesn't usher in a cadre of armed guards, I realize he is probably just a typical student.

Whom I nearly stabbed out of nowhere.

Damn it, Frey. I inhale raggedly and make it outside, only to jump as a dark car flits past. I know that I won't last an hour out in the open without a solid plan. Should I find Daze? Maybe. Though considering the fact that he was a suspect in the death of his son's mother, it might be better to take my chances alone.

Don't think like that, a part of me scolds. The last person on earth I should be doubting right now is the only one to show me any kind of loyalty. He nearly got his head caved in to protect me from Silas, let alone all the risks he took by evading my father's security just to meet me. That had to account for something, right?

Unless, that was his aim all along... Earn my trust while the entire time he was working with my father directly, spinning a web more convoluted than the one it seems like Father and Colton had in mind for me.

The paranoia winds my intentions into knots. I'm walking aimlessly, with no clear direction in mind, when someone approaches me from behind too quickly for me to suck in a breath—let alone grab the knife.

I lash out regardless—nails draw. My attacker grunts in alarm, biting out a curse—but his voice... I recognize it.

"Fuck! Don't move," he hisses, spinning me around to face him. "You've got a lot of explaining to do, missy. I suggest you start talking."

DAZE

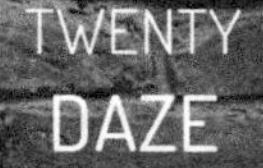

MY CELL PHONE is in my hand, but it takes me a full fucking minute to call just one number.

"Day?" Lyra asks, picking up on the first ring. "I've been trying to get a hold of your ass for days! I—"

"I know," I reply. "It wasn't safe, but I've got things under control and..."

"What do you want?" she questions, openly suspicious. "To warn me away from Silas? Trust me, I don't need that advice. I heard you two got into it again, and I want nothing to do with it. Sammy will not be used as a token in a pissing contest between you two. I refuse to allow it—"

"That's why I'm calling," I interject. "About Sam. I wanna see him sometime soon."

She pauses, and I hear what sounds like cartoons playing in the background. "Is this a ploy? Your way of playing tit for tat because Silas asked me to—"

"This has nothing to fucking do with him," I snarl. Hold up. "What did he want?"

I hear her curse under her breath. "If you don't know, maybe I shouldn't say. I told him no, for what it's worth, and—"

"Lyra. Tell me, what the fuck did he say?"

"Oh, alright! He wanted to know if I'd be open to selling dad's gym, since I'm technically part owner. He recommended this fancy construction company who want to turn it into a clinic for the homeless or something—"

"And you told him to go to hell, right?" My voice sounds so damn hard.

"Of course!" Lyra insists. "I know how much that place means to you, Day, though you'd never admit it. I would never agree to sell it without your permission."

"Maybe you should," I toss back. "At least then we could make some money off Marcus' supposed legacy."

"Don't talk like that, Day. Daddy had his problems, but they were *his* problems. That gym is in your blood. Don't be ashamed of that. Do you want to know something? Why mama even agreed to name you something as ridiculous as Daze in the first place?" She laughs, and it hits me how rarely I've heard that sound come out of her lately. "It was Daddy's idea. They wanted to name you Marcus, after him. Had baby crap with that name on it all picked out. Then, when you were born, Daddy took one look at you and said you were the only baby he'd ever seen come out of the womb swinging. Like you were born ready for a fight, and when there was no danger, you got this weird dazed look on your face. He thought it was hilarious. That's why he gave you that name. Angry Daze, always on guard, ready for violence, and shocked when someone doesn't want to beat the shit out of him. After seeing you grow up, I think it's fitting."

"Very funny," I deadpan. It isn't like her to be so damn nostalgic, but I don't remember hearing this story before.

"You want to take Sammy? Fine. He has a playgroup thing tonight, but I can bring him around after school tomorrow. Just as long as you promise me that you're safe. That he won't be in danger."

"I promise. Can... Let me talk to him."

She exhales harshly, and muffled noise comes from her end next. Then...

"Daddy?"

I grit my teeth at the sound of his voice. I didn't realize until now just how much I missed it. Missed him. Since Lyra took him in, I've kept my distance—and she's rightfully called my ass out about that. The truth is, I don't want to abandon my own son. Not ever. But looking into his eyes, knowing how badly I fucked up for both our sakes, stings like hell. I couldn't face it.

What changed? Maybe witnessing how easily someone else, like, say, a skinny little blond, could charm her way into his life without trying. Take care of him without batting an eyelash. Protect him, even though she didn't ask for the responsibility.

"Hey, little man. I've missed you," I finally say, dragging my free hand through my hair. The fingers shake, and I accidentally brush over a bruise. The fresh bite of pain snaps some sense into me. I clear my throat. "I'm gonna spend the day with you tomorrow after school. Would you like that?"

"Yes!" His excited shriek is so loud I have to hold the phone away from my ear. "Can we watch SpongeBob? And get ice cream. And—"

Another bit of muffled static chops off the rest of his request. "Yeah, yeah," Lyra says, apparently having taken the phone. "Just don't get his hopes up, Day. Promise me?"

"I promise," I swear back.

When we finally hang up, I can't describe how I feel. There's still the cartel shit to deal with, and Heywood, and Frey. Even so... I know my upper lip is quirked in a smile I don't feel the urge to suppress right away.

I return to the bar and find Ben tending the counter. At a glance, the place looks dead. Empty. I grit my teeth with worry over Frey, but I decide to spare Ben the third degree for now. He looks edgy, staring me down with a wary frown. "Well? How did it go?"

I tell him what happened. When I finish, I'm not sure if he believes me or not.

"Shit." He grabs a shot glass filled with whiskey and downs it in one go. "Your old man would kill us if he could see you now. Cutting a deal with the fucking cartel."

"I bought us time," I say in my own defense. "And I never gave much of a damn what he thought anyway."

"Well... I'll be honest, Day, I didn't think you could do it. Not without a pot to piss in anyway. You've proven me wrong." Ben chuckles to himself while pouring two more shots. One, he hands to me. "Now what?" he asks after draining his drink.

I stare into the amber-colored liquid writhing in my shot glass and shrug. "You tell me. Weren't you supposed to, I don't know, find someone while I was out?"

"We'll get to that." Head cocked, his expression pensive, Ben sets his glass on the counter. "Business first. You've scored yourself a warehouse, and a delicate house of political cards to play with. How in the hell do you plan on surviving this mess with your balls intact? We can't crash with Chris forever. It's only a matter of time before Silas figures out you're here, anyway."

"Exactly," I point out, turning my head to get a good view of the empty room. My first suspicion seems correct—there's no one else here. "While I was out playing the good little errand boy, you had one fucking job, Ben. Don't tell me you spent the afternoon sipping beer while I was risking my ass."

"A task?" Ben frowns and strokes his chin. "Oh, you mean finding your little girlfriend before she gets her ass dragged into another one of Silas' black vans? I think I managed to do that *and* get back here in time for plenty of beer. She's upstairs—" He nods to a hallway behind the bar. "I don't think she'll be very happy to see you, though."

"Bullshit." I head down the hall and up a narrow staircase. There's a landing with two doors at the top, and emanating from the one I've claimed is the faint sound of water running. Sure enough, when I get inside, I find the bathroom door closed.

Fuck. I can smell her through it. It's the intangible stuff preachers talk about when they bitch about goodness and innocence. Sweet. Light. Fragrant. She's a living embodiment of that purity, and I'm the one who plunged her into this hell.

Maybe I should feel guilty about that—a better man would. Instead, I just breathe her in and grip the doorknob, sensing her just beyond this fragile barrier. She must be in the shower, washing off whatever the fuck she's been through to escape her father's prison.

A good man would probably let her do so in peace, too. Let her recover and face me on her own terms.

I twist the knob and push the door open.

She's in the stall, her back to me, and her ass on display. Dripping wet, her pale skin glistening, she takes my fucking breath away. Then I step closer and note the variations in her skin that shouldn't be there. Angry, red lines slashing down toward her hip.

Son of a bitch. I see red. Someone hit her—no. They whipped her, like she was a goddamn animal. Silas or her father had to be the culprit, and for a second, all I know is rage.

Then she tilts her head back, and with that simple motion, she makes me do the one thing I rarely do—second-guess myself. A girl like that belongs in a fucking castle, or some manor downtown surrounded by an army of butlers. Anywhere but here, with me.

"You're staring." She has her face angled toward me, those green eyes wide as hell. As Ben suggested, she doesn't seem happy to see me. In the short time I've known her, I've come to recognize that look. The pouty, slightly angry one, as if she doesn't even know why the fuck she's so upset. She's used to plastering on a pretty little smile, denying she felt anything but perfect all the damn time.

It hits me now like a kick to the stomach—I don't want perfect.

"Tell me what you're feeling," I command her, stepping fully inside the room. "Spit it out. No beating around the bush. No sweet little words. Say it."

She sucks in a breath, but keeps her front contorted away from me. It takes all the restraint I have to stay put. But, fuck it, I take one more step, coming close enough to touch her if I wanted.

And I fucking do. She's shaking like a leaf, flinching at the slightest contact. I'm not the reason, though. She leans into me as if she can't stop herself, her eyes wide with confusion.

"I'm angry," she says.

"Wrong." I take another step and savor the way she inhales raggedly. It's sexy as hell, and she doesn't even realize the effect she has on me. "I said no sweet words. Tell me the truth. None of that shit you learned in finishing school. Tell. Me. How. You fucking feel."

"Fine." She shuts off the water, and faces me fully, her head tilted back. For a second, that naïve light leaves her eyes. She's suddenly a different person, a woman far too confident to take any shit from me. "I'm pissed. Happy? I'm so fucking pissed!" She lashes out, landing a blow on my chest that I barely feel. "You lied to me."

About that...

"You have every right to be upset," I admit, leaning against the outside of the shower stall. "But I owe it to you to explain myself. Will you let me?"

She crosses her arms. "It seems like all you know how to do is 'explain yourself.' Take your own advice. No more sweet words. I want the truth. About Silas. About Hale. About...Renna."

My guard goes up at the mention of that name. I can't help it.

"Fine. Renna died, but not by my hand like Silas insinuated before. And..." I pause for a moment to gather my thoughts. "I did lie. I looked you dead in the eye and told you I didn't know Hale, but I did. I knew he was investigating your father's church and thought it was connected to a string of murders downtown. I did what I could to help him and got myself thrown in lockup as a reward. While I was away, Silas took over the Saints, and Hale was murdered."

She sighs and inspects me from head to toe. Damn. The way she looks at me with those furtive little eyes makes my cock twitch. I've been in fully nude strip clubs and felt less.

"Explain," she says, squaring her chin. "Tell me exactly what happened."

"I'll tell you everything you want to know. All the dirty little details. But first, I need to feel you," I confess as I find myself inching closer, ready to...

Do what? Hold her, I guess. Wrap my arms around that tiny waist as she processes the full extent of the shit her family's been up to. The strange part is that just a week ago, she'd have needed that level of coddling. I'd have to spoon-feed her the dark, twisted answers and hope she didn't overdose on them.

But this iteration of Frey... She holds her head high and takes it all in without batting an eyelash—though she does flinch.

"No more lies, I swear on my life," I say as I look deep into her eyes. "Anything else, you can ask, and I'll tell you. I swear."

"Yeah," she says softly. Perhaps without realizing it, she copies my stance, leaning back against the wall of the stall, letting her hands fall, breasts on display. My cock reasserts itself, hammering against the inside of my jeans. I wonder if she can tell. When her eyes cut down to my waist and dart up again, I have my answer.

"Tell me why I should trust you."

Her voice does something to me when it's soft like that. So damn delicate. The look in her eye stops me from underestimating her, though. Her gaze is sharp as hell, honed to cut.

"Because I know what your trust is worth," I confess. "I don't take it for granted. Not for a second."

She juts her chin into the air. "What changed?"

"Nothing." I drop the patient act and step forward, taking in every inch of her body. She tries to raise her hands, but at the last second, seems to stop herself. She keeps her head held high and doesn't take her gaze from mine even for a second.

Damn, is it sexy.

"I just realized you aren't someone I want to piss off. I don't like it when you're angry at me."

I keep advancing, stepping into the stall, blocking her in.

"Do you want to know how I prefer you to look at me?"

She bites her lower lip, and I can't stop the sound I hiss out in return.

"H-How?"

No more games. I lift her wrists above her head, arching into her. At the same time, I rake my gaze over her body without holding back.

"Like you don't want to grab my hand and pray. You don't want to talk, either," I say, watching her chest rise and fall with every panting breath. "You look at me like all you want is for me to…"

She raises that defiant chin even higher, her eyes blazing. "What?"

"Do this—" I press my mouth to hers—hard. She wants the honest, real Daze? Well, she got him. He doesn't beat around the fucking bush, and he isn't much into taking things slow and gentle.

But I'm not the one who uses teeth first—she does, biting at the tip of my tongue the second it tries to slip between those plump lips. Then she turns the tables, kissing me back just as ferociously. They certainly didn't teach her that in bible study.

I let her wrists go in favor of cupping her breasts, drawing her into me. I savor the little gasp that rips from her throat, but it's already becoming a moan as I swipe my thumb along the tip of a nipple.

Screw talking and conversation. This is how we communicate best—she can't hide behind her polished grammar and manners. She's greedy and feisty, clawing at me just as hungrily as I grope at her.

We move like that to the back of the stall, where I grip a fistful of her ass and force her to straddle me.

She looks up, her eyes half-closed, her hair a mess. A question lurks behind those eyes, but it can wait.

"You can doubt me if you want," I tell her. "Think I'm still lying to you. But you can't deny this—I'm here with you now. No one can take that away. No one."

A tiny sound escapes her mouth. Maybe her attempt at trying to agree? Like it or not, we fit together. Meld together. Already, I need her so badly it hurts. My body takes on a mind of its own, and I can't get inside her fast enough.

I reach for my jeans one-handed, but she beats me to it, squirming out of my grasp to stand on her own. With a grace that makes me groan, she undoes the clasp with those delicate fucking hands and tugs them down. Then, a heartbeat later, she has me in the palm of her hand.

Fuck. I definitely didn't teach her that.

"Harder," I bite out, bucking into her silken grip. "You think you can handle me? Then do it—"

She curls her fingers around me, matching the natural rhythm I seek out. Nothing in the world compares to the feel of her skin. The way her eyes widen as she tries to take her cues from me. She's a quick learner—too quick. She tightens her grip, stroking back and forth. The entire time, she studies me, her lip trapped between her teeth. The sight makes me crave to learn what other skills she's picked up on.

"I think you got the hand job down," I tell her, gripping her wrist. "But how well can you work that mouth, Freylie? I'll show you mine if you show me yours."

She inhales, but before I can even process how quickly she moves, she's on her knees. Her breath sends a goddamn shiver down my spine. She takes her time, sizing me up, probably going through the steps in her head.

But when she opens her mouth, there's none of that sexy hesitation from the first few times I had her like this. She takes me like a pro, tilting her head back, so those eyes stare directly into mine.

"*Fuck—*" I rake my fingers through her hair, then seize a handful, catching her off guard. I feel her shiver as I use my grip to guide her mouth where I want it.

"Easy," I grate out when I feel her teeth tease the length of my shaft. "I'm not into masochism, baby." But I'm laughing anyway. I know what her intent was—don't command me. I'm in charge.

And even I can admit that, for the time being, she is. She takes me down as far as she can, watching me with those haunting eyes. Damn. This will be over too soon if I can't rein it in.

I push her back gently, ignoring the part of me that wants her to keep going. "My turn."

I yank her upright and press her back to the wall before crouching.

"Come on," I rasp. "Spread those legs for me."

She does, so slowly I'm gritting my teeth in anticipation. Some things haven't changed. She may be bolder when it comes to my body, but she's still shy when it comes to hers. I'll be damned if I know why.

"You're beautiful," I tell her. I mean it. Every inch of her is perfect, beyond compare. It isn't lost on me that I don't deserve to even look at her, let alone touch her.

But if lust is a sin, I'm not the only one of us on my way to hell.

She arches her back, bringing her pussy as close to my mouth as she can. Just by looking at her, I can tell she's wet. When I run a finger along her seam, she whimpers.

Fucking hell.

"You must love foreplay, beautiful girl," I tell her. "But I don't know if I can hold out any longer."

I cut to the chase, slamming my tongue inside her with a force that makes her groan. She seizes fistfuls of my hair next, telling me where she needs me the most.

Her taste is divine. It shouldn't be possible for anyone to feel this good. This goddamn perfect. As if she were made for me.

"I need you, Frey," I breathe into her. Then I pull her out of the shower and bend her over the counter. I sink into her slowly, inhaling her scent. Then instinct takes over.

I slam into her, driving every moan from her throat that I can. She's tense at first, clenching her jaw as if her entire church is lurking nearby, watching. Judging.

"No one's here," I tell her, slipping my arm beneath her and cupping a breast against the palm of my hand. "Look—" I angle her body until she's face up, watching herself in the mirror. Her eyes widen at the woman she sees—blond hair a mess, lips a sexy bitten red, her skin flushed, chest heaving.

"Look at yourself. Look at those pretty little eyes, how wide they go when I fuck you like this—"

Her inner muscles spasm, and it's a miracle I can keep talking.

"I think you like watching," I tell her. "So do I. So, watch, and let me hear you. I need to. No one's around, so tell me—"

She moans as another ripple of pleasure leaves her clutching the sink for dear life. I cup her breast with one palm and nip her ear lobe until I have her full attention. God, the way her eyes meet mine in the mirror's reflection... Only one thing keeps me from blowing the game here and now.

"I've got you," I tell her, flexing my fingers until her knees buckle, threatening to go limp. "I won't let you fall, so trust me. Let me have you, all of you. In return, you can have whatever you want from me. Come on—" I slam into her again and watch her knuckles whiten. She's biting her lip so damn hard, I bet it's bleeding.

Fuck.

"Scream for me, Frey," I hiss into her hair, drunk off her scent. "I need to hear you—" I press into her, forcing her to bend over the sink entirely. Her head goes down, and a bitten-off moan escapes her gritted teeth.

"Oh god—"

"Don't cry for him," I snap. "Cry for me. It's my name I want to hear come out of that sweet little mouth."

She whimpers, and I recognize the way her breathing hitches.

"You're close, aren't you?" I know she is. One good thrust will make her come like a fucking gusher. I rock my hips, but rather than give her what she craves, I threaten to pull out. "Naughty girls don't get rewarded, Freylie. Come on—"

"You're...a bastard." She raises her head, her gaze finding mine in the mirror. Real anger blazes there—obviously, Ben wasn't off base with his judgment of her mood. At the same time, she arches that beautiful body into me, hungry for a tip over the edge. "I hate you—"

"Liar." I give her another taste, thrusting into her shuddering grip, and she quivers, her mouth falling open. "You wouldn't be able to come all over my cock if you hated me that much."

"You're the liar," she chokes out, but her voice has already lost that bitter edge. She's practically melting into me, her eyes unfocused, her body trembling. "All you've done...is lie to me."

"Not true." I press my face to hers, watching us both in the mirror as I slam into her harder. "I care about you more than I want to. More than I should. More..."

"Daze." Her throat cords around a cry, making it clear that now isn't the time for this conversation. "Please... I can't..."

I run my fingers through her hair, gripping the back of her scalp. "Ask, and you shall receive, beautiful girl."

Then I pin her down and stop playing nice. I need her. More than I want to admit—so much it fucking aches. When her moans come freely, each one louder than the next, it's fucking kryptonite to any part of me that thought I was in control.

I'm not. She is, melting around me, commanding with every twitch of her body how fast to move. How hard to thrust. I'm nowhere near in control when I come inside her, bellowing out.

It's her. She has me in the palm of her fucking hand, even as she screams my name.

"Damn." I lean against the counter, still catching my breath. A smile plays on my lips. I feel like a fucking teenager, giddy after fooling around with the hottest girl in school—only she's different than that.

I size her up in a way I don't normally scrutinize people. Definitely not women. She's so damn small, barely a hundred pounds wet, but that look in her eye... It's penetrating, cutting me down to the goddamn bone. No one else on earth affects me the same way. I feel a silly need to express that to her. Make her realize the truth. Even beaten down and scarred from whatever shit her father put her through, she still has power, all her own, especially over me.

"You look way too serious," I taunt instead. "I don't know... Maybe I'm slipping. I think you should be breathless right now, murmuring something about how I have the best—"

"What are we doing?"

Her tone cools any remaining heat from that impromptu shower. Just like that, the real world intrudes on this sliver of the universe again.

"Doing." I chew over the word choice like I'm trying to decipher something meaningful from it. The truth is that I just want to stall. There isn't a good answer to that question. Not a single one. "What do you think we're doing?"

"I don't know," she admits in that small, wistful voice. It's the way she talks about her brother, like she's already on the verge of tears. Then she blinks and shakes her head. A heartbeat later, some resolve seeps into her gaze, and she's the woman who stared me down while I beat a man to death. Not quite an angel any longer. "You said you would tell me the truth about my brother. About everything. But..."

I stiffen. A good man would have a comeback ready. He'd insist that he did tell her everything and there were no more secrets between them. Nice, mushy, happy shit.

It would be a damn lie.

"There's so much about you that I don't know. *You*," she says. "Starting with your past, for one. Or your real issue with Silas. Or what happened to..."

She trails off, but I recognize that probing tone of voice. It's the same one people use regarding only one topic.

"Say it," I snap, sounding harsher than I mean to as I step a few feet back. "Say her name. That's what you really mean, isn't it?"

She winces, but keeps her chin high in the air. That's different. A few days ago, she wouldn't hold her own like this. A part of me hums in respect. I think I prefer this Frey to the entirely innocent one.

That doesn't mean I'll let her off easy, though.

"Say it," I prod when she remains silent. I step toward her and watch her throat jerk around a hard swallow. Some primal part of me loves that involuntary reaction—feeds off it. "Use those pretty words, Frey. I want to hear you ask me outright."

"What happened to her? Renna?" she demands. "Sammy's mother? And please don't give me the run around this time. I want to hear the truth. From you."

Damn. It's my turn to flinch. That look in her eye... She isn't the angel anymore. Her time with me has rubbed some of the shine off her halo. She's been tainted by the devil.

If anything, the thought makes her sexier.

I cock my head to take her in while running my tongue along my lower lip. As brave as she feels now, she can't disguise how unnerved the action makes her. Her breath catches, and it's the most beautiful fucking sound I've ever heard.

"Do you really?" I can't resist taunting her just a little bit. Though she's right.

I've put it off long enough.

With a sigh, I open the door and hunt for a pair of towels. All I can find are two bedsheets. Returning to the bathroom, I toss her one and leave the other slung over my arm.

Gathering up the nerve to meet her gaze is harder than it should be. When I do, she's already staring back as inquisitive as ever. "You want the truth? Fine. I'll give it to you, but unlike before... I won't hold anything back."

TWENTY-ONE

FREY

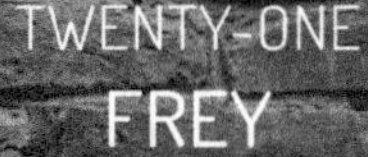

HE'S SO INTIMIDATING like this. His eyes take on that unnerving faraway look, and it's like he's a different person. Someone the sheltered Frances Heywood I used to be would never want to meet. A man who more than embodies the danger that Hale was supposedly investigating.

He leads me into a living room containing only a battered couch and an outdated stereo system. With a nod for me to sit, he claims one end of the sofa for himself. I squeeze in beside him while gingerly arranging my damp sheet around me.

For seconds, we linger in awkward silence—though I'm not sure if I should be the one to break it. After days of uncertainty, it feels so strange being alone with him again. An undeniable sense of anticipation lingers in the air, and when he finally opens his mouth, I realize I've been holding my breath.

"Like I told you, I've known about your father before we met, and not just because of his charming reputation as the resident pastor, either. A little over a year ago, I was in charge of the Saints, and I let greed and fucking cockiness tempt me into doing something I shouldn't have."

"What?" It isn't like him to bare himself like this. For once, his insecurities are on full display, and I can't deny that it only enhances his appeal to me. Confident, cocky Daze is mesmerizing, but honest, open Daze is even more intriguing.

"We had been on the decline for a long time. My old man had a gambling problem and used the Saints' accounts to leverage his debts. No one knew. The bastard went to his grave thinking I hated him, but I never even told the others of the shitstorm he left us in. Still haven't." He frowns, and I can tell how much the weight of that lie has bothered him. "We needed money to pay off the creditors he owed. Let me put it this way—they aren't the kind of men you want breathing down your neck. I needed profits, but I couldn't let the others in on the real extent of the trouble we were in, so I did the one thing I regret now more than any other dipshit mistake I've made in life."

"What was that?" I prod gently.

"I went to Silas for help," he says coldly. "The bastard had always gunned for power, but I stupidly thought that as Sammy's uncle, he might play nice for his sake."

"And you were dating his sister, weren't you?" I try not to remember the soft, aching way he said her name, as if it pained him just to recall it.

Even at the mention of her, he grimaces. "That too. Not that he was too happy about that, either. Silas was always a dick, but he had his fingers in the pots that my old man wouldn't touch with a ten-foot pole. I thought he could find a way to make cash quick without breaking too many rules. I thought wrong."

I draw my knees up to my chin and observe him. So far, he doesn't seem to be withholding the truth or outright lying to me—but there's a reluctance in his voice I don't miss. He may loathe Silas, but he hates this more—opening up to someone about his faults and mistakes.

"What happened?" I ask.

"Silas had the bright idea to use his contacts to find a bit of work I could do on the back end. None of the other boys would know, and it supposedly wasn't anything too illegal. A delivery, he said. For a wealthy benefactor. All I had to do was gather up some boys and wait at the docks for a shipment to come in. Supposedly it was a batch of counterfeit purses to sell on the black market. Nothing too hot. Then I was supposed to store that shipment in one of the warehouses the Saints control. When the client was ready to have the shipment moved, his men would take over from that point. Easy peasy, or so it seemed at the time. The money should have been my first clue, though."

"How so?"

He raises an eyebrow and lets out a coarse laugh. "Three mil cold. The kind of money that wouldn't be thrown around just to watch some counterfeit purses. I think I just didn't want to see the trap at that point. I wanted to settle the Saints' debts and move on, leading them my own way without standing in my old man's shadow. Things went to shit practically right out of the gate. As soon as the boat came into the docks, I got a glimpse of the real merchandise we were smuggling."

"Let me guess," I say softly. "It wasn't a handbag?"

"Hell no. It was heroin. Grade-A quality, right from Columbia—and not just your regular, run-of-the-mill shit, either. That stuff was the real deal. Supposedly we were being paid three million to guard it, but the stash they had us bring in was easily worth ten times that. The numbers didn't add up, and I confronted Silas about it."

"What did he say?"

Daze scoffs. "The bastard laughed right in my face. Tried to tell me that I didn't know what I'd seen and that if I wanted to keep the Saints from going under, I needed to be a good boy and see the job through to the end. By then, I finally got the sense to do the smart thing, and I had one of my men track him to see who he was really dealing with. You're not going to like the answer to that."

I take a deep breath. All along, I've been gearing up to face the truth about my father and Hale's death. Now that I'm on the precipice of doing so, I don't feel eager to see what lies on the other end of this twisted merry-go-round.

"Tell me the truth."

"I'd suspected Silas might have been working with the mob. Maybe even the cartel. Someone big enough to secure a shipment of that quality with that much money at stake. He certainly laid the groundwork to make it seem that way, but what he didn't account for was Ben. He tracked him around town, and one of his stops didn't make a lot of sense in the grand scheme. It wasn't to one of the mob casinos or the cartel's gambling dens, either. It was to some church soup kitchen in the squeaky-clean part of the city. Salvation."

I've been preparing for it, but I'm still not ready for the shock I feel. Silas at Salvation?

"Why?"

"I didn't know at first," Daze admits. "Ben thought it was his way of trying to throw us off his trail, but I know Silas. He isn't that smart. On a hunch, I decided to look more into the place. I did some digging and found out about your father, but I didn't make the obvious connection. Not then. It wasn't until a few days later, when everything went to shit, that I decided to put the pieces together."

"What happened?"

"The warehouse, the one with millions of dollars' worth of Columbian heroin? It got raided by the authorities overnight, and I didn't even see it coming. Just like that, the Saints went from being several grand in the hole, to several fucking million on my watch. That's not even the worst part. I thought my old man was a real fuckup, but as it turns out, I had him beat."

He sighs and leans back against the couch, threading his hands together. The look on his face tugs at me, urging me to my feet before I can help myself. With slow, deliberate steps, I cross over to him and cradle his chin with both hands.

Objectively he looks horrible. His bruises stand out in stark contrast to his skin, and a blind man could see the exhaustion pooling beneath his eyes in the form of purple bags. At the same time, there's no denying the strength he exudes. Despite being beaten and physically broken, I wouldn't count him out for a second.

"You aren't a fuck up," I tell him, parroting his coarse language. "You're not. You wouldn't care so much if you were."

"Ah, you do have a way with those pretty, little words," he murmurs. He reaches up, pressing his palm against my cheek. "Maybe save your judgment for when you hear the full story, huh? The truth is, I fucked up bad. Silas is a sick, fucking prick, but he has good reason to hate me. Maybe he even has the right to kill me should he ever get around to it—"

"Don't say that!" I press my finger against his lips. "And you're not going to go looking for him either. Promise me."

He smiles and gently shrugs me off. "Yeah, yeah. Let me finish first before you get all bossy on me, alright? Come here —" He takes both of my hands, stroking along the palms of them. I shiver at the contact. His callouses reflect the hard life he's lived and are a mere glimpse into the things he's had to do just to stay afloat. Do I believe unknowingly helping to smuggle in illicit drugs is the worst thing he's ever done?

Not for a second.

Holding my gaze, he pulls me onto his lap. Then he brings one of my hands to his mouth and presses a kiss against the knuckles.

"You look so damn sexy when you get all worked up, you know. Once I get this show and tell over, I might have to take advantage of that."

I swallow hard. Would he really be devious enough to try and distract me now? Probably. I do my best to resist and make my expression as serious as I can.

"Keep talking."

"Ben was following Silas, but I didn't realize that Renna was following me. I came home one night to find her asleep on the floor while Sam was screaming his head off in the next room—only she wasn't sleeping."

"Oh god." I don't know what to do other than withdraw my fingers from his and smooth them along his jaw before pressing a kiss to his forehead. "I'm so sorry."

"Silas blamed me," Daze admits. "But he was right to. I was so caught up in trying to keep the Saints afloat that I didn't even notice when she was too far gone. The raid happened soon after, and by then, I was in deep, deep shit. It was then that your brother found me. I thought he was just a junkie. I threatened to kick his ass, but he was persistent. A lot like you, actually."

I'm holding my breath. I thought I was ready to hear this part of the story, but tears still prickle behind my eyes anyway. "What did he say?" I croak.

"He was worried," Daze admits. "About you, and what your father might be up to. When he brought up Salvation, I realized it wasn't a coincidence that Silas had been seen there. Not only that, but Hale mentioned that after doing his own digging, he'd found a troubling pattern when it came to the people who applied for the employment outreach program."

"They wound up dead," I say. Hearing it all come together makes my stomach churn. I have to lean into him just to get my bearings.

Daze raises an eyebrow. "Yeah. Too many people to be a coincidence, either. When I looked more into the heroin shipment, I realized that it wasn't the first one of its kind, either. Not only that, but the Westpoint P.D. handled the bust. When the hell have you ever heard of that before? That a local department would take over an international drug bust and not the feds?"

He's right. It sounds highly unusual.

"I thought Silas would be pissing his pants. I wanted to leave town, but he said he had it all under control. That sounded fishy, so I kept working with your brother, and the more I learned, the shadier this whole thing got. Surprise, surprise, but trusting Silas turned out to be the wrong move. I got arrested, and while I was in, your brother wound up dead. By the time I got out, your father was already climbing the polls,

Silas was in charge of the Saints, and I had no proof to prove otherwise."

"And you stopped caring. That's why you were there at the bridge. Following me was the last lead you had."

He nods, and his lips quirk into a sad, wistful frown. "I knew the second you saw me that you didn't know a damn thing about your father's true nature. Call me a bastard if you want, but I didn't have the heart to dump all this shit on you. Not then."

"So why not later? Why not when I begged you to tell me if you knew my brother? Why string me along like that!"

"Because of this—" he nods my way. "I didn't want you to look at me like that."

"Like what? Like you can't be trusted?"

"Exactly that."

"So, what now?" I ask.

He inclines his head, and I can't read his expression. "You make a choice. You can go back. Or you stay with me, no matter what happens."

"And what do you think might happen?" I don't know how I manage to gather up the nerve to ask him that, but he takes the question in stride, seemingly unsurprised.

"If I know Silas and things are as bad as they seem, then to put it bluntly? Shit's going to hit the fan."

His honesty makes my stomach churn, but I prefer it to the sugarcoated lies everyone else in my life seems more than happy to placate me with. I might prefer this brutally frank, open side of him more than the charming mask he puts on for the rest of the world.

"What do you think I should do?"

He smirks, and my heart flips at the expression. "I think you should do something that I don't think anyone else has ever told you, princess. Do whatever the fuck you want to. I won't stop you."

As his words sink in, I'm startled by how much they affect me. He's right. No one else has ever given me that same freedom. Or maybe it's a curse. Even Hale didn't trust me with that power. He couldn't even tell me himself about all the horrible things he suspected our father was up to.

Speaking of which...

"It's my turn to come clean about something," I say. "I think I know what Hale was afraid of. And I think Renna didn't just die from an overdose."

He doesn't react as I tell him everything that happened. A part of me suspects that he already knew, but when I finally trail off, his expression is anything but smug or guilty. He looks...furious.

"It makes fucking sense. After all this time..."

"So, what does it mean?"

He looks at me sharply before he removes me from his lap as he stands, raking a hand through his hair. I scramble to draw my knees up to my chin, mourning the loss of his heat.

"It means that Silas got himself in deeper shit than I thought. The bastard will drag Sam and Lyra down with him if I don't do something. Fuck!" He forms a fist and smashes it against the wall. His body ripples with tension as he breathes in and out, his skin flush with anger. Then he sighs and meets my gaze from over his shoulder. "We need to find out what the hell they're up to. Who is this reporter you talked to? What does he know?"

I quickly fill him in on everything Jamie Colland told me, including my father's supposed involvement in Hale's death, before moving on to what happened in the library before I met up with Ben. Then I take a breath and add, "Long story short, he thinks whatever it is, is linked to Salvation. Is there more that you aren't telling me?"

He runs his tongue along his lower lip in a move that makes my breath catch. "No..."

I don't want any more secrets between us, so without thinking the action through, I turn around and drop my sheet to let him explore my back in full. I'm sure he already saw when he first came in, but he gives me enough grace to pretend like he didn't.

"My father... He's not himself," I say thickly. "And Colton, he's crazy. They... They want me to marry him, and I don't—"

"Crazy?" Daze spins me around and takes both my hands in his. "It looks like he fucking whipped you to make marks like that—" Suddenly, he rears back, his upper lip curled in utter disgust. "He did, didn't he? He whipped you like an animal. That sick son of a bitch." He drops my hands before starting to pace, his hands balled in fists, his mind no doubt racing with a million revenge scenarios starring my father. A few days ago, I might have cowered at the sight.

Now? I reach out and place my hand on his shoulder, stopping him in his tracks. "Don't. He wanted to scare me. Beat me into submission—" Literally, it seems. Sucking in a breath, I force myself to add, "They know about us. About you. Father probably thought that if he hurt me, I'd obey him and stay away. But it didn't work. I'm here—"

"And they can't have you. You're mine," Daze grits out, snatching my wrist. "And if they ever touch you again, I will fucking kill them, Frey. Do you hear me?"

Warmth shoots between us like an electric current, pinging up and down my spine. It's insane how even being near him affects me like this. So intensely I can barely suck in any air. One look at his eyes, and he drags me under his spell completely.

Suddenly, his lips collide with mine in a brutal claiming that flips my whole world upside down. Can this possessive devouring be called a kiss?

Before I know it, he's pulling back slightly and resting his forehead on mine.

"I learned my lesson," he says in a voice that makes my belly quake. "I won't ever lie to you again. Do you believe that, Frey? I swear on my life. I won't. But you can't lie to me, either."

My head swims at the heated promise. Has anyone sworn anything to me so fervently before? Maybe Hale, back when he promised he'd always protect me.

"Okay," I say shakily. "I—"

"No." He steps into me, brushing his lips across mine. "This is your first lesson on what it means to be outside of your daddy's influence. No more taking people at face value. If someone promises you something—anything—you make them prove it."

My heart flutters in my chest. I fight to choke out, "H-How?"

He chuckles low in his throat, and I feel his fingers ghost along my bare waist to settle against my lower back. "You do something that good little girls like you aren't taught in those fancy private schools—you make demands."

Demands. That word sounds so dangerous coming from him. Maybe it's even a twisted joke at my expense. My father and men like him are the ones who call the shots in my world. They train their followers like Colton to do the same. The wants and needs of those they oppress don't matter to any of them.

With one guttural statement, Daze turns that dynamic on its head. He makes it sound so easy to claim that power for myself. To take advantage of the wider world with only might and a few uttered words.

Holding his probing stare, I manage to gasp out, "How?"

He smiles in that devilish way. "I'll teach you." He leans in, moving his lips to my ear. Voice rasping, he says, "It's simple in practice, though it might seem alien to you sheltered little princesses. You look the man across from you in the eye—"

"Or woman," I interject, holding my breath as he cocks his head to meet my gaze. "It could be a woman I want to dominate."

His eyes flash, and he bares his teeth in another feral grin. "Or woman," he corrects. "Whoever they may be. You stare them down like this..."

He fixes those beautiful eyes on me, honed like lasers. It's not fair how easily he can inject a predatory intensity into every inch of his body. He radiates power like nothing. Dominating others comes naturally to him, and for a second, a terrifying thought sneaks in—how easy would it be for him to be lying to me still, playing me like a puppet on a string. Could I even tell the difference?

"Uh-Uh," Daze scolds, his eyes narrowing. "Don't do that. This is your second lesson. Doubt is forbidden. From now on, when you want something, don't hesitate. You don't give into fear, either. You go for it."

I feel like a broken record. "How?"

He laughs and then steps closer, jarring our bodies together. "It seems another demonstration might be in order. Listen up carefully, Freylie-Frey. I'll show you only one time. When you want something, you ask for it. Point blank. None of that pretty fucking language."

His hands return to my waist, smoothing over the skin with featherlight caresses. I'm so distracted by the contact that I miss the second his lips settle over mine, softly enough so that I can feel every movement of them as he speaks again, "For example... I want you to kiss me, Frey. For real. No holding back. Show me that you have what it takes to seize the reins. Think you can take control?"

His grated voice does something to me. In an instant, I'm bolder than I've ever been, infected by his strength.

"Yes," I tell him, gripping the back of his head with one hand. Then I kiss him hard, mimicking the movements he employed on me not too long ago. My fingers sink through his hair, angling his face to make it easier for me to slide my tongue along the seam of his mouth and slip inside.

He puts up little resistance, nipping at me once, but it isn't long before he surrenders to my rhythm, letting me set the pace.

He's right. There is something different in being on the receiving end of power versus taking it for yourself. Nothing compared to having another person in the palm of your hand at your whim. It's intoxicating.

Emboldened, I reach down between us, eager to test out that theory literally. My fingers brush over the zipper of his fly once, and his entire body stiffens in response. Rather than undo it, I press my palm against the bulge already straining at the material.

Yep. Having him under my sway figuratively is incredible, but nothing compares to this—feeling him straining with desire for me alone. I can't stop myself from stroking him, drawing a grunt from his throat.

But he isn't used to being at the mercy of someone else. I gasp as he captures my wrists and pivots, pinning me against the wall with my hands above my head.

"Not bad, Freylie," he praises in between pants. "But I think you can do better. Here's your next lesson—never demand more than you can handle."

He maneuvers to capture both of my wrists in one hand while trailing the other down my ribcage.

"Don't be greedy," he scolds, dragging his thumb over a nipple. I gasp out, and my hips twitch, testing his grip on me. "Use your judgment. Ask for too much? And you'll be in over your head, beautiful girl."

I shiver as his touch grazes my inner thigh. Fire pools in my belly, sparking a delicious heat that begins to creep through my veins. I can't escape a dangerous thought that blurts out of me, "But what if I want more?"

His eyes cloud over, and he leans in, pressing his forehead against mine. "You should. That's the catch when it comes to power. You always want more. The trick is knowing when to stop. But I'll let you in on a secret... The fun part is to not give a damn either way."

He seizes my mouth in a kiss that sends shockwaves through my entire body. Suddenly, I can't get enough of him. Not his mouth. His touch. I break his rule almost instantly—I want all of him, way more than I could ever possibly handle.

But I don't care.

I tug my wrists free and cup him again, exploring him in a way I would never dare just a few days ago. I can't get enough and hastily open his fly and push his pants to the ground. He's beautiful, so soft and yet as hard as steel at the same time.

"Fuck," he breathes out, his lips ghosting over mine. "You're catching on to this whole seizing power thing."

"But what does it mean?" I ask him. "If I have power over you now, what happens when this is over? Do we just go back to what it was like before? The games? The lying?" I don't even know where the questions come from. Deep down, I think I need some level of clarity, if only to keep my mind from wondering what could be. If sex alone isn't the only thing I could demand from him, but more...

"I don't know." He thumbs my lower lip, capturing the gasp I make. His hands are slick with a mixture of sweat, and me, and God knows what else, but I don't shy from the contact. He feels perfect. Smells perfect. Even the way he inhales my scent and bites down on his lower lip is just so perfect. "I don't. Sex comes easy to me," he admits. "Fucking is second nature. I'm not too good at the other stuff. Talking..." His gaze clouds over in that rare way that betrays just how intelligent he is beneath the carefree persona. Daze Keaton isn't a dumb brute, not by a long shot, but he prefers for people to see him that way. Not for the first time, I wonder why.

"That's what I want from you," I admit, pressing my forehead to his chest. With slow, savoring, deep breaths, I take him in. Every ounce of sweat and musk and his unique natural flavor. "I want to know it's more than just sex. I need to know that you..."

What, exactly? That he cares about me? Wouldn't risking his own life by breaking into my father's mansion merely to see me prove that? Or by taking on Silas, who already has it out for him?

"I need to know you," I say. "The real Daze. I need to know I can rely on you for more than this."

For a second, he's so quiet that only his heartbeat fills the silence, steady and pulsing. Then I feel his fingers rake through my hair, gathering the damp strands in a loose ponytail at the nape of my neck. Gently, he tugs once, making me look up. The expression I find on his face startles me. It's not the mocking or cocky smiles I'm used to. His eyes are focused, his mouth a stern, serious line.

"What do you want to know?" he asks, and my heart races with a mixture of relief and maybe some fear? I've never felt this connected to anyone else. Not like this. What do I want to know? He made it sound like such a simple question, but the truth is...

I want to know everything.

"Start with something simple," I say, surprised by how hoarse my voice comes out sounding. "What do you want to tell me?"

He sighs and leans in, pressing his forehead into my shoulder. My breath catches at the surprising intimacy. I can't stop myself from reaching up, and running my fingers through his hair.

"I'm not good at this shit," he says. "None of it. I tried with Renna, and it all went to shit."

Renna. Sammy's mother.

"Her brother would say she was too good for me from the jump, and it's the truth," he admits. "She was tough as nails. She was wild as hell, and liked to have fun. I met her when I was still with the Saints, feeling like a big shot. She had a way of knocking me right back down to earth. She was..."

He trails off, but I don't rush him. He sounds so different when he's speaking like this—from the heart and not with the aim to manipulate or confuse. I give him the time he needs to get the words out, smoothing my hands up and down his arms.

"She was good," he says thickly. With another heavy sigh, he tilts his head to meet my gaze head-on. His eyes are a brilliant gray, blazing with intensity. "Even when she got pregnant, most girls would have acted like it was the end of the world. Not her. She loved that little boy like hell before he was even born."

"What happened?" I ask, tempted to break my one rule. This part of the story, he seems more reluctant to tell, but he swallows hard, his gaze distant.

"I happened," he says. "I put all my time and energy into the Saints. I thought I had shit to prove. Maybe I wanted to show that I was better than my old man. Doesn't matter. I was so wrapped up in the bullshit that I didn't even notice when she started using again. To be honest, she was on the shit before Sammy, but she promised she'd stop after she found out she was pregnant."

"Drugs?" I ask, though I already knew at least a tiny bit of this part of the story.

He nods, his expression constricted. "Cocaine at first. Then heroin. One day I came home and found a tourniquet mixed in with the baby bottles."

I fight to hide my disgust. "That sounds awful."

"It was," he says, his jaw tight. "It was hell. I did everything I could to try and get her clean, though don't try to tell Silas that. I protected her for as long as I could, but it was never enough. Not me. Not even Sammy. When she died... I know it's wrong, but I won't deny that a part of me was relieved. Sam's too young to remember her by the end—and he will never know the truth if I can help it. He deserves to remember the person she was before. Not the mess she became."

"Even at her worst, I think... I know she still loved him," I say. He shoots me an odd look, but I don't shy away from the skepticism.

I know firsthand what it feels like to watch another person slip away, a slave to their own addiction. I know what it's like to hunt for love and affection beneath their indifference. I know what it's like to comfort yourself at night with a lie.

"If you ask my father about my mother, he'll tell you she died of cancer," I start. It's my turn to expose part of my past to him, but it's harder than I would have thought. I feel naked —stripped down in a way that a lack of clothing can't even achieve. At the same time, there's a thrill to baring myself to him that comes close to the pleasure I feel during sex.

"The truth was, she was an addict. Pain killers. She fell deeper down the hole every day, and my father threw himself into the management of the Collective rather than facing reality. Hale knew, though. In his own way, he tried to protect me, but he was just a kid. He couldn't fix everyone on his own."

"What happened to her?" Daze asks.

"She left," I say, hearing my voice break. The tears I've learned to suppress for the past decade threaten to break free, but I push them back. "My father told everyone she died of cancer, but that's not true. I saw her leave. Maybe she's dead now, I don't even know..."

"What do you mean?" Daze strokes his thumb along my cheek. Each gentle brush sends an electric shock down my spine.

"I saw her leave that night," I reiterate. "I thought that was the end of it. She just didn't want us anymore—but I have to believe she loved Hale and me. She did. These last few days... I think there is more to it. That my father did something to her soon after she left. Catherine, my stepmother, was insistent that she was really dead. Like she knew. Then Colton said something odd to me. That my father could teach him how to deal with an unruly wife. God, I don't even know what to believe anymore."

Daze frowns at the mention of Colton, but says nothing. For a long time, he looks at me in a way I can't decipher. Regardless, my heart feels heavy as he reaches out to smooth a stray piece of hair from my face. His touch lingers, tracing a path to my jaw.

"You believe what you have to," he tells me in a voice that makes my toes curl. "You have good instincts. Don't doubt that. I don't take your trust for granted, either. I mean that. I wasn't worthy of Renna, and I sure as hell am not worthy of you, but still... I want a chance, if you'll let me. I want to be whatever you want me to be. I want you."

My chest feels so tight I can barely speak. "I want you too," I admit. "When I'm with you, I feel... Stronger. I like that feeling. Even when you toy with my head. No one talks to me like you do."

"And how is that?" His lips come dangerously close to mine.

"Raw," I say. "Like you don't care if I can handle it or not. You give me everything all at once." My cheeks flame as I realize how else that statement could be interpreted.

For once, however, he doesn't seem to let his mind go into the gutter.

"You should give yourself more credit, princess," he scolds. "You're not as sweet and innocent as you pretend to be. You've got claws." He runs his fingers down my wrist, lacing his fingers with mine. "You've got bite. You're a hell of a lot stronger than you realize. You don't need me to tell you that."

"Oh really?" I counter. "Strong enough to turn the tables?"

I wiggle out from under him and pivot so I'm standing in the hallway, watching as he races to interpret what I'm saying.

"How so?" he asks, flexing his arms so the muscles jump against his skin.

"By setting the pace," I say, taking a step back as he steps out of his pants and advances one. "By letting me take the reins again."

He lets out a guttural laugh that makes me shiver. "I can do you one better. Play your cards right, and I'll let you be on top."

We move to the couch, where he lets me straddle him. Our hands interlock as our chests collide, and our heartbeats strive to match each other's. This position feels so intimate I'm overwhelmed. Dizzy, even. He isn't inside me yet, and still... I can sense his presence throughout my body, invading each pore and crevice.

I rake my hands down his chest, tapping my fingers in time to the heartbeat racing beneath them. He can be so violent at times, like a raging storm. The next second, he's soft and warm and submitting to my touch with gritted teeth as if it pains him to practice restraint.

I tease him, slowing my descent to a crawl around his belly button. "Are you okay?" I ask, sneaking a glance at his face.

"Hell no, I'm not. No one drives me crazy like you do," he admits, watching me through wayward strands of blond hair. "No one."

He sounds so serious. My belly flips. I can't breathe. This isn't a mocking game anymore. We're on the verge of something monumental—I can feel it. All it would take to tip over the edge is one simple question, and I fumble with my tongue to voice it. "What does that mean?"

He sighs and reaches up to grip the back of my skull in a fluid motion. With gentle pressure, he brings me in for a kiss that makes my toes curl. With our lips still meeting, he murmurs, "It means I'm so fucking whipped," his voice rasping. "And you're so damn innocent. You probably don't have any fucking idea what that means, do you?"

I don't, not that I care to confess that just yet. Instead, I nuzzle into him, pressing a kiss against his throat. And again, when he shivers at the contact. I mouth a trail down to the thatch of hair at the base of his abdomen. Then I look up to find him watching me, his upper lip skewered between his teeth.

"I want this," I tell him, letting my breath wash over him. He jumps, his cock already stirring to life with a virility that I sense isn't typical for most men, even dangerous, sinning ones. "I demand this. All of you. Can... Can I have it?"

He bucks against me, snatching my hips to drag me up, so our pelvises collide. Hissing through his teeth, he reaches between us and guides himself into me. Then he tugs on my hips, forcing me to rock. Move.

"Daze!" My eyes threaten to roll into the back of my head, but I push down, setting my own rhythm. Having him inside me in any capacity is an experience to remember, but this... Being able to stare down at him while his eyes glaze over, and pleasure radiates from every inch of his body is incomparable to anything else.

It's a taste of the power he taunted me with, and I want more.

More.

More.

With a mindless hunger, I rush to consume every ounce of Daze Keaton I can. Every inch. Every thrust. Every last drop.

TWENTY-TWO

FREY

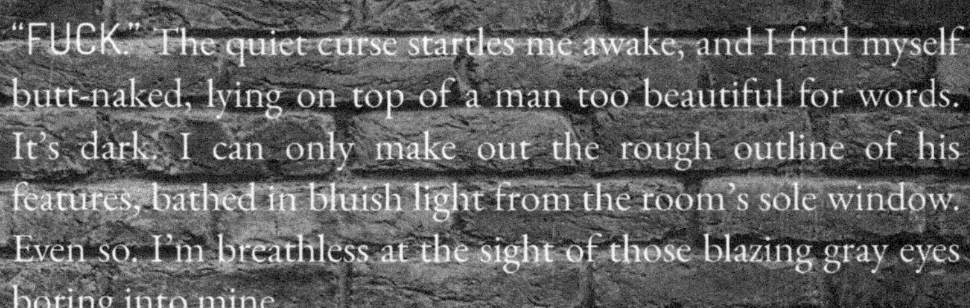

"FUCK." The quiet curse startles me awake, and I find myself butt-naked, lying on top of a man too beautiful for words. It's dark. I can only make out the rough outline of his features, bathed in bluish light from the room's sole window. Even so, I'm breathless at the sight of those blazing gray eyes boring into mine.

"We fell asleep," Daze says, explaining his apparent frustration. "So much for teaching you more ways to use that pretty little mouth. Turns out, I'm as bad a teacher as I was a student."

"It isn't like we don't have plenty of time to practice," I say, pressing my cheek to his chest. "I can't go back home." I don't know if I sound sad about that or resigned.

"As if I'd let those fuckers anywhere near you," Daze snarls, shifting so that he can sling his arm over my waist, providing a bit of warm protection from the slight chill in the room. Before I know it, he is lightly caressing the marks on my back.

"I hate that I couldn't be there for you when that fucker hurt you." He exhales before continuing, "You better get used to being on the run, princess. You aren't going any-fucking-where." We lay in companionable silence, both lost in thought.

"Though... Fuck." He sighs. "I asked Lyra to take Sammy today. She's bringing him over after school."

"I don't mind," I say, picturing Sammy's sweet little face. "He's a cutie. Way cuter than his dad."

"Very funny. It's been a long time since I've had him on my own. I don't even know what the fuck to do. And with Silas out for blood, I can't exactly take him to the park."

"My mom used to read us stories," I say, smiling at the memory. "I'm sure he'd love that. And watching movies. There's plenty you can do to entertain him here."

He lifts his head to shoot me a look that makes my heart flip. "And you'll help me?" He sounds so... Hesitant. Like he *needs* me to help him. I swallow hard and pull myself upright to face him.

"Yes," I reply hoarsely. "Of course."

"Good." He reaches up to run his fingers through my hair. I shudder at the contact, tilting my head to extend his touch for as long as I can. "That's not all I could use your assistance with. I won't take Silas' bullshit lying down. I'm striking out, forming my own crew. I could use a little angel on my shoulder, wishing me good luck."

My cheeks flame at his characterization of me. It's sweet. Yet, there's a subtle desperation lurking beneath his words. Like he's only partly joking.

"I'll do more than that," I say, licking my lips. "If you want to take down my father…" I trail off, weighing the consequences of telling him the full truth. Do I hate my father after everything he's done? No, I don't think I do. But can I just watch him continue to sow chaos and confusion in his wake? I only need to think of Hale to have my answer. "I think I know who can help. Remember the reporter I mentioned? We can ask him to investigate the company the college student recognized from the overdose locations—Higher Limit Construction. I think it might be connected to this mess."

Daze frowns and assists me in climbing off him so he can stand. "Never heard of it. But I'm not surprised that this shit goes deep. How do you know you can trust this reporter?"

I shrug, relieved by his non-bloodthirsty reaction. "He said I could contact him if I found anything new."

"Let's see him together. I want to size up this man for myself," Daze suggests. "We can get ready and contact him to set up a meet."

"Okay," I murmur, thinking of the day ahead of us. Daze breaks my train of thought when he grunts.

"You know, I just realized… I haven't smoked one cig since I lost you."

Staring him in his eyes, I tease, "I think you've found a new addiction."

Suddenly serious, he bends down to hover closer to me as he says, "I think I have, but it's more dangerous than nicotine. An innocent little angel with a naughty little temper."

Daze claims my mouth with a quick kiss. He withdraws, then says, "We better get up before we stay in bed all day." With an endearing grin, he extends his hand for mine. He leads me into the bathroom, and we shower together, stealing away as much closeness as we can despite the urgency surrounding us.

Once we're dressed, Daze returns to the couch, taking on that serious, thoughtful expression that warns he's thinking hard. "Once we set a location to meet, we'll take the back streets there," he says, thinking out loud. "Stay out of sight. You'll wear one of my hoodies, so you go unnoticed. Then we'll see if this reporter is legit enough to trust."

"I'm sure he is," I say in a rush. "And, I found some of Hale's notebooks. I'm sure there is an answer there—"

Suddenly Daze bolts upright, cocking his head. "Is that..."

He's referring to a distant commotion that must come from downstairs. Two separate shouting voices ring out at once.

"Where the fuck is he? Is he up there? Daze? Daze!"

"Lyra," someone pleads. Ben? "Just calm down. What the hell is this about—"

"Don't tell me to fucking calm down! Daze! Daze! Where the hell is he?"

"Damn it." Daze scrambles to his feet and bolts from the apartment, shouting down to Lyra. "I'm here. Damn it! What the hell, Lyra? What's going on?"

"Of course, you don't fucking know," I hear Lyra reply. Her voice breaks. Is she crying? "I've been trying to get a hold of you for a goddamn hour. Where the hell have you been? Though, looking at you, I can guess. Like always, fucking around is more important than your own son."

"Okay, you got that insult out of the way," Daze says with obvious restraint. "Where's Sam? What's going on?"

"Oh, God, Daze..."

Panic shoots through me at the sound of that name. Without thinking, I lunge for my shoes and pull them on before racing after Daze. As I reach the lower floor, I strain my ears to catch what Lyra says next.

"...he's missing." From my position, I can see her standing in the hallway beside Daze, her eyes bloodshot. "Someone picked him up from school early, but it wasn't me. Silas claims it wasn't him either. I hoped that maybe you—for once in your life—had decided to be a father, but... Oh god, Daze! He's just a baby—"

"What the hell do you mean he's missing?" Instantly, Daze transforms, losing any trace of the warmth he showed me seconds ago. He's cold, his body rippling with tension. "Lyra?"

"Someone picked him up from school not long after I dropped him off. A woman. The stupid secretary thought she was my sister! They couldn't even give me a license plate—"

"Did you call the police?"

The color drains from Lyra's face. "Silas… Silas told me not to."

"So that fucker is involved. What the hell is he playing at?"

"He said he'd handle it. That I shouldn't worry, but Daze, Sammy's just a little boy… He can't be involved in any of this mess."

"Now you think that?" Daze bellows. "Fuck, Lyra. I told you not to trust that son of a bitch!"

"You want to gloat? Find Sammy, and you can bitch at me all you want. Just find him, Daze."

"You don't have to tell me that." With a murderous expression, he storms over to where Ben stands behind the bar counter. "Give me your shoes," he demands, his hand outstretched. "And your jacket."

Ben complies, stepping out of his boots before handing them over. "You need to think carefully, Daze," he warns. "Don't go strutting around guns blazing. Silas doesn't need any excuse to have you jumped again—or worse. Just, chill for a second."

"You think I'm going to leave my son out there alone?" Daze demands in a vicious tone.

"N-No. Of course not." Ben blinks. "At least let me come with you. This could be a setup—" He shoots a wary glance in Lyra's direction. "No offense."

"I don't care," Daze snarls, already barreling toward the door. "If you want to come, fine, but don't think you can stop me." He pauses near the doorway and looks back at me. "Stay here."

A second later, he's gone, and cursing under his breath, Ben disappears into a back room—presumably to find another pair of shoes and then takes off after him.

"God, what the hell have I done?" Lyra buries her face in her hands and leans against the wall. Slowly, she sinks down to the floor. "Poor Sammy. This is all my fault..."

"What happened?" I take a step toward her as her shoulders begin to shake with silent sobs. Thinking fast, I circle around the counter and grab a handful of napkins that I bring over to her. She hesitates for a moment, then takes one and blows her nose before looking up.

With tears streaming down her face, she's night and day from the confident, bossy elder sister I'd met what feels like a lifetime ago while half-naked in Daze's apartment.

"I dropped Sam off at school like always," she says, staring into space. "Then I got a call about some 'make-up' assignment for classes he'll miss. When I asked what the hell they meant, they said he'd been picked up early by 'my sister.' He wasn't at the house or with Silas. I've never seen Daze look like that. Scared. God, if anything happens to that kid, I'll never forgive myself—"

"Your sister?" I ask.

Lyra shrugs and dabs at her eyes with the tissue. "That dumbass secretary should thank God that I didn't beat the answers out of her. I'm going to sue the shit out of that school. Do I even look like the sort of person who goes to church?"

"Church?" I crouch down to her level. "What does that mean?"

"That's what the bitch said," Lyra insists with a watery laugh. "That my 'sister from church' came to pick up Sammy for me. I should have rung that idiot's stupid neck. I just hope it was some overzealous weirdo, and he's okay. God, what am I even doing here? I should be out there looking for him." She tosses her used napkin aside and lurches for the door. "Tell Daze he can reach me on my cell!"

I watch her leave, frozen in place. *Sister from church.* My mind won't stop replaying those words over and over, and with every iteration, a new knot forms in my stomach. A woman who looked sweet enough to charm a school secretary into giving her custody of a child without question. Someone cunning enough to use religion as a tactic of manipulation.

It can't be...

I feel sick as I turn on my heel and retrace my steps into the apartment. I find my jacket and grab my bag. Something makes me stop and write a note to Daze, just in case...

I leave it on the coffee table before finally exiting the bar entirely. It takes three tries before I manage to convince a passerby to let me borrow their cell phone. Then I dial one of the few numbers I know by heart and wait, holding my breath with every toll of the dial tone.

I'm not sure what I expect. Maybe I'm praying to God that someone won't pick up, and my hunch is wrong. Please, don't pick up. Please...

"Hello?" The voice on the other end is deceptively sweet, but I can hear the trepidation in it.

It's like time slows down to a crawl as I gather the courage to choke out a single reply, "Catherine?"

A startled gasp resonates through the receiver. "Oh, Frances, I'm so sorry! I am so, so sorry. Please forgive me."

"Catherine... What did you do?" I can hear the panic in my voice, and I know the elderly businessman whose phone I'm using is watching me with concern.

Nothing else matters.

"Catherine, tell me! What did you do?"

"I had no choice," she croaks. "Your father said... He said that I needed to do my duty—that it was the responsibility of all of us to right your sins. If I didn't... I would wind up like her —I *know* what he did to her. He showed me. Frances, please come home. Please—"

"Where is he, the little boy?" I snap. That voice doesn't sound like me. Not sweet, innocent Frey. It's so harsh that Catherine gasps again. "Tell me! Where is Sammy?"

"I'm so sorry... I don't know. Your father said to say that you would know where. He said you have to go there alone. If not... Frances, what is going on?"

I just hang up, feeling sick to my stomach. Only a few days ago, there were plenty of things I would have thought beyond even my father. Sure, he was ambitious and could be cold at times, and perhaps he even had an unusual detachment to Hale's death. But I would have never thought him capable of this.

Using anything or anyone to get his way.

Someone gently taps my shoulder. "Miss? You, okay?"

I woodenly hand him back his phone and then take off blindly, unsure which direction I'm even heading in. I'm not surprised, though, when I find myself nearing Cherry Lane, just as icy rain droplets begin to fall.

With every step I take, a million different voices in my head start screaming for supremacy. I'm being stupid! I can't give in. Can't go back. I should find Daze and come up with a plan. I should. I should. I should...

One realization keeps those fantasies at bay, though. If my father was willing to let Hale die and watch me be beaten merely to prove a point, then he won't care about a four-year-old little boy with no connection to him. He'll hurt Sammy if he has to.

Or worse.

Numbed by that realization, I keep walking until the silhouette of Salvation finally comes into view. Against the backdrop of a dreary, gray sky, it doesn't resemble the warm haven of peace I grew up believing it was. The brick looks grim in contrast to the storm clouds, and the wide front doors seem like a gaping mouth ready to swallow me whole. Despite the supposed fire damage on the interior, the exterior is as welcoming as always.

At least in theory. Lurking behind that beautiful façade is a grim reality that I can't escape. Deep in my soul, I know that if I return now, I might never leave again.

But even though it's only been a day since the last time I was under my father's thumb, I feel like a different person. Someone who won't easily break against the threat of violence.

And someone who isn't without a plan.

I won't let fear stop me from saving a sweet, innocent little boy—and I won't be beaten into submission either.

TWENTY-THREE

DAZE

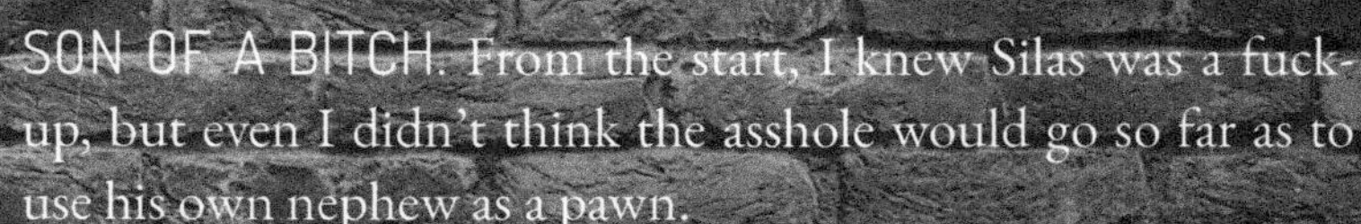

SON OF A BITCH. From the start, I knew Silas was a fuck-up, but even I didn't think the asshole would go so far as to use his own nephew as a pawn.

His actions deserve more than an ass-whooping this time. He deserves to have his fucking throat slit. By me...

"Daze!" I look over my shoulder to find Ben sprinting down the street toward me.

"Have you lost your fucking mind?" he demands. "What's your plan, huh? You just barge in there and cause a scene. That if someone does have Sammy, they won't hurt him just to get to you? Daze, you need to think!" He slams his hand into my chest, knocking me back a step.

"What the hell else am I supposed to do?"

Ben taps his temple. "Use your brain," he snarls. "Think! If you go off like a fucking psycho, you'll just be playing into

Silas' hands, don't you see that? You'll be making it easy to flush you out and finish you off without having to lift a finger."

I shove him off and keep walking. "If you think I'm just going to sit around and let that son of a bitch use my son as a pawn…"

"No, Daze! I'm asking you to not fuck up a good thing for once in your life. You can still find Sam without getting your brains blown out… What's wrong?"

He nearly runs into me as I stop short with my eyes on the building up ahead.

"Something's off." The street is too quiet. All of the Saints' bikes are still in the rack, and the lights are on in the club.

"Now you realize that?" Ben snaps. "Spit it out. What are you thinking? But can we not stand in the fucking open, for fuck's sake?"

We both back into a nearby alley with a better view of the street. From here, it's more obvious that the mood in the club isn't the typical raucous atmosphere Silas usually lets simmer. It's too quiet. Too still. As if those motherfuckers are all waiting for something. A cue?

"This is riveting, I must admit," Ben says near my ear. "But do you mind telling me what the hell is going on? I know that look. You're using that brain of yours for once. Talk to me."

"Silas never hunkers down like this," I admit. "Not when he's cocky that he has the upper hand. If he did take Sammy, he would be parading him out in the open. He'd be daring me to come and get him. Hell, he'd probably have it plastered on a sign that he took my kid and won't ever give him back. This... This is different."

"Like I tried to tell you," Ben snarls. "Silas is stupid, but even he knows what lines not to cross. He may have snatched your little girlfriend from under your nose, but he won't do the same with Sam. I know you don't like hearing it, but he does care about that kid. In a sick, selfish as fuck way, of course."

"Silas doesn't give a shit about anyone but himself," I counter. "But... You might have a point. He's lying low for a reason. Almost like..."

"Like he isn't the one calling the shots this time," Ben suggests, picking up my train of thought. "Maybe he doesn't know about Sammy, or maybe he isn't the one behind it. He's just waiting."

"Probably for me," I admit. "I don't think you're being paranoid after all, Benny. I think someone tried to set me up."

"Do you think Lyra is in on it?"

"No." I shake my head. "She wouldn't ever play around with Sammy. Not even to stay on Silas' good side. Whatever happened, she isn't in on it. But..." Something he said sticks out to me, gnawing at the back of my mind. "Frey—"

"I shouldn't have to say this, but don't you think finding your son is a bit more important than babysitting your girlfriend?"

"No. Something's wrong?" I spin around to head back to the bar.

Ben shrugs in confusion. "What do you mean? I think she stayed behind with Lyra, not that it should matter until we find Sam—"

"Fuck. What if Sam was just a decoy? Shit," I shout to him before taking off. I don't wait around to see if he's following.

How could I be so fucking stupid? Silas is an ambitious prick, but Ben was right when he said that he wouldn't use Sam, not even to get to me—which means that someone else did. Someone whose aim wasn't to get to me after all, but to the one person who could send his whole twisted empire crumbling down.

Shit. Shit. Shit.

I reach the bar and race inside, calling her name. Damn it, I just hope she wasn't stupid enough to leave—or that Silas wasn't bold enough to come for her a second time.

"Frey!" She isn't in the apartment, but I search like hell for her anyway, tearing through every last room. Ironically, it isn't until my third trip around the living room that I see what she left for me to find.

Trust someone like her to leave a fucking note behind. I rip it open, ready to read some heartfelt bullshit about how I should respect her choice and not come for her.

Instead, I find two short sentences that nearly knock me off my fucking feet.

First, *I'm tired of being weak.*

Then, *I'm ready to fight. If you want to help me, then go to where we first met.*

TWENTY-FOUR

FREY

I DON'T KNOW how long I linger outside the perimeter of Salvation before I finally approach the main entrance.

Alarm bells go off the closer I come to the glass façade. For one, father's army of armed guards isn't in sight. No SWAT officers are ready to tackle me at a moment's notice, either. The entire building seems far too quiet, almost peaceful.

But I would be a fool to fall for it.

Without realizing it, Daze taught me something way more vital than merely learning how to make my own demands. He made me trust my gut and learn to see beneath the obvious surface to the unrest beneath.

I can sense that Father is probably inside this building, and he isn't alone. Colton might be with him, and they both conspired to ensure I would come to them alone.

I could write it all off as my father wanting to control me and Colton craving some power in Salvation's hierarchy, but there has to be more to it than that.

What could my marriage garner my father that he couldn't otherwise have?

My gut tells me that the answer to that question is somehow interconnected with everything else. I don't know how long I stand there, frozen on the front walkway, before the doors open and someone steps out. Though he's dressed in a formal suit, I recognize him instantly. Colton.

"Come home, Frances," he says, his arms outstretched. "Please. Everything will be forgiven if you just come home—"

"Where is he?" I demand without taking a step. "I know what you did. Was it really that important to lure me here? You'd have to resort to kidnapping?"

My voice breaks, but as I watch Colton's expression shift and raw fury transform his features, I have my answer.

"Don't be ridiculous, Frances," he snaps, letting his arms fall to his sides. "Have you truly been led so far astray?" He looks at me in that condescending way my father eyes Catherine. Like I'm too stupid to know up from down without his guidance. I used to be blind to the open revulsion in that expression—but now I know what lurks behind it.

Apathy. He doesn't give a damn about me apart from the superficial image we would create as a married couple—me as his property.

"Bullshit," I say, letting my voice ring out. "Where is he? I'm not doing a damn thing until you show me he's okay—"

"Enough."

I'd been so focused on Colton, that I didn't even notice the other figure, lurking just out of sight within the church's entrance. Father. He steps forward, his hair gleaming in the overcast daylight, his eyes like blue hellfire.

"So much like your mother," he says, his voice soft but sharp enough to carry on the wind. "Defiant until the end."

I shudder at the insinuation. "And like her, you won't ever let me go, will you?" I ask. God, I want him to cringe at the suggestion. Flinch. Deny it outright. Something.

Anything other than stare me down coldly without an ounce of emotion on his face.

"You need more stability than I alone can provide for you, Frances," he says, after a long moment. "Agree to return now. Marry Colton tonight, and you may be able to begin to atone for your transgressions. Should you refuse..."

He gestures behind him, and two more figures exit from the lobby. One of them bounds to me, his blond curls bouncing.

"Ms. Lady!" He's smiling as he throws his tiny arms around my waist.

"Are you okay, honey?" I smooth my hands along his shoulders, hunting for any sign of injury.

"Yeah." He giggles. "Can we go see my daddy now? I'm hungry."

"Will he, Frances?" my father asks. In his shadow, Catherine cowers, her face streaked with tears. "I suggest you think carefully."

I feel a lump in my throat as I crouch down to Sammy's level and smooth the hair back from his face. "You'll see your daddy soon," I tell him. "But I have to stay here for a little while."

He frowns. "Okay. But you'll come later, right?"

"Of course." I force a smile and then face the three once-respected figures in my life, standing like my executioners.

Slowly, I stand and approach them, holding Sammy's hand in mine.

I'm no longer the naïve innocent I was. I just have to trust that Daze knows that.

TWENTY-FIVE

DAZE

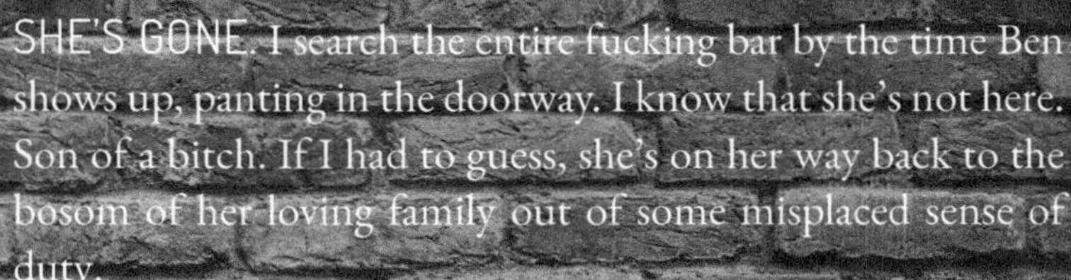

SHE'S GONE. I search the entire fucking bar by the time Ben shows up, panting in the doorway. I know that she's not here. Son of a bitch. If I had to guess, she's on her way back to the bosom of her loving family out of some misplaced sense of duty.

"Fuck!"

"I take it, your girlfriend split yet again?" Ben asks. "If you want my advice, you should focus on Sam—"

"Don't you fucking see? Sam was just a distraction. To get to her."

"Why?"

I don't fucking know, but I don't intend to stick around twiddling my thumbs trying to figure it out.

"If Heywood wants a fight, then fine. He got one—"

I start for the door and nearly run into someone attempting to enter from the other end.

"Thank God," Lyra says. "You weren't answering your phone —again. Despite everything that's going on. But I still wanted to make sure you knew—"

"Knew what?"

"Sammy's safe," she says with a sigh. "Someone dropped him off at the house. It must have been some kind of stupid mix-up. He seems fine."

"Where is he?"

She nods behind her. "In the car. He's a little worn out, but there isn't a scratch on him, thank God. Silas said it was probably just some stupid housewife who had one too many martinis before picking up the kids from school."

"Oh, I bet he did," I snarl, but I'm already outside, heading for Lyra's SVU parked along the curb.

Sam's in the back seat, his eyes half-closed. "Daddy?"

"Hey, little man... What happened today? Your Aunt Lyra said you had an adventure?"

"I went to see Ms. Lady," he says sleepily.

"Who? Your teacher?"

"No. Ms. Lady," he insists. "A lady picked me up from school and said she was going to take me to see Ms. Lady. We went to a weird place to wait." Sammy yawns and starts to doze off.

"Hey, buddy, what happened next?" I carefully prod him. I don't want to scare him any more than he already is.

"Then Ms. Lady came to see me. She gave me a big hug and some ice cream and told me everything would be okay."

"Maybe Lyra was right," Ben says near my ear. "Or maybe I'm a monkey's uncle."

"Sleep tight, buddy."

I kiss his forehead, then pivot on my heel.

"Well, that's a good thing, right?" Ben asks, keeping pace. "He wasn't hurt. Silas wasn't behind it. No harm, no foul."

"What if I wasn't the target of this little stunt?" I ask.

"Huh? What are you talking about?"

"Silas stood down because he didn't have a fucking choice," I say, thinking out loud. "This wasn't his fight, and Sam was just collateral."

"For what?"

"Her. Frey."

And like an idiot, I let her go skipping right back into the fire.

"Shit." I take off in the vague direction of that church. Heywood will probably have his private army ready, but so be it.

"Daze! Daze, wait!" Ben grabs my shoulder from behind, spinning me to face him. "Where the hell do you think you're going? If you think I'm going to let you prance right up to Heywood's front door after everything I've risked to help you pull off this crazy fucking plan, you've got another thing coming. This isn't just your neck on the line, anymore. Do you realize that? I'm in this, too, not to mention the other dumb fucks who signed up to join your new outfit. I know you hate the comparison and all, but you should stop resenting your old man and try to be more like him."

"Oh really? So, I should skip town and leave you all high and dry?"

"No," Ben says, suddenly serious. "You should do the one thing he was good at—lead. Slow down. Think. Do you even hear what I'm saying?" he shouts as I keep walking. "Stop letting your dick guide the way and just use your actual brain—"

"She just sacrificed herself for Sammy. I can't just leave her there—"

"That's because you're balls fucking deep in love with her," Ben cuts in.

Spinning around to face him, all I can do is stare. Is he right? Am I in love with Frey? The realization of it all hits me hard. "Fuck," I groan, feeling as if the wind has been knocked out of me. "Maybe I do. I just know... I won't leave her there." Or, in other words—I'm completely fucking whipped. Frey Heywood has me wrapped around her finger.

"All the more reason to use your head—"

"I hear you, Ben," I admit. "I think you actually said something for once that makes sense."

"What's that?"

"She left me something," I tell him, taking off once more. "A note. I think it was her way of telling me the same thing you have."

"What do you mean? If you're not going to Heywood, then where?" he shouts after me.

"Where she told me to," I call back.

It takes ten minutes to get to the bridge, and when I do, it's already dark. I nearly miss a tiny bundle looped around one of the poles in the railing. A bag, hers.

Inside it is a bunch of shit I don't understand the significance of—a tablet, a reporter's card, and an old journal. However, I do find a note with delicate handwriting that makes my heart twitch as I read.

Trust me. Hale tried to tell me the truth, and I owe it to him to get him justice. Don't come after me yet—I'll come to you. I can handle myself. After all, I learned from the best. —Love, Frey.

Love.

The word *love* replays in my head, and I recall what Ben said. Damn, since when have I turned into such a whipped, corny bastard?

Part of me is impressed by how quickly the little princess has grown a set of balls. The overwhelming majority of my brain, on the other hand, scoffs at her request.

I need to tell her how much she means to me. I need to show her. Prove to her that she and Sammy are worth risking every-thing for.

But most of all, I need to tell her I'm in love with her.

And if she thinks I'll let her go without a fight, she has another damn thing coming.

~ Daze and Frey's story continues in Wild Devil ~

ABOUT LANA SKY

Lana Sky is a reclusive writer in the United States who spends most of her time daydreaming about complex male characters and parenting her Cockapoo Joey. She writes dark, twisted romance across several genres. Her titles include everything from mafia romance to vampires.

facebook.com/AuthorLanaSky

twitter.com/lanasky101

amazon.com/author/lanasky

pinterest.com/lanasky101

goodreads.com/lanasky

instagram.com/lanasky101

bookbub.com/authors/lana-sky

tiktok.com/@author_lana_sky

ALSO BY LANA SKY

For more titles by Lana Sky, please visit:

https://www.lanaskybooks.com

www.ingramcontent.com/pod-product-compliance
Lightning Source LLC
Chambersburg PA
CBHW071206210726
48293CB00002B/306